BROOMSTICKS AND BONES

A Spellbinder Bay Cozy Paranormal Mystery - Book Two

SAM SHORT

www.samshortauthor.com

Copyright © 2018 by Sam Short

All rights reserved.

No part of this book may be reproduced in any form or by any electronic or mechanical means, including information storage and retrieval systems, without written permission from the author, except for the use of brief quotations in a book review.

v.1

❦ Created with Vellum

For Katie. A metal detecting fan and all round good egg.

Chapter 1

*B*eing careful to avoid the delicate flowers, whose lilac petals peeked through the dune grasses which whipped her bare calves as she ran, Millie Thorn wove a lazy path through the dunes, heading for the beach below the sea-front cottage she called home.

Reuben flew in lazy circles above her, his complaints making an irritating soundtrack to accompany her run. "I told you," panted Millie, her trainers sinking into the soft sand. "Exercise is good for us. We've been lazy since I moved into Windy-dune Cottage."

The Cockatiel swooped low, his wingtip brushing Millie's face. "*We've* been lazy? It's not me whose bottom has got bigger," he squawked, gaining height again. "I keep myself svelte. I think it's good to have pride in oneself."

Millie veered left, following a new trail which

would take her directly onto the sweeping expanse of beach. "I do have pride in myself, Reuben," she said. "The last four months have been hectic, that's all. You try moving to a new town and then finding out you're a witch. *Then* finding out your dead mother was a witch, too — a secret she'd kept to herself! It was quite a shock. No wonder I turned to junk food for a brief period."

Reuben dive-bombed her again. "I'm a demon who spent six human lifetimes in a terrible dimension known as The Chaos before I was brought to this world by a kindly witch who placed my spirit in the body of a bird. That's incalculably worse than what you've gone through, and *I* didn't turn to vices to help me through life. I think it's good that you've taken up running, though. Your bottom looks a lot bigger from up here than it does at ground level."

Millie picked up speed as the downward gradient steepened. "You may be my familiar," she said, "but must you be *so* familiar? Say something nice, Reuben, or the pizza I promised you for tonight's meal is off the menu."

Reuben's concerned squawk carried on the wind, startling a passing seagull, which changed course and headed towards the ocean. "Something nice?" he said. "Erm... your hair is the colour of the finest mahogany burnished by a tropical sun, and your eyes are velvet pools of melted chocolate — set in a face which even the angels covet — despite the slight bend in your nose and the cleft in your chin."

Millie smiled, wiping a bead of sweat from her brow. "That was actually very nice. The nose and chin part aside," she said. "I'll pretend you meant it." She slowed her pace as the soft sand of the dunes gave way to the firmer sand of the beach. "I haven't heard you mention angels before," she said. "Are they real?"

Reuben laughed as he flew in circles above his witch. "Seriously?" he said. "Are you seriously asking me if angels are real?"

"Of course I am!" snapped Millie. "I don't see what's so funny about the question. Four months ago, the weirdest thing in my life was my landlord, and since then I've learned that witches, ghosts, vampires, werewolves and mermaids — to name a few, are real." She stopped running, and looked up at the little bird. "Of course my question was serious!"

With a soft beating of wings, Reuben landed gently on Millie's shoulder. "In answer to your serious question," he said. "No. As far as I'm aware, angels are not real."

"Thank you," said Millie, surveying the storm-ravaged beach. "That's all I wanted to know."

"That really was some storm, wasn't it?" said Reuben.

Millie nodded. "The worst in a century according to the meteorologists," she said.

The breeze swept a strand of hair into her eyes as Millie took in the sight before her. Huge swathes of sand had been pushed aside by powerful waves which had battered the shoreline, and in some areas of the beach the underlying hard-packed gravel which had once been covered by sand, was now visible.

Plastic, wood and other debris had been pushed far up the beach, the high-tide line having encroached further inland than it had done for a very long time, or would do again.

Reuben took off, gaining height as Millie began running. Her thigh muscles cramped and tight, she promised herself once more that running wouldn't become one of those fleeting hobbies she'd taken up in the past, only to drop a week later. Learning to play the flute being the most short-lived.

"There's a man dancing!" shouted Reuben from above. "In the sand dunes. He must be some sort of weirdo. Spellbinder Bay *does* seem to attract them."

Millie squinted her eyes in order to see through the harsh glare of the morning sun on the wet sand. Reuben was right. There was a man, visible in the steep valley between two tall dunes — and he did *seem* to be dancing. It wasn't much of a dance, certainly not the sort of dance you'd see in a nightclub at two-o'clock on a Saturday morning, but the man was doing his best — punching his hands vigorously into the air above his head as he lifted his knees high, his head bobbing from side to side. Changing direction, Millie made a beeline towards the man — he looked like he could be fun, and she needed some fun.

Noticing Millie's approach, the man ceased dancing and bent down to pick something up from the sand. Recognising what the lengthy piece of equipment in his hand was, Millie's interest increased a notch or two. She slowed to a walk as she neared him, and put a cheery smile on her face. "You're a metal detector!" she said. "Did you find something? Is that why you looked so happy?"

The man adjusted his hat, folding the peak so it shielded his eyes from the sun. "I'm not a metal detector," he said, his wrinkles deepening as he smiled. He tapped the long piece of equipment in his hand, a large disc at one end, and an electronic box fitted below the handgrip at the other. "*This* is a metal detector. *I'm* a metal detectorist. I only took this hobby up last month, but even I know that's an important difference to establish from the outset."

"I'll start again," said Millie, gazing into the hole the man had dug using the shovel at his feet. "You're a metal detectorist! Did you find something interesting?"

The man's eyes widened as Reuben fluttered from the sky and landed on Millie's shoulder. "That's amazing!" he said. "It's a cockatiel, isn't it? It's beautiful."

"An astute fellow," whispered Reuben into Millie's ear. "I like him already. We should invite him back to the cottage for coffee and some of those muffins you baked. Not the lemon-fancies, though. There was nothing fancy about those — believe you me!"

Millie smiled, ignoring her familiar's insult. "Yes," she said. "He's a cockatiel."

"Does he talk?" said the man.

"Don't you dare," hissed Millie, sensing that the

bird was about to prove just how well he could speak. She nodded at the detectorist. "He knows a *few* words," she said. "Ask him who's a pretty boy."

The man took a step closer to Millie, and increased the pitch of his voice by an octave or two. "Who's a pretty boy, then? Who's a pretty boy, then?"

Millie winced as Reuben's claws dug into her flesh. "I suppose I am, although I prefer the term handsome, but in answer to your question — Reuben is a pretty boy! Reuben is a pretty boy!"

His eyes widening and his smile transforming into a worried frown, the man stared curiously at the cockatiel. "What did he say?" he asked. "That was… out of the ordinary. He didn't even sound like a bird."

Millie sighed. "It's just learned behaviour," she said. "It's his party trick."

"Well, it's a heck of a trick," said the detectorist. "That was very curious. Very curious indeed."

"He's a curious bird," said Millie, crouching to get a better view of the hole the man had dug. "Now you've seen my curiosity — how about you show me yours? Did you find something exciting, or do you always dance around holes you've dug in the sand?"

The man gave Reuben another intrigued look, and turned his attention to the hole. "If I tell you, do you promise you won't tell anybody else?"

Millie made the shape of an X on her chest. "Cross my heart. I won't tell a soul."

Dipping into the pouch which hung from his waist, the man withdrew a circular yellow disc which glinted in the sunlight. "Gold!" he said. "It's only my third time metal detecting, and I've found gold!"

"What is it?" said Millie. "A coin?"

Rotating the disc between his fingers, the man smiled. "Yes. And there's another in the hole I've just dug." He pointed to the hard-packed sand which made up the walls of the small excavation. "Look," he said. "Sticking out of the side."

Sure enough, peaking from the sand was the rim of a coin, the yellow metal vivid against the dark sand. "It's your lucky day," said Millie. "Two gold coins."

"There's no luck involved," said the detectorist. "That storm cleared inches of sand from the beach and shifted a lot of sand from the top of the dunes, too. Metal that was too deep to find in the past can now be detected. I used my head, though — while all the other detectorists are searching the areas of the beaches where the tourists drop their jewellery and money, I came to this empty stretch of beach. I checked the history books — this part of the coast was notorious for shipwrecks before the lighthouse was built. Some of the ships were said to have been carrying great wealth, and it seems I've found some of it — and I'm sure that's not the last of it, either."

"Shipwrecks up here?" said Millie. "We're standing in sand dunes. Even a very high tide won't reach this spot."

"The history books say there was a superstorm," he said. "Hundreds of years ago. The sea pushed two galleons almost a mile inland and smashed them to smithereens. Most of their cargo was never retrieved, and one of those boats was said to have been carrying French gold. It seems the storm we've just had has made it possible to find some of that gold. This piece of beach might make me rich." He paused. "I shouldn't have said that, should I? Now you'll want some of the gold to keep my secret." He gave a deep sigh. "How does twenty-percent sound? You don't tell anybody about what I've found, and I'll give you twenty-percent of my finds."

Millie laughed. She didn't want to tell the man exactly how much money she'd inherited from the generations of witches who'd inhabited Windy-dune Cottage before her, but she did want him to feel safe in the knowledge that she wasn't about to blackmail him. "I don't want any of your gold," she said. "It's all yours, and I crossed my heart — your secret is safe with me."

The man narrowed his eyes. "You don't want gold? What sort of person doesn't want gold?"

Millie smiled. "I had a bit of luck myself," she said. "I was left an inheritance from a family I never knew I had. You keep your gold. I don't need it."

Tension visibly leaving his shoulders, the man bent over and prised the gold coin from the wall of the hole. He placed it in his pouch, and stared along the beach. "If I want to find more," he said. "I'd better get moving. Eventually the wind will replace the sand which the storm removed, and make the gold impossible to find again, but before that, other detectorists are certain to be along. I need to work quickly — so if you don't mind…"

"Rude," whispered Reuben in Millie's ear. "Forget the muffins. Definitely give him a fancy."

Millie smiled at the man. "Of course," she said. "I'm Millie, by the way. Millie Thorn. I live in Windydune cottage — the cottage you can see up there, above the sand dunes."

"I've heard of you," said the man. "You inherited the lighthouse, too, didn't you? After Albert Salmon had committed suicide. He left it to you."

Millie nodded. The fact that Albert had been murdered was not common knowledge, and the fact that he'd written his suicide note and changed his will *after* he had died, was *certainly* not common knowledge — the human population of Spellbinder Bay would probably not have reacted well to the fact that ghosts walked among them. Especially ghosts who changed their wills after shrugging off their mortal coils. She smiled. "That's me," she confirmed.

"I'm Tom," said the man. "Tom Temples, and I live alone in a tiny rented apartment on the outskirts of town. I'm hoping this gold will change that, though. I'm not getting any younger, I retired last year, and my pension isn't good. This gold may be the chance I need to finally own a home."

"Well, Tom," said Millie, breaking into a gentle jog. "I wish you luck!"

"Cheerio," said Tom, "and thank you for

promising to keep my secret. Some of those other detectorists can be very jealous. Very jealous indeed. Especially when a beginner finds gold. Some of them have been doing it for decades and never had a whiff of the yellow stuff. They'd contract the dreaded gold fever if they heard about this spot! And who knows what that could lead to?"

Chapter 2

Millie allowed the makeup brush to drop from the air, where it hovered next to her cheek, as Reuben fluttered in through the open roof window and landed on the bed next to her.

The cockatiel looked up at his witch. "I saw you!" he said. "You were using magic to control that brush! You said you'd never use magic for frivolous tasks! You said that witches like Judith, who use magic for the simplest of jobs, are lazy! Hah! Caught you red-handed, you lazy witch!"

"I was practising," countered Millie. "That's all. Anyway, you can't accuse *anybody* of being lazy. You spend most of your life in front of the television."

Reuben hopped along the bedcovers. "Not today! I've had a wonderfully exhilarating day on the beach, watching Tom Temples digging up treasure. He found loads more after you left — coins and jewellery. *And* he shared his lunch with me. I think he found it odd that a cockatiel would enjoy chicken sandwiches. He murmured something about cannibalism, although I fail to see how he came to that conclusion. Chickens and cockatiels are very different creatures! I can fly, for a start!"

Millie narrowed her eyes. "You didn't speak to him, did you, Reuben?"

The cockatiel looked away. "I may have offered the suggestion that mayonnaise would have livened his sandwiches up a little, but that aside — no. I didn't say much. Not much at all."

"You'll get us in trouble, Reuben!" warned Millie. "You shouldn't speak in front of non-paranormal people!"

"Relax... take it easy, witchy woman," said Reuben. "The concealment spell covering Spellbinder Bay will make him think there was absolutely nothing out of the ordinary about discussing the merits of a petrol engine over a diesel engine with a cockatiel."

"The concealment spell —" Millie paused and took a deep breath. "Wait! What did you say? You discussed engines with him, too?"

"Yes. TV shows, also. He likes Springer, I like Kyle. We agreed to disagree," said Reuben. "Although I know who's right. Springer is a has been. Kyle is the present *and* the future of cringe television."

"I hope that concealment spell works as well as it's supposed to. For your sake," said Millie, retrieving her makeup brush from the floor.

"It works as well as that stuff you're plastering on

your face to conceal that pimple which burst into life overnight," said the bird. "I can hardly see it! Your fake face works wonders, Millie. Your vampire date will never know what despicable horrors lurk on your chin."

"Two things," said Millie, gathering her hair into a ponytail. "One — it's not a fake face. It's *my* face, with the best features enhanced. Two — I'm not going on a *date* with George. I'm going to a pub quiz in The Fur and Fangs, and Judith will be there, too. We're a team. It couldn't be further from a date!"

"Oh yes," said Reuben. "The famous pub quiz team. *The Dazzling Duo* — although there are three of you."

"There was only two of us when we named ourselves," said Millie. "And when George joined us, he thought we should keep the name. He thinks it's ironic. Or something." She shook her head. "I don't know. I think we should just change duo to trio."

"Wouldn't work," said Reuben. "You'd need to change the word *dazzling* to one beginning with the letter T." He paused. "Wait. I've got a better idea. How about *The Dazzling Duo and the tag along vampire who only became interested in pub quizzes when he discovered the witch he fancies partakes in the Monday night activity herself.* It doesn't exactly roll off the beak, but it's an accurate representation of the situation."

With a low laugh, Millie threw the makeup brush at Reuben, who chortled and flew to the bedside table. "Then he's a vampire with taste, *if* that is the case," she said.

Reuben fluffed up his plumage, and gazed at the envelope propped up against the lamp next to the bed. "Are you ever going to open it?" he asked.

Butterflies bloomed in Millie's stomach, as they did every time she thought of the letter. "Eventually," she said. "Maybe, I mean."

Reuben cocked his head to the side. "Don't you want to know what your mother had to say? Don't you want to know who your father is? Henry said he still lives in Spellbinder Bay — it could be anyone."

"Don't you whisper a word of that to anybody," warned Millie. "Only me, you and Henry know about the letter. I want to keep it that way. Until I've come to terms with things."

"I promised I wouldn't," said Reuben. "My word is my honour… but if I was you — I'd open it. I'd want to know."

Millie slumped onto the bed, her unfinished ponytail falling free. "I spent my whole life thinking my conception had been because of a short-lived fling my mother had with a man she hardly knew. She told me that she couldn't find my father to tell him she was pregnant. Then I find out that it was all a lie, *and* I find out it was a lie from a building masquerading as a man, who my mother called to her deathbed. I wish she'd told me, not some magical man building."

"Henry's not a building, Millie," said Reuben. "He's the manifestation of the magic contained within Spellbinder Hall — the human face of the building, if you will. You must understand? It's hardly genius level magic."

"And that's all you got from what I just said?" asked Millie. "A debate on Henry Pinkerton's status as a building or a man? Which I understand perfectly well, thank you very much."

"What do you want me to say?" said Reuben. "You tell me how upset you are about it on a weekly basis. It's all very sad, but I wish you'd just open the letter. Prising open that envelope is the only way you'll get closure."

Millie gazed at the ceiling. "You and Henry told me that my mother's energy is contained within the walls of this cottage."

"In the coven cavern beneath the cottage, to be more precise," said Reuben. "And to be even preciser, in the cauldron in the cavern, but yes, your mother's energy, along with all the dead witches who have ever lived in this cottage, is contained within these walls."

"That's why I won't open the letter," said Millie. "I can feel her presence here, and I…"

Reuben hopped onto Millie's chest, and gazed into her eyes, his head leaning to the left. "And you what?"

Millie smiled. "I talk to her, Reuben. I ask her if she can hear me."

"Maybe she can," said Reuben. "I don't know how dead witch energy works. All I know is that I can feel Esmeralda's energy here, too. It's comforting, isn't it? To feel the presence of somebody you cared for. And who cared for you."

Running a fingernail over the bird's grey plumage, Millie smiled. "It is, Reuben," she said. "I just wish she could answer me when I speak to her."

"What would you ask her?" said Reuben. "If she appeared in front of you right now."

Millie closed her eyes. "Before I asked her who my father was, I'd ask her if she regretted becoming pregnant with me. I'd ask her if I was conceived from love, or from… something else. I'd look into her eyes as she answered, and I'd know the truth. Her eyes always told the truth, even when she tried to tell me her illness wasn't going to kill her. I can't get honest answers like that from a letter, Reuben. All I can get is the name of a man who doesn't even know he's my father, and probably doesn't want to be. Maybe the letter is best left unopened. Maybe it will cause less pain that way. Less pain for me, and less pain for the man who's my father."

Reuben ran the edge of his beak along Millie's finger. "I'm sorry," he said. "For trying to persuade you to open the letter. I don't think things through sometimes. It's my weakness. I won't mention it again. I promise. I hope I haven't upset you."

"Don't be silly," said Millie. "You haven't upset me. But I could do with your help?"

"Anything," said Reuben.

"My red heels or my new comfy biker boots?"

"With jeans?"

Millie nodded. "And a white t-shirt."

"The biker boots," said Reuben. "The bloodsucker will love them, seeing as he rides a motorbike."

"I'm not dressing for George," said Millie. "I'm dressing for me. Maybe I'll wear the heels."

George winked. "Nice boots!" he said. "Hoping for a ride with me, were you?"

Millie tossed her ponytail over her shoulder. "In your dreams," she laughed. "I put them on without thinking. They're comfy. That's my only reasoning behind wearing them!"

Her blonde hair bunched high on her head, Judith pushed a pint of beer across the circular table top towards Millie. "You're a drink behind us. George and I have been googling capital cities. There's always one of those in the quiz."

George put his phone in his pocket and shuffled along the upholstered bench, which formed a semi-circle around the small table. "Venezuela — Caracas. Sit down and drink your beer," he said. "The quiz begins in fifteen minutes. You always do better after a pint."

Sitting down next to George, Millie brought the glass of froth topped amber liquid to her nose, and took a sniff. "Vampire's Vengeance?" she said.

Judith shook her head. "No. This is a new beer from the not so world famous Fur and Fangs microbrewery — it's called The Wandering Witch. It's nice. Very malty. Try it."

Millie gazed around the pub as she took a sip of the potent liquid. The pub owners, Stan — a werewolf, and his vampire wife, Mary, couldn't have made the pub more traditionally British if they'd tried. A place where paranormal folk mingled with normal people — the latter oblivious to the fact that they shared their little town with all manner of species — the Fur and Fangs harked back to a time in which Millie sometimes wished she had lived.

From the tall open hearth stone fireplace, decorated with horse brasses and old military badges, to the solid oak bar, behind which hung a row of pewter tankards — each belonging to one of the locals who took their real ale more seriously than the average customer, the pub oozed community spirit.

With no televisions interfering with the friendly hum of conversation, The Fur and Fangs was a pleasant place to spend some time, and Millie licked her lips appreciatively as she swallowed her beer. "Very nice," she said. "It's got a fruity tang to it."

"That's good to know," said a deep voice from her side. "That's the sort of response I was hoping for. I'm glad you like it."

Millie smiled up at Stan, who held a full pint in his hand, his thick beard dotted with beer foam. "You've done a great job," she said. "It's really tasty."

"I hope you've got room for one more," said Stan, placing the fresh glass in front of Millie. "This is a gift from the gentleman at the table next to the window over there. He wanted to buy you a drink, and I took the liberty of choosing another Wandering Witch. He didn't want to interrupt you and your friends, so he asked me to bring it over. He told me you'd know why he bought it for you. He said it was a thank you."

George picked up a cardboard beer coaster, and tore at the edges. "She's got a male admirer, huh?" he said, surveying the room. "Which one was it, Stan?"

"The elderly chap at the small table," said Stan, making his way back towards the bar. "The one with the big smile on his face."

George dropped the coaster, and grinned. "An elderly admirer? How lovely."

Millie looked across the room, and waved. "He's not an admirer," she said. "He's just a nice guy who I promised to keep a secret for."

"What secret?" said Judith.

"The clue is in your question," smiled Millie. "It's a secret." She stood up. "I'm going to go and say thank you to him."

"The quiz is starting soon," said George. "Hurry. We have a good chance of winning this week. Two of the Spellbinder Starlets have gone down with food poisoning, so the rest of the team have pulled out of the quiz, too. They tried to blame it on the nursing home kitchen, but I went out for a drink last night with one of the nurses who work there, and she told me that some of the residents have been bringing in kebabs from that horrible greasy place on Harbour Street."

"Oh," said Millie. "Sounds awful. Poor women, I hope they get better soon." She lifted an eyebrow. "Who's this nurse, then? The one you went for a drink with?"

George tapped the side of his nose, the glint in his hazel eyes matching the mischievousness of his smile. "You've got your secret. I've got mine."

"Fair enough," said Millie, turning her back on the table and weaving a route through the crowd, towards the man near the window. She wasn't jealous. Of course she wasn't. *Was she?*

"Tom," she said with a smile, as she reached the table. "Thank you for the drink. I really appreciate it, but you wouldn't have been interrupting anything if you'd brought it over to me yourself."

"I didn't want to go ruining you young folk's fun," he smiled. "Are you three a team in the quiz? You, your boyfriend and the young blonde lady?"

"What?" said Millie. "Yes. No!"

Tom narrowed his eyes.

"I mean, yes, we're a team," said Millie. "But, no… he's not my boyfriend."

"Oh," said Tom. "The way he watched you when you walked over here gave me the wrong impression. I do apologise."

Millie glanced over her shoulder. George was busy studying Judith's phone with her. Looking up more capital cities, no doubt. "No problem," she said. "Anyway… how did your search go today? Did you find much more gold?"

Tom's face broke into a wide smile. "That's why I'm in the pub on a Monday night!" he said. "I'm celebrating! I found a lot more, but the less I say about it in public, the better." He leaned across the table, and lowered his voice. "The walls have ears."

"Oh, right, of course," said Millie. "I won't mention it again."

"I'll tell you one thing, though," said Tom, his voice still low. "There's plenty of gold in that sand! I found a woman's gold ring, too. I handed it in to the sergeant at the police station in case it was lost recently. I'll get it back if it's not claimed within a few months. He didn't seem too interested, though, that sergeant — he just took the ring from me and scribbled a few notes on a sheet of paper."

"I'm sure he'll take care of it," said Millie. "I know Sergeant Spencer quite well. He's busy with other matters at the moment — he's taking a look at unsolved cases which occurred before he moved to the town, I'm sure he'll get around to filing the ring away properly."

Tom sat back in his seat. "A busy man. I can accept that." He took a sip of beer. "That little bird of yours didn't follow you straight home, did he?"

"Erm… no," said Millie, heat rising in her cheeks. "He's well trained, though… he always flies home eventually."

"I seem to recall having an interaction of some

sort with him," said Tom. "But when I try and remember, it all goes fuzzy.... must be the gold fever, hey?" He smiled. "Or my age."

Or the concealment spell, thought Millie, with a hidden sigh of relief. She smiled. "He probably squawked so much, he sent you mad," she laughed. "He likes the sound of his own voice."

"Odd, though," said Tom, staring into his pint. "When I try to recall the image of him, all I can think of doing is changing my old diesel car for a petrol version. They're far better for the environment, you know? And the power difference is remarkable!"

"Oh, right," said Millie. "Well, thanks for the drink, Tom, but the quiz will be starting —"

"Excuse me, Millie," said a voice from behind her. "I've got an order for this table."

Millie stepped aside, and Mary placed a plate loaded with sandwiches on the table in front of Tom. "Chicken sandwiches," she said.

"With mayonnaise?" asked Tom.

"Plenty of it," said Mary, "just the way you asked for."

"Funny, isn't it?" said Tom, when Mary had scurried back to the bar. "How does a man get to my age without trying mayonnaise in a chicken sandwich? I've had a terrible craving for it since I left the beach today. I've never so much as considered it as a sandwich option before... must be the salt air, hey? It makes a man hungry."

"Indeed," said Millie, silently cursing Reuben. "Thanks again, Tom, but I must be going —"

"Ah! There you are, Tom Temples!" boomed a voice, as the door slammed shut behind the man who'd burst into the pub. "Or should I say Tom Midas? The man with the golden touch?"

Tom looked up at Millie.

"I didn't tell a soul!" said Millie. "I promise!"

Chapter 3

"I know you didn't," said Tom, turning to face the doorway. "You've got an honest face."

"Celebrating are you, Tom?" said the newly arrived man, his greying hair combed in a way which managed to conceal half of the fact that he was balding, but left the other half proudly reflecting the lights hanging from the pub ceiling. "Celebrating your gold coin find?"

Tom looked at the contents of the table top. "Celebrating with a sandwich and a pint? That's hardly pushing the boat out, is it?"

"You usually have a half-pint!" spat the man, approaching the table and invading Millie's personal space. "I've seen you in here before, sitting alone in the corner sipping your lady's drink! They say the first sign of somebody coming into wealth is a change in their habits!"

"What makes you think I've found gold coins, Eric?" said Tom. "And if it's the one-pound-twenty price difference between a pint and a half, then that's hardly evidence, is it?"

Eric folded his arms and narrowed his eyes, his bushy eyebrows forming a snowy mono-brow. "I popped in to see Pawn Shop Pete tonight. I wanted him to look at the Roman coin I'd found, but Pete told me that a certain man visited him this evening asking for a rough valuation of the gold coins he'd found. When Pete informed this particular gentleman that he would be rich when he sold them, he left the shop with a spring in his step and a wobble in his buttocks — Pawn Shop Pete's words, not mine!" He glanced at Millie, and gave a quick shake of his head. "Certainly not my words."

Millie smiled. "Why are you so angry?" she said. "So what if Tom *has* found gold? You should be happy for him. Not that I'm saying he has, of course."

"We detectorists are a close-knit bunch," said Eric. "We like to keep each other informed about the forgotten treasures we discover beneath our little piece of England!"

Tom laughed. "Surely you mean the detectorists in your little club are a close-knit bunch, Eric. The little club which is full to capacity, and *definitely* has no room for one more person — especially a beginner who owns a top of the range detector, which just so happens to be better than everyone else's in the club, giving him the chance to outshine the veteran members and embarrass them with his superior finds!"

Eric took a deep breath in, and puffed out his chest. "It was nothing to do with the fact that you had purchased a Garrett ATX Extreme Pulse Induction metal detector, Tom Temples! The club was full when you applied to join last week. The Spellbinder Sand Diggers was at full capacity, Tom! The committee had a meeting, and decided they couldn't allow you to join due to overpopulation in the ranks, not because you own a machine which costs the same as a small used family car!" He glanced at Millie, and lowered his voice. "It *is* a good machine, though. I'll say that much."

"Full to capacity? Committee meeting?" laughed Tom. "There's only three of you in that club, you daft old sod!"

Eric shuffled his feet, and looked at the floor. When he lifted his face, he was forcing a smile. "Tom Temples," he said. "I'm here on behalf of The Spellbinder Sand Diggers. It would be my pleasure to offer you a place in our club! We've made space for one more member! Welcome aboard, old chap!"

Millie spotted movement through the window behind Tom, the uppermost portion pushed open to allow a cooling breeze into the room.

A checkered flat cap and a bright red baseball cap ducked out of sight as Millie smiled at their owners. "Are they with you, Eric?" she said. "It seems like they are."

Eric waved a frustrated hand at the window. "I told them to stay out of sight!"

"Well, I'm glad the whole club is here," said Tom, turning in his seat and rapping on the glass with his knuckles. "Hello?" he yelled, "are you there? We know you are!"

The two caps appeared slowly, the flat one adorning the head of a pensionable aged gentlemen, and the baseball cap teetering on the skull of a younger man with curly black hair. They nodded in unison.

"Can you hear me from out there?" demanded Tom.

The two heads nodded once more. "Just about," said the older man. "I'd appreciate it if you could speak up just a little, though. My ears aren't as good as they once were. The doctor says it's age related, but my wife insists some warm olive oil will sort it out."

Tom sighed. "Try the oil." He stared at Eric. "Thank you for the offer, members of The Spellbinder Sand Diggers," he said, his voice raised. "But I'd rather douse my testicles in cheap brandy and set fire to them, than join your club of losers! You'll never know where I found my gold, and there's plenty more where it came from, too! I didn't tell Pawn Shop Pete where I'd found it, so good luck searching — it's a very big beach, and I'll have emptied the hot-spot of gold before you get anywhere near it!"

Eric bristled with rage, and Millie took a nervous step away from him. "How dare you!" he yelled.

"You'll regret not taking us up on our offer! We'll find out where you found that gold, Tom Temples! You mark my words! You've messed with the wrong club! We're not the softies from The Bexington Beach Burrowers — we're The Spellbinder Sand Diggers! And we don't mess around! You'd better watch your back!"

"Okay! That's enough," said Stan, hurrying across the pub floor and grabbing Eric's elbow in a large hand. "We can accept a little shouting in The Fur and Fangs, but we do not accept threats towards our patrons! It's time for you to leave!"

"You get a badge, Tom — when you join!" urged Eric. "And a free cup of coffee or tea, with a biscuit, at meetings! A homemade biscuit! Often with a choice of raisins or chocolate chips! Sometimes both, Tom. Sometimes both!"

"No thank you," retorted Tom. "I can buy all the biscuits and badges I like from now on!"

Eric allowed himself to be escorted to the door as the rest of the customers looked on. As Stan pushed the door open, and guided the grumbling man through it, Eric gave one final warning. "Watch your back, Tom Temples! Watch your back! You've been warned!"

"Sorry about that, ladies and gents," said Stan, as the door slammed shut. "Now he's out of the way, let's have a little quiz!"

"Gold fever," said Tom, over the excited chatter of the other customers. "An awful thing."

"Are you okay?" said Millie. "You look a little shaken."

Tom smiled. "I'm fine. Now off you go, and enjoy your quiz, young lady. I'll finish my sandwich and go home for an early night — I'm going back into the dunes at sunrise tomorrow, before those idiots *do* manage to find my spot."

"I KNOW IT!" SAID MILLIE. "I ACTUALLY KNOW IT!"

George scratched his nose. "Are you sure? This could win it for us. I haven't seen any of the other teams write an answer with any confidence."

Millie took a gulp of beer and wiped her mouth. "I spoke to Aunty Hannah on the phone yesterday," she began.

"In Australia!" said Judith.

"Yes," said Millie, "and after I'd spoken to her and Uncle James, they put Peter on the phone! He's settling into his new country wonderfully, and he loves school! He's only six, but he's really bright — he told me all about what they were learning regarding the history of Australia, and he was very proud that he knew the name of the first Prime Minister!" She cupped her hand around George's ear, and whispered. "Edmund Barton. Write it down."

George put pen to paper, his pupils dilating as he looked at Millie. "Are you sure? This could win it for us."

"I trust my little nephew," said Millie. "Write it down. We'll win the star prize! We'll win the turkey crown from Edward and Son's Butchers, and the free pint of ale each from the Fur and Fangs microbrewery range — prize not transferable to outside brewery supplied ales."

George scribbled on the paper. "Say what you want, but it's better than last month's prize — a basket of scented candles and a sandwich each."

"Prize not transferable to the hot food menu!" laughed Judith.

"I'm glad we didn't win last month," smiled George. "But I'd like tonight's prize."

George lifted his head as a girl seated at a table near the fireplace called his name. "Got the answer?" she teased. "How about you share it with us? We'd make it worth your while!"

The four women at the table burst into laughter, making George smile. "I'm sorry ladies," he said, "you're on your own — I want the prize tonight! You know I'm a wee bit partial to a nice plump bird!"

The girls broke into another round of laughter, their eyes fixed firmly on George. Millie had become accustomed to girls taking a fancy to George, but for a reason she couldn't *quite* put a finger on, she didn't much like it.

She stared at George. "What terrible flirting. That was embarrassing. And probably sexist. Is one of those girls your *nurse*?"

George displayed his white teeth in an over-exaggerated grin, his eyes dancing with fun. "Wouldn't you like to know? Like I said earlier, you have your secret, and I have mine."

"You all heard my secret!" said Millie, fixing George with a scowl. "The whole pub heard the argument about Tom's gold! That *was* my secret."

Running a hand through his thick dark hair, George sat back in his seat and handed the team's sheet of paper to Mary as she passed their table, collecting quiz answers. "Maybe I like having a secret," he said.

Millie narrowed her eyes. "Fair enough," she conceded. "Keep your secret. I don't care."

George smiled. "I know that stare, Millie Thorn," he said. "Are you trying to read my thoughts?"

"No, George Brown," she said, quickly tuning out of the signals she was receiving from numerous sources in the room. "I promised I wouldn't attempt to read anyone's thoughts unless it was important. Your thoughts are safe in your head." She gulped two fingers of beer. "They're probably better off trapped inside that thick skull than they are let loose in public, anyway."

George drained the last of his beer, and laughed. "Good," he said. "I don't want my *juicy* secret getting out."

"Children!" snapped Judith. "Quit the bickering. Stan's about to read out the answers and announce the winners."

Stan stood at the bar reading out the answers, to

groans and excited muttering from the assembled teams, and when he announced The Dazzling Duo as the winners, the other teams gave a polite round of applause as Judith collected the turkey crown and three vouchers for a free pint of beer.

"Thank you!" she shouted, as she made her way back to the table, plopping the wrapped meat in front of Millie as she sat down. "There," she said. "You take it home… that fridge of yours needs some healthy food in it, and I thought maybe you'd like to invite your fellow pub quiz team members for a meal at your cottage?"

"That would be nice!" said George. "Will there be roast potatoes?"

"And cranberry sauce?" said Judith. "You can't have turkey without cranberry sauce."

Rolling her eyes, Millie smiled. "Do you two fancy coming to mine for a meal on Wednesday night? I'm doing turkey with cranberry sauce and roast potatoes."

"That would be splendid," said George. "I'll put it in my diary."

"Diary!" laughed Judith. "Since when does a man who spends most of his days whizzing around the countryside on his motorbike need a diary? People with jobs and responsibilities need diaries — not wealthy vampire gallivants!"

"Don't pick on me," smiled George. "Anyway, Millie could be accused of the same thing. She hasn't done anything meaningful with her life since arriving in Spellbinder Bay!"

Millie tossed a beer mat at George. "Apart from solving a murder," she said. "That was pretty meaningful. And the very fact that I live in this town is the reason that the door to The Chaos remains sealed. My magical energy is quite *meaningful*, it seems."

"You don't need to *do* anything, though," said George. "The door to the other dimension remains sealed because you come from the same bloodline of witches who sealed it in the first place. It takes no effort on your behalf. And anyway, it's never been *fully* sealed… things still sneak through every so often. When I say meaningful, I mean… meaningful — as in something that will fill your life with meaning."

"I've been learning magic," said Millie. "That's meaningful. I've spent hours in the cavern beneath my cottage, trying to fix the magic I broke in Lillieth's dress."

"Any progress?" said Judith.

"I think so," said Millie. "But I need Lillieth to come back to the bay before I can test it. Mermaids are rare, it's not like I can fish one out of the sea, ask her to try the dress on, and see if she grows legs."

"She'll come back when she's ready," said George. "Then you can test her dress, and offer her your newly acquired lighthouse to live in, which is a very kind gesture in my opinion."

"I feel sorry for her," said Millie. "We accused her of murder, and I ruined her magic dress, *and* she said even when she wears the dress, she never feels safe enough to venture far away from the sea. What better place for her to live in than a lighthouse which is as close to the sea as you can be without being *in* it?"

"It's very kind of you, Millie," said Judith. "I'm sure Lillieth will be grateful, but George has a point — you have all that money, yet the only impressive thing you've bought with it is a car, and you spend your days in your cottage or on the beach. I think it would be good for you to have a purpose. Have you thought any more about what Henry suggested? Joining me?"

"Being a part-time teacher in Spellbinder Hall?" said Millie. "I don't know. You enjoy doing it because you've had your magic for a lot longer than me, Judith. You're better at it. What can I possibly teach paranormal kids that their own parents haven't already taught them?"

"It's not just paranormal stuff they learn," said Judith. "And it's not just witches you'll be teaching — they don't all need to learn magic. You have plenty of life experience which would benefit them, and you make a mean cake. You could teach them how to bake! The school has the facilities for cookery lessons, but they haven't been used in years. Not since Marjory Timkins developed witch dementia and turned herself into a soufflé mix in front of a class of nine-year-olds."

"Oh no!" said Millie. "Was she okay?"

"She would have been," said Judith, her eyes

dropping to her drink. "But one of the kids thought it would be funny to put her in the oven. Gas mark seven. She was in there for eleven minutes before another teacher popped into the classroom and removed her. It was too late to save her, though."

"How awful!" said Millie.

"Did she rise?" said George.

"George!" said Judith. "That was horrible of you, but I doubt she rose after just eleven minutes."

"Not long enough," confirmed Millie. "You'd need at least twenty minutes in a hot oven for a decent risen soufflé."

"So?" said Judith, smiling at Millie. "Will you do it? Teach baking at Spellbinder Hall?"

Millie drained the last of her beer. "After that horror story?" she said. "Really?"

"Yes, really," said Judith. "Or at least promise you'll consider the idea."

With a sigh, Millie relented. "I'll think about it," she said, standing up and tucking the turkey crown under her arm. "But right now, I want to go home. I've drunk way too many beers, and I want to be up early for my run along the beach."

"After your run," said Judith, "would you mind coming to the police station? Dad has asked for my help with something, and I'm sure he'd appreciate your help, too. He thinks you're some sort of Sherlock Holmes type since you solved Albert Salmon's murder."

"Not another murder?" said Millie. "I haven't heard anything about a murder."

Judith shook her head. "No. There are no mad murderers running around the bay," she confirmed. "I think he wants help with his cold cases. There seems to be a lot of unsolved crimes in the Spellbinder Police records. Too many for him to get through on his own."

Millie shrugged. What George had said was true. She *didn't* have anything meaningful to do with her days, and since dragging herself from the junk food devouring doldrums she'd found herself in during the past few months, she needed something to focus on. She nodded. "Okay," she said. "I'll help."

"Great!" said Judith. "It's a date! I'll meet you at the police station at eleven o'clock."

Chapter 4

Her head sore and her stomach protesting, Millie had quickly given up arguing when Reuben had announced that he wasn't joining her for the morning jog. Upon insisting he had more important things to do, Millie had left the cockatiel to his own devices, and forced herself out of the front door and into the sea air.

It seemed that Wandering Witch beer had quite the bite in its broomstick, and Millie struggled to get up to pace as she wove a route through the sand dunes and onto the beach.

Her lungs full of revitalising air, and a cool breeze on her face, it didn't take long until she felt a little better, and settled into an acceptable running rhythm, following the base of the sand dunes towards the end of the peninsula a mile away.

With firm sand beneath her feet, warm morning sun on her face, and the rolling ocean to her left, her head cleared further as she covered more ground, nearing the spot where she'd met Tom Temples the day before.

It was with little surprise that Millie noticed Tom as she edged around the curve of the shoreline. He'd said he was going back to the dunes at sunrise, and it seemed he'd been true to his word. Hunched over a hole dug in the sand on the slope of a dune, his shovel and metal detector laying amongst dune grasses and flowers, Tom remained motionless as he gazed into the hole he'd dug.

"Found something?" said Millie, approaching Tom from behind, her feet sinking into soft sand.

Tom moved quickly. Using his hands and forearms as scoops, he began refilling the hole with the pile of sand he'd excavated. "No!" he said, glancing over his shoulder. "No! This is an empty hole. There's nothing to see here!"

Standing behind him, Millie peered over Tom's shoulder. "When somebody says there's nothing to see — there's always something to see! What is it, Tom? What have you found?"

Tom scooped more sand back into the hole as Millie craned her neck for a better look. "I saw something!" said Millie. "Something white! It looks like a bone! What is it, Tom? What have you found?"

His face red, Tom looked up at Millie and sighed. "Okay," he admitted. "I have found something. Something I think might be very important, but what I've found needs to be reported, and *if* I report it, this section of the beach will be cordoned off and I won't be able to recover the rest of the gold which I know is still here."

Millie knelt in the sand next to Tom. "Now I'm really interested," she said. "What's in the hole, Tom?" She gasped. *Bones. Of course!* "Is it a body?" she whispered.

Tom reached for his shovel, and began excavating the hole again. "No, of course not," he said. "Well, not a human one, anyway. These remains are much older than a human. A lot older — I'd hazard a guess that they're from the Jurassic Period, considering the fact that Spellbinder Bay is on the Jurassic Coast."

Millie crouched lower, and began helping Tom excavate the hole, the sand cool against her hands. "A dinosaur?" she said. "Seriously? How exciting!"

Tom stopped digging and threw the shovel aside. "Not really," he said. He frowned, and shook his head. "No, that's not what I meant. It *is* exciting, and had I found it at any other time, I'd have been ecstatic. It's just that if I report it, all the gold in this area will be lost to me. The people who excavate this whole area looking for more dinosaurs will either pocket the gold or give it to a museum. Either way… it won't be mine."

Millie continued moving sand aside, widening the hole. As her fingers made contact with the cold hardness of bone, she brushed away the final layer of sand, and stared in morbid fascination into a sand-filled eye socket of the skull which had been partially revealed.

She stood up and grabbed the shovel from beside Tom, and began widening the hole further. "I'm sorry, Tom," she said, being careful to keep the sharp edges of the shovel away from bone, "but you *have* to report this. I've always been fascinated by dinosaurs — I loved them when I was a child. I had loads of books about them — and I've never seen anything like this in any book I've read." She threw the shovel aside, and knelt at the edge of the hole, staring at the huge skull. "I think you may have found a new species of dinosaur, Tom. This is very important! You *have* to report it, and if you don't, I will." She raised an eyebrow. "Who knows? If it is a new species, maybe they'll name it after you."

Tom stared at Millie. "Really?" he said. He tilted his head, and gazed at the skull. "Tomosaurus," he murmured. "It does roll off the tongue, doesn't it? Are you sure it's a new species?"

Millie stood up and took a step backwards. She estimated the hole to be a metre in diameter, and the skull filled most of it. At the base of the wide skull, the upper portion of the creature's spine was visible, and if the whole of the skeleton lay beneath the sand, Millie guessed the complete remains would be at least fifteen metres long. "Well... I've never seen anything like it," she said. "Look at it. Look at the size of the teeth compared to the head. You'd expect an animal which was this big to have had huge teeth, but these teeth are small, and they look sharp, and there must be hundreds of them!"

Tom stared at the creature. "And it has horns!" he said. "Tiny horns. Horns which look too small for such a huge head!"

Millie nodded her agreement. "It looks terrifying! I've never seen anything like it in all the books I've read. I think you've discovered something special here, Tom! How did you find it? Your metal detector won't find bone."

Grabbing the little pouch which hung from the belt on his waist, Tom gave it a shake. "Hear that jangling?" he asked. "I found all that gold this morning. Two of the coins were in this hole. That's how I found it."

"So, you've found plenty of gold?" said Millie. "Do you really need any more?"

Tom smiled. "I don't think you can ever have *too* much gold," he said. "But I get your point. I'll report the dinosaur remains to the relevant authorities. I'll come back and look for more gold when they've finished doing what they'll need to do."

"You'll report it today?" said Millie.

Tom reached into his pocket and withdrew his phone. "Right this moment," he promised. "You can wait with me until somebody arrives, if you like."

Judith greeted Millie at the front desk of the

police station, a stack of paperwork in front of her, and two mugs of coffee alongside her phone. "On time as always," she said with a grin. She glanced at her phone. "Actually, it's two minutes to eleven. You're early." She pushed one of the mugs towards Millie. "I was so sure you wouldn't be late, I made you a coffee knowing it wouldn't go cold."

Millie grabbed her mug and blew steam from the hot liquid. "I almost was late," she confessed. "But that's what happens when you discover the bones of a dinosaur previously unknown to the scientific community."

Puzzlement etched on her face, Judith stared at Millie. "What? You've done what, now?"

Millie laughed. "Tom Temples found it," she confessed. "While he was looking for gold coins on the beach, but I was there when the guy from the museum turned up. He was very excited! He says he's never seen anything like it. It's an unknown species, he reckons. A predator of some description, he thinks. He measured the skull and believes that if the whole skeleton is present, it could be the length of a bus!"

"How exciting!" said Judith.

Millie grinned. "That's exactly what I said. Tom wasn't as excited as me, though. He wanted to finish searching the area for gold, but he's got no chance of doing that now. He had to leave so he could take his car to the garage to have some work done, and the man from the museum has already begun some sort of legal procedure to get the area sealed off so they can begin digging. He told us we had to vacate the area immediately. Nobody's allowed anywhere near the site."

"And there was me thinking my morning was exciting because I managed to fry two eggs without any oil spitting out of the pan and burning my arm," said Judith.

"And very nice eggs they were, too," said Sergeant Spencer, appearing in the office doorway behind Judith. "My daughter keeps me well fed, I must admit."

"Good morning, Sergeant," said Millie.

Sergeant Spencer frowned, the laughter lines around his eyes forming deeper furrows. "Come on, Millie," he said. "I've told you before… you don't need to keep calling me that. Call me Dave, or David, at least."

Millie looked away. "It feels weird," she explained. "I called you Sergeant Spencer when I first moved to the bay, and it's hard to break the habit, especially while you're wearing your uniform and we're in the police station. It feels unprofessional."

Sergeant Spencer gave a bellowing laugh, and stared around the small area. "Unprofessional?" he said. "You don't work for me. Everything you do to help me is from the goodness of your heart. I'm the only copper in this town, and my little police station consists of two cells, an interrogation room, my office and the front desk you're standing at. The fact that the concealment spell keeps the rest of the police force from interfering in town business makes what I do here *far* from professional by normal policing standards. I think you calling me Dave is hardly going to break any more important guidelines!"

Millie smiled at the big man. "I'll try," she promised.

"Good!" said the sergeant, placing his hat on his head. He grabbed his fluorescent jacket from the back of a chair and glanced at his watch. "I'm sorry, girls," he said. "I can't help with the cold cases this morning. I've just received a phone call — it seems my services are required elsewhere. I've explained to Judith what I'd like you two to help me with, so I'm sure you won't need my input."

"Where are you going, Dad?" asked Judith. "Off to solve an urgent crime, or give Mrs Raymond a lift home from town with her shopping again? That woman takes advantage of you. She might be in her eighties, but she's as sharp as a razor-blade. She only hobbles around with that stick when it suits her. I've seen her power-walking along the cliff top with the rest of the pensioner's fitness club! I've even seen her walking through the sand dunes, and that's hard going by anybody's standards. Even if she *did* struggle to walk, she could afford a taxi home with her shopping… she's rich, Dad."

"And lonely," said Sergeant Spencer. "That fitness club is the only place she goes to socialise, and that's only a couple of times a week. I know what she's up to, but I don't care. I'm not just here to throw people in jail. I'm here to help, too." He snatched his car keys from the front desk, and winked at Judith. "Anyway, it's neither of those two things, clever-clogs. Mrs Raymond hasn't asked for my help all week. Somebody has discovered some sort of dinosaur skeleton on the beach, and I've got to waste my time setting up a cordon to keep people away. I've got far better things to be doing with my time. Bloody fossil hunters. What sort of boring person gets off on digging up long-dead animals? A sad sort of person — that's who!"

Millie cleared her throat and hid a smirk. "Actually," she said, "it was a metal detectorist who found it, and it was me who made him report it. I'm the person responsible for wasting your time, and I happen to think that dinosaurs are incredibly interesting."

His cheeks turning crimson, Sergeant Spencer nodded. "Yes, I suppose they are quite interesting, in their own peculiar way. Well done, Millie. You did the correct thing by making him report it to the relevant authorities." He glanced at a sheet of paper on top of a filing cabinet next to his office door. "It wasn't Tom Temples who found it by any chance, was it?" he asked.

"Yes," said Millie. "It was Tom."

Sliding a small potted plant aside, Sergeant Spencer picked up the sheet of paper, and a small white envelope next to it. He placed them on the front desk, next to Judith. "He was in here yesterday with a ring he'd found while metal detecting on the beach. I've been meaning to file the details and put the ring in the lost property cabinet. Could you do it for me, Judith? The ring is in the little envelope, and all the details of where he found it are written on the paper."

"Yes," sighed Judith. "I'll do that, as well as working through the big stack of cold cases you want my help with. I don't mind in the slightest. It's not like I'm your daughter helping you out for no pay, and not a fully paid police officer."

"Sarcasm?" said Sergeant Spencer, hurrying towards the door.

"A little," said Judith.

"Well, it's not like I'm your father allowing you to live in my house rent free, and not some wealthy landlord charging a fortune for the privilege of living beneath my roof," countered Sergeant Spencer, unable to disguise the humour in his eyes.

Judith picked up the little white envelope. "Consider it done," she said.

Sergeant Spencer exited the room, his laughter leaving with him. "Thank you," he called. "I'll see you two girls later! And remember to give Millie her identification card!"

"Identification card?" said Millie. "As in police identification?"

Judith smiled and slid a black leather wallet across the desk. "Your card and badge are inside," she said. "I have one, too. As far as everybody is concerned, you're now Detective Constable Millie Thorn. Don't ask me how he got them done, but I do know it had something to do with Henry Pinkerton, a magic spell and a box of doughnuts. They're totally legitimate. When you help Dad out in the future, you'll be able to pass as a police officer."

As the sound of the police car's engine roared into life outside, Judith opened the little envelope and tipped the contents onto the desktop. "I'll file this ring away for him, and then we'll go and interview some people," said Judith.

"We're going interviewing people?" said Millie. "I thought we'd be stuck in here doing paperwork."

Judith picked up the gold ring and held it to the light. "We're interviewing the families of missing people," she explained. "Not people who are suspected of crimes. Dad just wants to find out if any more information has come to light since the people went missing." She spun the ring between two fingers. "This has an inscription on the inside edge," she said. "Write this down, would you, please? It's in a foreign language. French, I presume."

Millie plucked a pen from the chipped mug masquerading as a stationary pot. "Go on," she said, the pen poised over the sheet of paper Sergeant Spencer had given Judith.

When Judith had finished painstakingly spelling out the words on the ring, Millie read them out loud. "*Je t'aimerai pour toujours*," she said. "I can't remember any of my French from school, but considering the ring has a heart on it, I'd say it's a romantic phrase, whatever it means."

Judith slipped the ring back into the envelope.

"Somebody will be sad that they lost it," she said. "Give me ten minutes to file it away safely, and we'll go and do some interviews. Let's see if we can shed some light on some of Dad's missing person's cold cases. We'll take your lovely little car, I presume? Dad's taken the only police car we have." She looked away briefly, and picked at a thumbnail. "I bet your car is really nice to drive, isn't it? I bet it's *really, really* nice to drive with the roof down?"

Millie fished the car keys from her pocket and placed them in front of Judith. "Would you like to drive? It's really nice."

Judith smiled. "You've had that car for two weeks. I thought you'd never ask!"

Chapter 5

The first person on Judith's list of interviewees still lived in the same home she'd shared with her husband when he'd gone missing almost three decades ago. The large house occupied a few acres of land, built high on one of the steep hills overlooking the town.

The narrow winding lanes which led to the property gave Judith ample opportunity to enjoy Millie's car, and she laughed with pleasure as the wind ruffled her hair while she took the final sweeping bend and turned into the gravel driveway.

"Did you enjoy it?" said Millie, getting her own hair back under control.

Judith brought the car to a halt next to a vibrant flowerbed, and applied the handbrake. "Did I enjoy driving a nineteen-seventy-two Triumph Spitfire, painted in original damson red, with the roof down, on the very type of British road it was originally designed to navigate? Let me think..." She gave a huge smile and pumped both fists above her head. "Hell yeah, I enjoyed it!"

Still laughing, Millie climbed out of her car and headed for the house. "We'd better wipe the smiles off our faces," she suggested. "We've come to speak with Mrs Danvers about her missing husband. I think we should appear more solemn."

Judith swiped a hand over her face, her smile replaced by a frown. "How's this?" she said.

"Very solemn," said Millie. "I like it."

"Can I help you?" came a voice from Millie's left. "I heard that awful sports car from a long way away. I hope there's a good reason for this interruption of my peace? I was enjoying a book in the back garden. One of the classics — The Wind in the Willows."

Millie turned to see the stern face of a woman who she estimated as being in her sixties, peering around the corner of the red brick building, her makeup perfect and her silver hair cropped short. She offered Mrs Danvers an apologetic smile. "I'm sorry for the interruption," she said. "We've come to talk with you about your missing husband. I believe Sergeant Spencer telephoned you and asked if it would be convenient?"

"Oh," said Mrs Danvers, looking the two girls up and down. "You must be plain-clothes detectives?" She gave the girls another look, her lips pursed. "Very plain-clothes indeed."

"No," said Millie. "We're not —"

Judith stepped past Millie. She opened the black wallet in her hand, and showed Mrs Danvers the badge inside. "Yes, Mrs Danvers. We're detectives. Could you spare some time to speak with us, or would you like us to return at a time more convenient to yourself?"

Mrs Danvers nodded. "Yes, of course I have time. Anything to get to the bottom of what happened to poor Colin. Would you mind following me around the back of the house — to the garden? I never allow dirty shoes in my home, and I'm not sure asking you to remove them would suffice. It's a warm day, and socks can become very sweaty. Who knows what manner of bacteria you might infest my beautiful wool Wilton with."

"The garden is fine," said Judith, casting a glance at her scruffy trainers. "We shouldn't need to take up too much of your time. We need to keep our records updated, and unless you can provide us with any more information since you spoke to the police after Mister Danvers initially went missing, this is purely a formality, so please don't get your hopes up."

Millie followed Judith and Mrs Danvers along the pathway leading behind the house, and into the large garden, populated by mature trees growing from the well-kept lawn.

Cast iron garden furniture filled a portion of the paved patio area adjacent to a small pond, and Millie took a seat next to Judith as Mrs Danvers plucked a half-finished wine bottle from an ice-bucket on the table, and filled her empty glass. "I'd offer you some, but you're on duty," she stated. "Some say it's too early in the day for alcohol, but I say as long as it's approaching noon — it's wine time."

"Indeed," said Judith, flipping open her file and removing the case paperwork pertinent to Mrs Danvers. She studied the paper for a moment, and looked up. "It says here that on the fourteenth of May, nineteen-eighty-nine, you came home from an evening with friends to discover your husband, a Colin Danvers, missing — along with a large proportion of his clothing, and the car. Is that correct, Mrs Danvers?"

Mrs Danvers sipped her wine, and gave a soft sigh. "Yes," she said. "It was awful. Whoever kidnapped him and stole our car *and* his belongings, did an awfully good job. There was no sign of a struggle, and the police failed to find any forensic evidence of an intruder."

"Kidnapped?" said Millie.

Mrs Danvers nodded. "Yes. Of course! The police didn't agree with me — they believed Colin had simply upped and left, but that was impossible. Absolutely impossible!"

"Why?" asked Millie, allowing her mind to tease a few of Mrs Danvers's emotions and thoughts from the violent barrage which spewed from the tormented woman's mind. Millie filtered the thoughts quickly, and focussed on the ones which would allow her a glimpse into how the real Mrs Danvers operated.

Her heart sinking with sadness, Millie softened her expression and gave Mrs Danvers a gentle smile. "Why was it impossible?"

"Because he hadn't finished his chores," said Mrs Danvers. "Colin wouldn't have left the dishes unwashed, and the clothes in the dirty laundry basket — no way! He enjoyed pleasing me, and he knew full well that not finishing chores was a sure-fire way to enrage me." She took a long swallow of wine, and shook her head. "No. Colin didn't just up and go! He was kidnapped — probably by a jealous man who wanted my heart for his own. But it hasn't worked — I've never taken another man, and I never will. Colin needs me to be strong for him. Colin is out there somewhere, wishing he was at home with me, cooking my meals and nurturing me. I'll wait for as long as it takes until he's found!"

Millie tuned out of Mrs Danvers's thoughts as another despairing salvo of emotions crossed the space between them. "I'm sorry," she said, trying not to concentrate too hard on the dejected eyes disguised by cheery bright blue eyeshadow. "I'm sorry he was kidnapped, and I'm sorry we couldn't find him."

Judith shifted in her seat, and scanned the paper she was holding. "Erm, Millie," she said, quietly. "We don't think he was kidnapped, it says here that the police who investigated at the time believed without doubt that he had left his —"

"But now we believe he was kidnapped," interrupted Millie. She glanced at Mrs Danvers. "I'm not sure we'll ever be able to find him, but I'm certain that wherever he is, he knows you're waiting for him, and that's giving him the strength he needs to go on. He'd want you to be happy, though, so make sure you try to enjoy your life, Mrs Danvers."

Her face crumpling, Mrs Danvers placed her glass on the table with a trembling hand, stood up, and stumbled towards Millie, bending at the waist and wrapping both arms around her. "Thank you," she sobbed. "You're the first person who's ever understood. I'll never forget you."

The older woman's tears hot against her cheek, Millie returned the hug. "Try and move on," she said. "Colin would want it."

JUDITH REMAINED QUIET FOR MOST OF THE SHORT journey to the next appointment, but as Millie parked the car outside the small terraced house, she broke her silence. "What happened back there?" she said. "That was strange."

Millie switched off the engine and closed her eyes. "Poor woman," she said. "I tuned in to her thoughts —"

"You said you were only going to do that in extreme circumstances," said Judith, with a frown.

"I know," said Millie. "And I've learned my lesson. I won't be doing it again in a hurry. I feel so sad. Mrs Danvers knows Colin left her, and she lives with that fact every waking minute of her life. She can't admit it to anybody, though, and it's breaking her — I could literally feel her despair. I could feel her emptiness — her will to live almost gone. She knew she'd treated Colin badly, and she regrets it. She's one of those people, though — the sort who can never be wrong, and I think she's totally lost her grip on reality."

"But she's living a fantasy," said Judith. "Surely that's not healthy?"

"It's healthier than fully admitting to herself that she was such a terrible wife her husband left her," said Millie. "I sensed that all she wanted was for somebody in authority to tell her what she wanted to hear. To tell her that her husband had been kidnapped, and that he had no choice in leaving her. She knew I didn't really believe it, but the words were enough to calm her mind. It may have been wrong of me, but I don't care — she's punished herself for twenty years, maybe she'll have a few easier years ahead of her. I hope she will — her mind is a very tormented place at the moment."

Judith put a hand on Millie's arm. "Don't tune into people's thoughts, Millie. It's not good for you."

Millie smiled. "I won't. I'm officially tuning out from this second on." She opened her door. "Come on, let's get this interview over with, so we can go home."

Judith stepped out of the car and consulted the paperwork in her file. "This should be simple. The mother vanished thirty years ago, both the police and the family believe she moved abroad, but no solid proof was ever found. This won't take long. It's another formality — we'll be in and out, and then maybe we could head back to your cottage and enjoy some wine on that lovely little patio of yours which overlooks the sea and is always in the sun — not that I'm jealous, of course."

Millie laughed. "You know you're welcome whenever you like, but yes, wine on the patio sounds like a grand idea!"

"So let's make this quick," said Judith, knocking on the door and taking a step backwards.

Within half a minute, the door was opened by a smiling man holding a dog's lead. He barked an order at the little dog at his feet, and the terrier stopped its yapping immediately, sitting dutifully as it stared up at the two visitors. "Yes?" asked the man. "Can I help you?"

"We're here to speak to you and your wife about the disappearance of your wife's mother," explained Judith. "I'm assuming you're Mister Harris?"

"Oh yes!" said the man. "But call me Chester, please. The sergeant phoned Jill last week and asked if it would be okay." He looked over his shoulder and lowered his voice. "I explained to the sergeant that Jill took a long time to come to terms with the sudden disappearance of her mother, so I'd appreciate it if you didn't raise her hopes about ever finding her."

"You have our word," said Millie. "This is purely a formality. We're here to see if you or your wife have any additional information we can add to the case notes — we're not here to deliver any fresh information of our own."

The man smiled. "Well, come on in. I was just about to take little Harry here for a walk, but that can wait."

"It won't take long," said Judith, following the man into the house, bending to pat the dog on the head. "Just a couple of quick questions."

Chester led them through the house and into the kitchen, where a woman wearing casual clothing stirred something on the stove. Chester went to her side and put a hand on her arm. "These young ladies have come to speak to us about your mother, Jill," he said.

"Oh! I wasn't expecting you today. The sergeant didn't give us a date," said Jill, placing a lid on the pot and wiping her hands on a tea-towel. "I'd have been a bit more presentable had I known you were coming, and I certainly wouldn't have been cooking!"

Millie sniffed the air, her nostrils tingling. "Curry?" she asked.

"Chester's favourite," Jill confirmed. "Lamb vindaloo. Not for the faint of heart." She moved an open newspaper from the table in the centre of the room. "Take the weight off your feet," she offered. "Tea, coffee? A cold drink?"

"No thank you," said Judith, sitting down. "We won't take up much of your time. This is just a formality. We need to keep our records updated."

"Naturally," said Jill, pushing at the little dog as he jumped up at her knee. She glanced at her husband. "Harry needs his walk," she said, taking a seat next to Millie. "I can deal with this. Why don't you take him out and see if you can get a glimpse of the monster on the beach?"

Chester shook his head and sat down. "No," he said, squeezing his wife's hand. "I'll take him later. He's been out once already today. This is important. The *so-called* monster can wait."

"Monster?" said Millie.

"That's what Mrs Jordan is calling it," said Jill. "She was walking her dog and managed to catch a glimpse of it before they cordoned off the area and hid it beneath a tent. The expert at the beach told her it's just a dinosaur, but Mrs Jordan telephoned me and said that men dressed in black arrived in a black van with tinted windows, and apparently people aren't allowed within half a mile of the skeleton. They wouldn't do that for a simple dinosaur skeleton, surely? It's all very exciting."

"We've been busy," said Judith, glancing at Millie. "We hadn't heard about all the fuss."

Chester tutted, his heavy eyelids drooping as he rolled his eyes. "It's just a dinosaur," he said. "We're on the Jurassic Coast. I'm sure there are plenty of monsters buried on that beach, and I'm sure it won't be the last one they find. The sooner they dig it up and take it away, the better. We don't want Spellbinder Bay turning into some sort of monster hunting carnival attraction! Not just that, either — there are rare protected flowers growing next to that beach — it would be a shame to have fossil hunters digging in the dunes and damaging them. It's illegal, too — those flowers are not to be disturbed! They're protected by law! They're more important than old bones."

Jill flicked a strand of long brown hair from her face. "You and your rare flowers!" She smiled at Millie. "Who'd have thought that such a beefy man would be so fond of seaside flowers? Well, I think the monster is exciting," she said. She looked at the file in front of Judith. "But I'm sure you've got far more important things to be doing than talking about monsters," she said with a smile. "Please carry on, and ask what you need to ask."

Judith opened the file and looked at the case notes. "I just need you to run over what happened, and tell me if there's anything more you need to add."

"No. There have been no more developments," said Jill, looking down. "My mother simply vanished. She lived here with me and Chester." She glanced around the kitchen. "This was her house. *Is* her house. Chester and I were married young — in our twenties, and when Chester lost his job we couldn't afford a home of our own, so Mum took us in. She was kind like that. *Is* kind like that."

Chester placed a big hand over his wife's. "She was very kind to me. Like you are."

Jill smiled. "I knew she was speaking to a man," she said. "A *married* man. A Canadian chap. They'd met when he was over here working, and had stayed in touch by phone and letters when he went home. He would send her gifts, too. I think she loved him. I'm sure she loved him, but I never expected her to just up and leave to be with him. Not without telling me, at least."

Judith scanned the case notes. "It says here that a suitcase full of clothes had gone from her bedroom, along with her passport. The police believe she moved to Canada to be with the gentleman in question, but failed to track him or your mother down. There was no record of her passport being used, but in those days security wasn't so tight," she said. "She could have left the country without leaving a trail."

"Mum was ill," Jill said. "Mentally ill. We're sure she suffered from bipolar, but back then the doctors still referred to it as manic-depression. It wasn't a nice thing to be diagnosed with, so Mum never saw a doctor about it. We think she had it, though. *Has* it. Some of the choices she made in life must have been down to an illness. They'd have made no sense otherwise."

"She was always making rash decisions," said Chester. "I wasn't surprised that she would just move to Canada without informing anybody. She could be very cunning, too — when in the grip of a manic phase. She could have sneaked out of the country easily. I *really* wasn't surprised that she'd done it."

"Me neither, if I'm honest," said Jill. "It would be nice to know if she's okay, though. She'll be in her seventies now. I'd like to know how she is. She had terrible rheumatoid arthritis. It was bad back then, poor woman. I'd imagine she's in an awful lot of pain these days."

"And there's been no more information in the years since?" asked Millie, tickling Harry's head beneath the table, smiling as the little dog licked her hand.

"Nothing at all," said Jill. "We've got used to it. I don't think about it as much as I once did. I try and keep it out of my mind. I just hope she's happy."

Judith closed her file. "I won't ask you any more about it. We'll leave you both to enjoy your day. I don't want to drag up the past unnecessarily."

Jill smiled. "Thank you for your time. It's nice to talk about her sometimes." She glanced at Judith's folder. "If you update the case notes, could I have a copy? I sometimes need proof that Mum is missing when official letters arrive for her. In the year she reached retirement age, I had some problems with the people from the pensions office. She's never been declared as dead, you see. And for a good reason."

"Of course!" said Judith. "We'll only be adding the fact that we've spoken to you again to the records, but we'll hand deliver a copy to you when the sergeant you spoke to on the telephone has updated them."

"Thank you," said Jill. "I appreciate it."

Millie drew to a halt at the entrance to *her* track leading to *her* cottage. She stared at the man standing in the road, who was ordering her to stop with an outstretched arm. "What does he think he's doing?" she said.

"I'll ask him," said Judith, standing up. With no roof impeding her progress, Judith stood with both hands on the top of the windscreen and shouted at the man. "Oi!" she yelled. "What do you think you're doing?"

The man lifted the brim of his black baseball cap and levelled his sunglasses in Judith's direction. "Nobody is allowed past this point," he said.

"What do you mean?" said Millie. "I live in that cottage over there. In fact, I own all this land, all the way to the lighthouse! You're standing on my land, trying to stop me entering my own property!"

The man approached the car, speaking into a radio as he walked. "The owner of the cottage is here," he said. "She's with somebody else. Should I let them through?"

"Yes, let them in," came the crackling reply. "I'll come and speak to them myself."

Stepping aside, the man waved Millie through. "Sorry about that," he said. "This area is off-limits to the public. A sergeant from the local police force cleared access for you and anybody accompanying you. A very nice sergeant. Very polite."

"Where is my dad — I mean, where is Sergeant

Spencer?" asked Judith, dropping back into her seat as Millie allowed the car to creep forward.

"He's with my boss," said the guard. "They'll be along to speak to you right away. I'm just the guard. I don't really know what's going on, if I'm honest. I never do these days."

Millie thanked the man with a smile, and drove slowly along the track. As she neared her cottage, a black van followed by Sergeant Spencer's police car approached from the direction of the lighthouse, and parked on the patch of gravel next to Millie's home.

Drawing her car alongside the two vehicles, Millie raised an eyebrow in Sergeant Spencer's direction as he approached her. "What's happening?" she said. "What are they doing on my property?"

Sergeant Spencer shook his head and gave a frustrated sigh. "Think of the most outrageous thing you could imagine happening on a normal Tuesday," he said. "Then multiply it by ten. You still won't be close to guessing what's happening." He headed towards the cottage door, pointing at the man climbing out of the black van. "Come on, let's get inside. He'll explain what's happening. I don't think I quite believe it."

Chapter 6

Millie stared at the man standing in her living room. Dressed completely in black, he seemed a formidable presence, but Millie wasn't about to feel intimidated in her own home. She pointed at the sofa. "Have a seat," she said. "And you can remove your baseball cap and sunglasses if you like — there's no sun in here, my roof does a good job of keeping it out."

Sergeant Spencer coughed, the sound hiding his laughter, but unable to conceal the mirth his wide smile exposed. "It's his *uniform*," he explained. "He's from a —"

"I'm quite capable of explaining who I am, and what organisation I represent, thank you, Sergeant," said the man. He smiled at Millie and Judith. "I'm Mister Anon, which is a clever pseudonym, of course — I like to keep my real identity a secret. I *have* to keep it secret. I represent a group known as the Alien Search Syndicate and Hazard Alert Team."

"Erm," said Judith. "You're from a group called ASSHAT?"

Mr Anon sighed. "You're quick at working out acronyms. Very good. Most people don't pick up on it. The group was named before I joined it. That mistake would have never slipped past me if I'd been in charge at the time."

"You could change it?" said Millie.

"Too late," said Mister Anon. "We've got headed paper, business cards — the works. We don't have the funds to make such sweeping changes."

"Funds?" said Millie. "Don't you work for the government?"

"No," said Mister Anon. "We're a non-governmental organisation which specialises in the search for extra-terrestrial life. Extra-terrestrial life on *this* planet."

"What an alien hunter is doing standing in my cottage, aside," said Millie. "If you're not from a governmental organisation — why on earth do you think you have the right to cordon off a huge chunk of the beach, and have a guard preventing people accessing my property?"

Sergeant Spencer stepped forward. "Because if we don't allow them access, and the right to keep the beach cordoned off, they'll call in the *real* authorities to look at the skeleton which Tom found," he said. "And if that happens, this town will hit the headlines all over the world." He raised an eyebrow in Millie's direction. "And we don't want that. *Do we?*"

Millie swallowed. The concealment spell was good, but could it disguise the paranormal inhabitants of Spellbinder Bay from the whole of the world's press? She doubted it.

"No, you don't," said Mister Anon. "You'll be flooded with tourists — and not the sort of tourists who will be a financial boom for the town, but the type whose own mothers would describe as a little eccentric, and possibly even dangerous if provoked."

"But the *real* authorities were called," said Millie. "Tom reported it to the museum, and a man came. I was there! He said the skeleton was probably an unknown dinosaur — a predator to be precise."

Mister Anon smiled. "Luckily for the Alien Search Syndic—"

"Luckily for ASSHAT," said Millie.

Mister Anon pursed his lips. "Luckily for *our group*," he said, with a scowl, "the man who Tom Temples reported his find to, is a friend of mine, and when he saw what it was that Tom had dug up, he sent me an urgent message. I dropped what I was doing immediately and called the rest of the team right away."

"Rest of the team?" said Judith. "How many of you are there?"

"It's a small team," said Mister Anon. "It's really just me and Mister Incognito — the man who was guarding the entrance to the track."

Judith giggled. "Another clever pseudonym?" she asked.

"Are you laughing at me?" spat Mister Anon, ripping off his glasses, to reveal piercing blue eyes. "You'd better not be! This is an important matter. There's an alien skeleton laying in the sand in the dunes below this cottage, and you think this is an appropriate time to be ridiculing me and my organisation? You should be more concerned as to whether the dead alien was a random visitor to our planet, or a member of the first line of an outer space invasion force! And believe me, aliens won't be coming here for our jobs or women, they'll be coming to make humans extinct — so they can take over our planet!"

"What?" said Millie, raising an eyebrow in Sergeant Spencer's direction. "You think the skeleton is an alien? Of course it's not an alien! It's a dinosaur."

Mister Anon gazed upward as Reuben fluttered in through the open roof window and landed on Millie's shoulder. "That's your bird, is it? It's been circling us since we got here. It even tried to get into the tent I've erected over the site of the alien's remains."

"It likes people," said Millie. "He's friendly, that's all. I wish you would stop referring to the skeleton as an alien, though. That's quite a claim to make. It's a dinosaur. We're on the Jurassic Coast!"

"When you saw it, Miss Thorn," said Mister Anon. "It was barely visible. You probably saw an eye socket and a few teeth, but since we've excavated it further, it looks nothing like a dinosaur!"

"I must say," said Sergeant Spencer. "It does look a little strange. Like the skull of the Cheshire Cat placed on the body of a meerkat. Very creepy."

Mister Anon withdrew his phone from his pocket. "Here," he said, turning the screen towards Millie. "Does that look like a dinosaur to you?"

The screech which Reuben emitted sent shockwaves through Millie's skull, and she put a hand to her ear in an attempt to stop the high-pitched ringing reverberating in her head. The cockatiel screeched again, and launched himself from Millie's shoulder, flying in frantic circles around the room, before zooming through the open roof window.

"What's wrong with him?" said Mister Anon.

"I'm not sure," said Millie, studying the photo on Mister Anon's phone. "Maybe it was the picture that scared him. It does look a little…. freaky. I saw the top of the spine when Tom and I dug out the hole, but I had no idea it would be so short."

"It doesn't look possible," said Judith. "The body is tiny. How could it possibly hold the weight of a head that large?"

"And that's the question which proves that it is extra-terrestrial in origin," said Mister Anon, with a satisfied smirk. "The gravity on this planet would not allow such a creature to evolve here." He tapped the screen of his phone with a dirty fingernail. "This creature comes from a planet where gravity works very differently than on Earth. And look at those teeth. They make no sense. There are at least four rows, and I counted over a hundred individual teeth in one row alone. What manner of prey must it feast on to require such gnashers? Ladies and gentleman, you are looking at an alien. Quite probably one which was extremely dangerous in life."

"What happens now?" said Millie, as Mister Anon slipped his phone back into his pocket. "What will you do with it?"

"Today, we'll do nothing," he said. "We require some specialist equipment which myself and Mister Incognito will be collecting overnight — we rushed here when we got the message from our informant at the museum, and we've arrived with a lack of equipment. The skeleton may be radioactive, and until it's been tested for such dangers, nobody is to approach it. Including myself. We may already be contaminated. Sergeant Spencer has promised to keep the area cordoned off until our return in the morning, and as your cottage overlooks the site of the skeleton, I'd be obliged if you would keep an eye on the area for me, too."

"Erm, yes. I suppose so," said Millie. "But what will happen to the skeleton when it's been fully excavated? If people find out it was discovered here, Spellbinder Bay, and my property in particular, is never going to be the same again."

"We shall remove it from this area, and never reveal where it was found," said Mister Anon. "I have big plans for that skeleton, and they don't involve this tiny town. You have no need to worry."

Millie nodded. "Okay," she said. "We'll make sure nobody goes near the skeleton while you're gone."

Mister Anon placed his sunglasses back on his face. "Then we shall leave. Mister Incognito and I will return tomorrow morning, at which time we'll begin a proper investigation into the origin of the specimen, and set about removing it from Spellbinder Bay. I thank you all for your cooperation. It's far better that you keep this situation away from the authorities, and in my capable hands. The authorities would force you to abandon your cottage, and would probably cordon off the whole of the town, which is not a situation anybody would like to find themselves in."

"Don't worry," said Sergeant Spencer. "No authorities higher than myself will hear anything about this. The skeleton will still be there when you return in the morning."

"Untouched?" said Mister Anon.

Sergeant Spencer sighed. "Untouched."

With an approving nod, Mister Anon muttered his goodbyes, and let himself out of the cottage. No sooner had the door slammed behind him, than a loud sound like a cracking whip filled the room, and Millie's hair brushed her cheek as a draft blew over her face.

A brief flash of light in front of the fireplace quickly morphed into the shape of Henry Pinkerton with Reuben perched on his shoulder, causing Judith to jump with fright. "What the hell?" she said. "Give us some warning!"

"Forgive the intrusion," said Henry, pushing his little round spectacles higher up his nose. "It's highly important, though. Reuben came to me with grave news, and when he took me to see the skeleton beneath the tent in the dunes — I realised the news is graver than even Reuben described it — and he was panicking so much he's left feathers all over my office. It's lucky I don't have any letters to write – it will take me some time to find my quill."

"I'm sorry, Henry," said Reuben. "I was scared."

"I didn't know you could do that," said Judith. "I know you travel along beams of energy, but I didn't know you could bring somebody else with you."

Henry smiled. "It's easier to travel alone," he said. "But yes, if the need arises I can bring somebody along for the ride. And Reuben's panic made it quite clear that this was one of those occasions. Anyway, Reuben is so small I hardly noticed him draining any of my energy."

"Sorry I left like that," said Reuben, fluttering to Millie's shoulder. "But when I saw that photograph on the phone, I had to act quickly, and I couldn't say anything about my concerns in front of that strange alien hunting man."

Millie ran a finger over the cockatiel's chest. "What is it?" she asked. "What scared you so much?"

"It's awful news, Millie," said Reuben. "I'm so scared that I discovered I can fly almost four times faster than I imagined I could. I made it to Spellbinder Hall in record time!"

"What's happened, Reuben?" said Millie. You're shaking."

"Allow me to explain," said Henry, beginning to pace in front of the fireplace. What Henry lacked in height, he made up for in confidence, and the smart tweed three-piece suit he wore embellished him with even more authority.

Everybody remained silent as he spoke. "Reuben arrived at Spellbinder Hall in quite the panic," he said. "He insisted I came with him right away, so I moved quickly. We went to the sand dunes first, and had a look at the skeleton for ourselves, and as soon as the gentleman dressed in black left, I came straight here. With bad news, I'm afraid. Troubling news."

"What is it?" said Sergeant Spencer.

"The skeleton on the beach is neither a dinosaur *or* an alien," said Henry.

Reuben's claws dug into Millie's shoulder. "It's far worse!" he squawked.

"Indeed," said Henry. "It is far worse. The skeleton on the beach is the remains of a demon. A particularly nasty type of demon. And a recent arrival."

"Recent?" said Judith. "It's a skeleton."

"If a demon manages to pass through the dimension gate below Spellbinder Hall, it will pass through as invisible energy, allowing it to evade detection," explained Henry. "If it does not find a suitable human host quickly, it will revert to its physical form and die. It cannot survive in this environment, and it will decompose remarkably quickly."

"We call the type of demon in the sand dunes a *scurrier*," said Reuben. "They were my biggest fear when I lived in The Chaos. We called them that because they scurried around on those tiny legs, causing pain and untold misery with that huge mouth and those sharp teeth."

"A demon got through the gate?" said Millie. "I thought my magical energy was keeping the gate to The Chaos closed? How could a demon have come through?"

"The gate is never fully closed," said Henry. "But I believe it was weakened by the recent storm. The electric in the air must have interfered with the magic, weakening the force-field."

"That's not the worst of it," said Reuben. "Scurriers never travel alone. They only ever travel in pairs. Where there's one scurrier, there's *always* another one right next to it. With no exceptions! Had both demons died, they would have died side by side, and the fact that there is only one skeleton in the sand leads to only one conclusion."

Henry removed his glasses and rubbed his eyes. "That the other one managed to find a human host, and possess the unfortunate person." He put his glasses back on, and stared at everybody in turn. "There is a person possessed by a demon present in Spellbinder Bay. We paranormal people needn't worry. It won't try and harm us, unless threatened, and it is no stronger than the person it possesses, but people like Sergeant Spencer — humans, may be at risk. The demon may not be strong, but it will be vicious and uncaring — capable of extreme violence. We should keep our eyes and ears open. People may be in grave danger."

"What about those alien hunters?" said Sergeant Spencer. "I don't trust them. I'm sure they intend to publicise the find, and if people ever discover that demons exist — which they will when that skeleton is examined properly, the paranormal community will be in danger of discovery."

"Shouldn't the concealment spell work on them?" said Millie. "If the skeleton is the remains of a paranormal creature, shouldn't the spell have made them lose interest in it? I thought it was designed to draw people's attention away from paranormal events?"

Henry sighed. "The sort of people who become alien hunters are the sort of people who thrive on conspiracy theories and rumours. The concealment spell uses gentle magic which nudges people's thoughts away from anything paranormal. They simply don't register it as strange, and move on. A conspiracy theorist's mind is too well trained for spotting the unusual — too resilient to the effects of Spellbinder Hall's concealment spell. It will work to an extent, but those two men will smell a rat eventually. We'll need to come up with a different plan to put them off the scent."

"We could just move the skeleton," offered Judith. "When they come back tomorrow morning we could tell them they imagined it. They'll have no proof."

"They have photos," said Millie. "But I suppose if we did move the skeleton, the photos would mean nothing without any physical evidence to back them up. People are always faking photographs."

"No," said Henry. "The skeleton mustn't be disturbed any further. Although by human standards the demon is dead, there's still a danger that some of the demon's residual energy remains within its bones. When it failed to find a host, it was likely drawn to this area by the magical energy emitted from your cottage, Millie, and when it realised it was dying, it burrowed into the sand in a futile attempt to reach The Chaos. It would have died quickly, and begun decomposing at a very fast rate. A very fast rate indeed. The bones will take a little longer to decompose — maybe a week, and until they are dust, nobody must touch that skeleton. It can be looked at, but nobody must lay a hand on it. It is not yet fully dead as we understand it — simply in an enhanced form of dormancy."

"And still able to take a human host if disturbed," said Reuben.

"Yes," said Henry. "So, until no bones remain, humans must be kept away from it — especially those alien hunters."

"How do we do that?" said Judith. "With magic?"

Henry fiddled with his cufflinks and shook his

head. "No," he said. "It's not wise to use magic in front of conspiracy theorists. You'll have to come up with a plan which doesn't involve spells or potions, and remember — a human in Spellbinder Bay is already possessed by a demon. I'll do my best to hunt it down, but they hide well. I'll warn the other members of the paranormal community, but we should all be on high alert. This is a dangerous time. Be on your guard. All of you."

Chapter 7

With the warm onshore breeze blowing in their faces, and the moon accentuating the white tips of distant waves with silvery light, it was hard to believe that the bones of a demon lay in the sand a few hundred metres away.

Judith sipped her wine, and reached for an olive from the Mediterranean platter which Millie had served on the patio table. "Isn't wine wonderful?" she said. "Earlier today, when Henry was warning us about people being possessed by demons, I must admit to having been quite nervous, but a few glasses of wine later, and all I want to do is put some music on and dance!" She glanced at Millie. "Where is the music?"

Millie laughed. "I did ask if you wanted music," she said. "You said the sound of the waves crashing on the beach and the wind in the dunes was the perfect soundtrack for a glass of wine and some antipasto."

"You did," said Reuben, pecking at a slice of chorizo. "I can confirm it."

"That was half a bottle of wine ago," said Judith. "Now I've changed my mind. I want music."

Millie stood up. "Then music you shall have," she said. "I've got just the Spotify playlist for this sort of occasion. Lots of classic eighties and —" She paused as something caught her eye. *Light in the sand dunes.*

"What is it?" said Reuben. "What are you looking at?"

"I think I saw something," said Millie, stepping through the open patio doors and into the kitchen. She switched off the light which bathed the patio in a bright yellow glow, and stared out over the sand dunes, searching the darkness. Then she saw it again — an unmistakable beam of dim torchlight. "There," she said. "Somebody's in the dunes with a flashlight!"

"At this time of night?" said Reuben. "It's almost midnight. That's not normal."

"No," said Millie. "Especially when the person is in the same area as the demon skeleton. We'd better go and look — we all heard what Henry said — that skeleton mustn't be interfered with. We have to go and see who it is, and find out what they're doing."

Reuben tucked his head into his chest. "What if it's the human who's possessed by the other demon?" he said, "come back to find its partner? It's not safe!"

"Henry said demons won't harm paranormal people," said Millie. "And that includes you, Reuben. Anyway, if the worst did happen — Judith and I will look after you."

"Henry said a demon wouldn't try and harm paranormal people *unless it was threatened*," said Reuben. "Do you really think you two could help us if we're attacked? If I'm attacked? I doubt it."

Judith stood up quickly, her glass tipping and soaking her jeans with wine. "Oh yeah we can!" she said. "No demon's gonna mess with our little Reuben! Let them try!"

"You two are drunk," said Reuben. "Drunks think they can take on the world! Would you approach those sand dunes if you were sober? If you thought there was a demon in the body of a human out there in the dark?"

Millie smiled. "I think I would, but let's not wait until we're sober to find out. Come on — who's coming with me?"

MILLIE LED THE WAY, WITH REUBEN ON HER shoulder, and Judith following. As her eyes became accustomed to the moonlight, she followed one of the tracks she ran along each morning, heading in the direction she'd seen the light coming from. The direction in which lay the remains of a demon.

Reuben's claws tightened on Millie's shoulder as the group ventured deeper into the dunes, and they almost pierced her flesh as the frightened shout of a man echoed across the sand. "What the hell? What are you—"

The heavy thud following the man's last word sent cold chills through Millie's veins, and she turned quickly to look at Judith. "Did you hear that?" she said.

"*I* did," said Reuben, a tremble in his voice. "It was the sound of violence!"

Judith grabbed Millie's wrist. "I heard it, too," she said. "That was the sound of something hitting a human head! It had to be!" She stared across the dunes, her moonlit eyes betraying her fear. "Hello!" she shouted. "Who's there? What's —" She spluttered as Millie placed a hand over her mouth. "Get off!" she mumbled against her friend's palm.

"Keep quiet then," whispered Millie. "We don't know what's going on! We don't know who's out there!"

"It's the demon!" hissed Reuben. "We should turn tail and run. There's no shame in retreat."

"Somebody might need our help, Reuben," said Millie. "The only way I'm running is in the direction the shout came from. You two go back to the cottage if you want. I'm going to see what's out there."

Judith took a deep breath and released her grip on Millie's wrist. "No," she said. "I'm no coward. I'm coming with you."

Reuben gave a low squawk, his claws relaxing on Millie's shoulder. "I'm coming too, I suppose," he said. "But I'm not providing air-cover! I'm staying right here, on the shoulder of my witch."

"Okay," said Millie, staring into the night. "Let's go, but keep quiet."

Moving as quickly and carefully as possible, Millie led the way through the dunes, managing to stifle a scream as a large square shape loomed out of the darkness. "It's the tent," she whispered. "The one that ASSHAT put over the demon's bones."

"Are you going to look inside?" said Judith.

"Why?" said Millie. "Should I?"

"Why else would somebody be in this area at this time of night?" whispered Judith. "It must be something to do with the demon's bones."

"It's too dark," replied Millie. "I won't be able to see anything, and anyway, the shout came from further on."

Judith wiggled her fingers. "I've got something which might help," she said.

"No," said Millie. "You can't cast an illumination spell — it can be dangerous to use magic after drinking too much alcohol."

Judith shook her head, and reached into her pocket. "I meant my phone," she said, fumbling with the screen until the built-in torch burst into life. "Here," she said. "You have a look inside the tent. I'll keep watch out here."

"I'll help Judith," said Reuben, hopping from one

witch's shoulder to the other's. "Four eyes are better than two."

"Fine," said Millie. "I'll do it. Alone." She paused for a few moments. Did she really want to look inside the tent? Obviously not, *but she had to*.

She took the phone from Judith and used it to illuminate the green tent's closed doorway. Four Velcro strips held the two fabric flaps in place, and she winced as she pulled them apart, the angry ripping sound amplified by the quiet night air.

Slowly, she peeled the flaps apart, and peered inside, the phone held out in front of her. She quickly verified that the tent was empty, and with no hiding places available from which somebody might leap out, she stepped inside, and pointed the light at the hole in the sand.

She couldn't stifle the screen which slipped from her mouth this time, but she managed to cut it short by placing a hand over her own mouth, and taking a deep breath.

The door behind her made a rustling sound as something pushed through it, and she ducked as Reuben flew in circles around the small interior of the tent. "Get off my witch!" he squawked. "Nobody hurts my witch! I'll peck you to death!"

"Millie?" shouted Judith, pushing through the door behind Reuben. "Are you okay? You screamed!"

"Yes," said Millie, regaining control of herself. "Everybody calm down. I had a fright, that's all. When I saw the skeleton." When she'd last seen the remains, most of them had been concealed by sand, but since the partial excavation, it was apparent that the creature in the sand had never been a dinosaur. Illuminated by the light from the phone, the permanently snarling skull had taken on an evil quality which made Millie shudder inside. "It looks scarier than in the photograph Mister Anon showed us," she said.

Judith put a hand on Millie's. "Come on. Let's get out of here. Henry said the demon's bones could still contain energy. I know he said it's okay as long as we don't touch them, but I don't like it in this tent."

Millie nodded. "I think you should phone your father, Judith. That shout we heard was a shout of fear, and I dread to think what the thud was." Knowing exactly what the thud had been, but hoping against hope that the sound like the crack of metal on flesh-covered bone may have been caused by something less sinister than the images which spiralled out of control in her mind, she passed the phone to Judith.

"Thanks," said Judith, tapping at the screen as they exited the tent. She spoke in urgent tones when her father answered, and ended the call with a promise. "I give you my word, Dad," she said. "We won't put ourselves in any danger." She looked at Millie. "He's on his way. He told me we should wait for him to get here before we do anything else."

"No way," said Millie. "Somebody might be lying

injured in the sand. Somebody might need our help. We can't afford to wait."

"My thoughts exactly," said Judith. She switched the phone's torch on once more, and moved the light left and right over the dunes in front of them. "Stay close to me," she said. "I'll lead the way."

A group of tiny moths fluttered around the phone as Judith scoured the sand ahead with the dim light, and a ground-nesting bird startled Millie as it burst from a large patch of dune grass and gave a panicked cry.

Millie followed close behind as Judith ventured left at the base of a steeper dune, and stopped in her tracks as the beam of light glinted back at her, reflected by a familiar object lying in the sand. "Over there," she said. "Look."

Millie approached the object first, and Judith bathed it in light. "A metal detector?" she said.

"Yes," said Millie. "And I recognise it. It's Tom Temples's."

Reuben let out a low moan. "Then that man lying in the sand over there must be Tom Temples," he said.

Following Reuben's gaze, Millie gasped. "Quick," she said. "Shine your light on him, Judith."

Millie reached the man's side first, and put both hands over her mouth as Judith gave a shriek, and Reuben fluttered to the sand. "Poor man," said the cockatiel.

Kneeling beside Tom, Millie placed a trembling

hand on the man's throat, and using two fingers, felt for a pulse. The deep bloody gash which ran for inches across Tom's scalp, and his lifeless staring eyes could have spoken for her, but Millie still felt the need to say the words. "He's dead," she whispered.

"And there's the murder weapon," said Judith, pointing a few feet to the right. "A shovel. It's got blood on it."

"I don't want to sound insensitive," said Reuben. "I liked the man, but I think we should be more troubled about the fact that his murderer may still be nearby, than the fact he's dead — for the moment, anyway."

Millie wiped a tear from beneath her eye. "Reuben is right," she said. "Look at that gash in Tom's head. The shovel penetrated his skull. He had no chance. He wouldn't have felt a thing. No amount of first-aid is going to help him. We should get back to the cottage and wait for your father, Judith. There's nothing we can do for Tom. There's nothing anybody can do for him."

Light peeked over the horizon by the time Sergeant Spencer had finished inspecting the area for clues, and Tom's body had been transported to the morgue.

Henry Pinkerton sighed as he stared out over the sand dunes. "A terrible thing," he said. "But that's what happens when demons pass through the gate — people get hurt."

"Killed," corrected Millie.

"You think it had something to do with the demons which came through the gate?" said Judith.

"We can't be sure about anything," said Henry. "The fact that Tom was found dead next to his metal detector almost certainly verifies Millie's speculation that Tom had sneaked back to the area under the cover of darkness, knowing it had been cordoned off, but desperate to find a few more gold coins. His empty pouch would suggest that he either found no gold, or was killed soon after arriving. Sergeant Spencer found his car parked half a mile away in the nature reserve car park, too far away for you to hear engine noise from your cottage."

"And he sneaked into the dunes," said Millie. "To look for gold, but finding only death."

"He would have sneaked onto the dunes from the direction of the lighthouse," said Henry, placing a gentle hand on Millie's shoulder. "I don't see any reason why anybody else should have been there with him. I can only speculate at this point that perhaps the second demon came back to this area, to search for its partner, unfortunately for Tom. It's new inside its host, and probably can't control its anger yet. It will learn with time, but if it did kill Tom, it would have required no motive other than the rage it experienced when it discovered Tom in the same area in which its partner had perished."

"It could have been gold fever," said Millie. "Maybe it wasn't the demon."

"Pardon?" said Henry.

"It's what Tom called it," said Millie. "The urge to find gold. There were other people interested in finding out where Tom had been discovering his gold coins. Perhaps somebody *did* find out, and perhaps it was that person who killed Tom. Maybe it had nothing to do with a demon. Maybe that's why his pouch was empty — maybe his gold was stolen."

"We'll look at it from all angles," said Sergeant Spencer. "While Henry attempts to track down the second demon, I'll treat the murder as if it were committed by a human, with a human motive to kill. Either way, whether it was a demon or not — we'll be looking for a human, it's just that in one of those scenarios the human will have an unwanted guest within him or her."

Henry nodded. "Treat the murder as you would any other. Focus on finding a human, whether possessed or not," he said. "And now this area is a murder scene, Sergeant Spencer, which allows you to cordon it off further. You no longer need a plan to keep those alien hunters away from the skeleton. When they come back, you'll have every right to keep them from approaching the demon's remains. Hopefully, the bones will be dust by the time they're allowed access to the site again, and then any photographic evidence they have will be worthless — they'll be labelled as fakes, and Spellbinder Bay won't become a town visited by conspiracy theorists from the world over."

"Good point," said Sergeant Spencer. "In fact, Mister Anon left me a business card. I'll ring him and explain what's happened. Maybe I can persuade ASSHAT to stay away altogether for a few days. It's worth a try." He glanced at the crimson horizon. "It's dawn. I suggest we all have some strong coffee and some breakfast, and then we'll get on with the task of finding out who, or what, murdered Tom Temples. I'm assuming you two girls will want to help me?" he said, looking at Millie and Judith.

Judith nodded. "Of course."

"Try and stop me," said Millie. "I liked Tom. I *really* want to find out what happened to him."

Henry Pinkerton adjusted his cufflinks and gave a nod. "You have a plan, it seems. I shall bid you farewell. Please keep me updated on any progress you make, and I shall do likewise with any progress I make," he said. "Be wary of everybody. Remember — a demon inside a human will appear from the outside as just another person, and with time will gain the ability to control its rage and mingle seamlessly with the rest of the human race. Some of history's worst dictators were humans possessed by demons. We don't want this demon to gain that level of notoriety. It must be found."

Before anybody had time to answer, a whip crack echoed across the dunes, and Henry had vanished, leaving only the faint smell of ozone, and a sliver of white light hanging momentarily in the air, before that vanished, too.

Sergeant Spencer took a deep sniff of the crisp morning air. "I'm hungry," he stated. "We should have breakfast before beginning a murder investigation."

Chapter 8

Millie served a simple breakfast, greatly appreciated by Judith, Sergeant Spencer and Reuben — who pecked at a crispy strip of bacon fat discarded by Judith, making appreciative squawks and whistles as he ate.

Eating a bacon sandwich, Millie watched the father and daughter laughing together as they shared a meal. She hated envy, but she couldn't shake the jealousy which wormed its way through her belly — not a malevolent jealously, but unwarranted all the same.

The fact that she'd never shared a breakfast with her father, didn't give her the right to envy anybody else's relationship. She helped herself to another slice of bacon and shook the idea of opening her mother's letter from her mind, butterflies rising in her stomach. *She wasn't ready*. Not Yet. Not ready to learn who her father was, and not ready for the potential hurt which might accompany his identity being revealed. She put a smile on her face. "Has everybody had enough to eat?" she asked, as she refilled coffee cups.

Sergeant Spencer patted his belly and gave a big smile. "I'm stuffed to the rafters," he said. "You're a fine cook."

"Me too," said Judith. "Thank you, Millie. Breakfast was delicious."

Reuben looked up, his beak smeared with egg yolk. "Very nice," he said.

"It's weird watching you eating an egg, Reuben," said Sergeant Spencer. "It doesn't seem right."

"I didn't lay it," said Reuben. "A hen did. What's weird about it, anyway? I can't even lay eggs. I'm a man-bird. It's rude of you to make such comments."

"I apologise," said Sergeant Spencer. "It was just an observation."

The bird nodded, and dipped his beak into the egg yolk on the plate in front of him. He gave a contented whistle, and moved his attention to a sausage.

"Remember to eat some seeds, Reuben," said Millie. "We had a deal. I let you eat what you like, but you supplement your diet with seeds. The vitamins in them keep your plumage looking nice and healthy."

The cockatiel swallowed a piece of sausage. "I know," he said. "I'll have some today, while you're out investigating Tom's murder. I promise."

"Oh?" said Millie. "Are you not coming with us? I

thought you'd enjoy it. You like putting your beak in other people's business."

"Very funny, but I've got other things to do," said the bird. "I was hoping you wouldn't mind me spending some time in your cavern again?"

Millie raised an eyebrow. "Of course I don't mind you being down there, Reuben," she said, glancing at the door to the left of the fireplace. "But what is it you're doing in there? You missed our run yesterday so you could be in the cavern, and I found you down there when I came back from the pub quiz on Monday night."

"You told me I was allowed," said Reuben.

"You are!" said Millie. "I was just wondering what you were doing."

"Looking through the big spell book," said Reuben. "Nothing exciting. It's taking some time because I don't have hands. Turning heavy pages with a beak and claws is quite hard going."

"Do you need help?" said Millie. "Are you looking for anything in particular?"

"What do you want with spells, Reuben?" asked Judith. "You can't use magic. Can you?"

"No, I can't use magic," said Reuben. "But I can be interested in it, can't I? That is allowed, isn't it? Everybody complains that I watch too much TV — I thought you'd all be happy that I've got my head in a book instead. A bird can't win, it seems! Damned if you do, and damned if you don't!"

"Blimey, Reuben, chill out," said Millie, beginning

to clear the table. "Spend all the time you want down there, just be careful, okay?"

Sergeant Spencer looked up. "An engine," he said. "Somebody's here. I bet it's ASSHAT. When I spoke to Mister Anon on the phone, he said he'd be here by eight. He didn't sound very happy when I told him the sand dunes were now a murder scene, and he couldn't access the skeleton. I think he swore before he ended the call."

Millie rushed towards the front door as it swung open, bringing with it the angry face of Mister Anon, with Mister Incognito close behind him. She stared at the two men. "I'll let you off this time, but never do that again," she warned. "You knock and wait to be invited in next time, do you understand?"

"Oh. Sorry," said Mister Incognito. "Should we go out and try again?"

Mister Anon turned on the spot, and faced his partner. "No, Mister Incognito. We will not go out and try again. We're angry, remember?"

Mister Incognito took a step backwards. "Okay Graham, I'm sorry. I —"

"Don't call me that!" hissed Mister Anon. He turned to face the room. "Did anybody hear that?"

"Hear what?" said Sergeant Spencer, his stomach shaking as he repressed laughter. "I don't think any of us heard anything."

"I didn't," said Millie.

"Me neither," said Judith. "What did we miss?"

Mister incognito peered past his partner. "I called Mister Anon by his real —"

"Stop talking, Mister Incognito!" snapped Mister Anon. "Just stop talking, would you?"

"I'm sorry," said Mister Incognito, bowing his head. "My lips are sealed."

"Good," said Mister Anon, adjusting his cap and turning to face the room. "Now, what's this I hear about a murder being committed in almost the exact same spot in which my alien skeleton was found?"

"Precisely that," said Sergeant Spencer, "and for the foreseeable future, you won't be allowed anywhere near the skeleton. The scene of a crime, *especially* a murder, is of more importance than the alleged remains of an alien for the time being. The site needs to be preserved until it's been searched thoroughly for clues." He looked at Millie, and winked. "And that could take some time. "Possibly a week."

"At least let us check the skeleton before you begin your investigation," said Mister Anon. "It's important!"

Sergeant Spencer shook his head. "Nobody is allowed near a scene of a crime. You might contaminate it. The alleged alien remains won't go anywhere, and nobody will go near them."

"It's not an *alleged* alien!" said Mister Anon. "Stop saying that! It *is* an alien! And what if the skeleton is radioactive? You don't want to be going anywhere near it until it's been tested."

"I doubt it's radioactive," said Millie, resisting the

urge to inform the men that it was not an alien, nor radioactive.

"It might be," said Mister Anon. "I'd rather be on the safe side."

"Yeah," said Mister Incognito. "Radioactive with *space* radiation. It's much worse than Earth radiation isn't it, Gra — Mister Anon? It can make your skin turn blue and your eyes go a bit mad, can't it, Mister Anon?"

Mister Anon sighed, and removed his sunglasses. "Yes, Mister Incognito. Space radiation *may* make your skin turn blue, and it's possible your eyes might go... a bit mad, but at the moment, that's mere speculation. It's never been proved." He stared at Sergeant Spencer, his top lip curling. "I'm sure you wouldn't like to be the first person to test the hypothesis? Maybe it's best if you stay away from the skeleton, while you investigate your so-called murder."

"So-called?" said Sergeant Spencer.

"It's a little convenient, isn't it?" spat Mister Anon. "We leave the area for one night, and when we come back we're told there's been a murder at the very site we came to investigate, and that we're not allowed near the skeleton! Very convenient, I'd say!"

Mister Incognito removed his glasses and narrowed his eyes. "Very conventional indeed," he said.

"Convenient, Mister Incognito!" said Mister Anon. "The word is convenient!"

Mister Incognito smiled. "It is, Mister Anon. Very convenient indeed."

"Never mind, Mister Incognito," said Mister Anon, removing his hat and running a hand through his thinning brown hair. "Never mind." His shoulders slumped as he looked at Millie. "I trust you'll allow us to park our vehicle on your land? While we wait until this *murder* has been solved. I want to make sure we can see the tent covering the alien's remains, twenty-four-seven. I don't want anybody going near it! I won't be responsible for an outbreak of blue skin and, or, mad eyes!"

Millie studied the two men. No longer as intimidating as they were the day before, the men's confidence seemed to have deflated — especially Mister Anon's, whose worried eyes waited for Millie to answer. "Okay," she said. "You can stay on my land, but is that little van of yours really equipped for sleeping in?"

"Oh, we didn't come back in that van," said Mister Anon. "When the sergeant telephoned me this morning, I assumed we'd be here for longer than expected."

"We came in the mobile home," said Mister Incognito. "Didn't we, Mister Anon?"

"We did," said Mister Anon. "We'll park it in a spot which gives us a clear view of the alien's position. Nobody will get near that skeleton without us knowing about it!"

"Nobody," confirmed Mister Incognito, removing his sunglasses and narrowing his eyes. "Not even me."

Mister Anon gave a frustrated sigh. "Try and be a little more professional would you, Mister Incognito?"

Millie headed for the door. "Follow me. I'll show you where you can park your mobile home. I don't want it right outside my cottage, thank you very much."

She pushed past the two men, and as she opened the door, she suppressed a giggle. ASSHAT funds must have been *really* tight if their transportation budget could only provide them with the vehicle which stood outside. "It's smaller than I thought it would be," she said. "You can park it alongside my cottage, on the right, where it won't be in my way."

"It's a classic," said Mister Anon, opening the rust-spotted driver's door. "It's a nineteen-eighty-one VW T25, and it's inconspicuous — nobody will suspect we're alien hunters. It's perfect for our requirements."

Sergeant Spencer slipped his notebook from his chest pocket and began writing in it. As the campervan's engine sprang into grumbling life, a plume of dark grey smoke billowing from the rattling exhaust pipe, he spoke to Millie and Judith. "As you can probably imagine," he said. "I don't trust those two. There's something very weird about them. I'm going to run the vehicle registration through the system and see if I can find out just who those characters are. I'm staying here while you two begin trying to find out what may have happened to Tom — I don't trust that they'll stay away from that demon, and the last thing we need is one of them becoming possessed."

"I'll stay here if you like," said Millie.

Sergeant Spencer frowned. "No. Even though you have the badge I gave you, I sense that Mister Anon won't accept that you have any authority over him. As Henry said, he's a conspiracy theorist. It's better that I stay and guard the murder scene. I'll look for clues here, can you two think of anywhere you can begin asking questions? Is there anything Tom might have said or done that might give us a non-demon suspect?"

"We should begin with the members of the Spellbinder Sand Diggers metal detecting club," said Millie. "They seemed very angry that Tom was finding gold and they weren't. One of them, Eric, even told Tom to watch his back. He sounded very threatening. Stan had to throw him out of the pub."

"Where is the metal detecting club?" said Sergeant Spencer.

"I don't know," said Millie. "But Eric mentioned he'd been to a pawn shop to have a Roman coin appraised, the same shop Tom had visited — it seems the pawn shop owner is the go-to person for detectorists who find rare items. We could start there. The shop owner will probably be able to point us in the direction of the metal detectorists."

Sergeant Spencer nodded. "I know the shop, and I know the man who owns it. He's got a colourful criminal history — nothing serious — receiving stolen goods, that sort of thing. But yes, that sounds like a good idea — start there. Ask him where he was last night, too," he said, watching as Mister Anon struggled to reverse the campervan. "I'll find out who those two alien hunting clowns *really* are. If it wasn't for the fact that they'd bring all manner of unwanted attention down on our town, I'd have thrown them off your land already, Millie. With any luck, I'll be able to soon enough."

Chapter 9

As Millie prepared to enter the pawn shop, Judith tapped her on the shoulder. "Oh, my gosh! Look," she said, her voice raised to compete with the roar of the black motorcycle which zoomed past them, the rider raising a gloved hand in greeting, and his passenger giving them a wide smile from the open-faced helmet she wore. The same helmet Millie wore when *she* rode on the back of George's bike.

"What?" said Millie, gripping the door handle in a knuckle-whitening grasp, and wincing as her teeth dug into her bottom lip. "It's just George taking a ride. It's nothing I haven't seen before."

"With a blonde bombshell on the back of his bike?" said Judith. "I haven't seen *that* before. You're the only female I've seen on the back of his bike since you moved to town. Who do you think she is? Do you think it's that nurse he mentioned?"

"It's nothing to do with me," said Millie, her

stomach churning as she caught a final glimpse of the bike negotiating the corner at the end of the road, the shapely blonde pillion passenger clinging tightly to George's waist. "Nothing to do with me at all. I don't care what George does! Or who he does *it* with!"

"Are you okay?" said Judith. "Your cheeks are red."

Millie span to face her friend. "I'm fine! It's a warm morning!" she said. "Okay? I'm fine."

Judith lifted both hands in mock surrender. "Okay. Okay. You're fine. I get it. I won't mention it again. I won't mention *her* again."

"Good," said Millie, pushing the shop door open. "Anyway, that blonde girl won't be smiling so much if George has a crash. I doubt a mini-skirt is going to offer her much protection."

"Or those high heels and tight t-shirt," added Judith, following Millie into the shop.

Millie took a deep breath and closed her eyes, ridding her mind of the unwelcome image of George and the... *woman*. When she opened them, she focused on the smells of the cluttered shop, enjoying the scent of old vinyl record sleeves, and the fragrant aroma of whatever the polish was the long-haired man behind the counter was massaging into the body of a guitar.

Millie smiled. "Is that a Gibson Hummingbird?" she asked, admiring the flame red and honeyed amber of the wood, decorated with an engraved pickguard featuring its namesake feeding from a flower.

The middle-aged man stood up, looking Millie up and down. He placed the guitar gently on the counter and wiped his hands on his denim jacket. "It is," he drawled. "This one's a real beauty. You know your guitars."

"My mother played," said Millie. "That was her dream guitar."

"Oh?" said the man. He traced a thin finger over the curves of the instrument, and ran the tip of his tongue across his moustache sheltered upper lip. "This one sings like a bird," he said. "If you know how to treat her right. If you treat her like a lady, that is. And I know how to treat a lady. I know how to treat a lady real —"

"Okay!" said Judith, rolling her eyes at Millie. "We get it! You're a ladies' man!"

The man frowned. "Why do you say that? I'm just trying to sell a guitar to the young lady. She seemed interested." He smiled at Millie. "It's a bargain at two-thousand-nine-hundred-and-ninety-nine. With spare strings, a case *and* a strap."

"You were flirting," said Judith. "Quite obviously."

"Sex sells," said the man. "And I wasn't flirting. I was using sensual imagery to encourage a sale. I learned it from an online course."

"I hope the course didn't cost too much," said Judith. "Because either you're misinterpreting the material you were taught, or you've accidentally been studying a course aimed at teaching losers how to pick up women."

The man ran a hand over his stubbly chin. "Can I help you at all? You seem like a very tense young lady. I've got a massage chair out the back. Only two-hundred quid. I have a feeling it might help you."

"I don't want a massage chair, thank you very much," said Judith.

"Then what *do* you want?" said the man, sitting down. "I'm busy."

"Are you Pete?" asked Millie. "Pawn Shop Pete?"

"That's what they call me," he said, nodding slowly. "Those that need to. Who's asking?"

"We're here on police business," said Judith. "Important police business."

Millie had never witnessed a face drain of colour before. She'd read about it, and had always assumed it was simply an author's way of expressing a character's state of shock, but watching Pete's face literally drain of colour from the forehead down, was quite the sight.

Pete bent down, and fumbled with something beneath the counter, before attempting a smile. "Oh. Now I recognise you. You're Sergeant Spencer's daughter," he said, speaking to Judith.

"I am," said Judith.

"How can I help you?" said Pete, a bead of sweat forming on his forehead, and the corner of his left eye twitching. "I keep records of everything I buy from people. It's not my fault if they stole those items, is it? How could I possibly know?"

Judith smiled. "We know about your criminal record, Pete," she teased. "And it's quite obvious that you have something under the counter that you don't want us to see, but we're not here about such trivial things. We're here about a murder."

Pete's face whitened further, and his cheeks seemed to sink, making his bony jawline more prominent beneath his scruffy stubble. His mouth slowly dropped open, and he placed both hands on the counter to steady himself. "Murder?" he said. "What murder? You don't think I did it, do you? I wouldn't hurt a man — or a woman. It could be a woman, couldn't it? Was it a woman? Who could do such a thing to a woman — not that I know what was done to her, of course! Was it strangulation? A stabbing? Electrocution? Blunt force trauma? Poor, poor woman — oh my, what has Spellbinder Bay come to, if a woman can't —"

"Stop talking, Pete," said Millie. "You're babbling! Calm down and take a deep breath."

Pete nodded, both hands on his chest and his lips forming a circle as he blew out a slow breath. He gazed at Millie with frightened eyes. "Underneath this counter, I have two laptops which I'm sure are the proceeds of a house burglary. I'll hand them over to you, but you must believe me when I say I'd never hurt a fly — literally! My house is full of them in the summer! They only have a twenty-eight-day lifespan. Who am I to shorten it any further?"

"You sound like a very kind man, Pete," said Judith, glancing at Millie. "But before we go any further, I'm afraid I'm going to have to ask you where you were last night? Between the hours of eleven, and one o'clock this morning."

"At home!" said Pete. "I'm always in bed before midnight!"

"Can anybody confirm that, Pete?" said Millie. "A wife, a partner?"

"Of course," said Pete. "My mum can confirm it! She saw me go to bed, and if I'd sneaked out at night, I'd have woken her — she's a very light sleeper!"

"Your mum?" said Millie.

"Yes," said Pete, picking his phone up and tapping at the screen. "I'll ring her right now, you can speak to her!"

"That won't be necessary, just yet," said Judith. "We came here to ask you some questions about gold. Specifically gold found by Tom Temples."

Pete stood up and hurried around the counter. "I've got his gold! It's safe — in my safe. It's in my office, come on, I'll show you. Do you suspect he murdered someone? I'd be shocked if he had — I've only met him once or twice, but he seems very nice. Certainly not the killing type." He paused. "Unless he got the gold fever. That can lead a man to violence."

Guiding them through the door next to a shelf displaying an eclectic mix of old vinyl records on one side, and a glass cabinet containing jewellery on the other, Pete glanced over his shoulder. "Well?" he said. "Have I got a murderer's gold in my safe?"

Millie followed Pete into the cluttered office. "I'm afraid it's not like that," she said. "I'm sorry to have to tell you that Tom is the victim. He was killed last night."

The colour draining from his face again, Pete dropped to his knees in front of the large safe standing next to a parched potted plant.

He fumbled with the combination wheel and gave a heavy sigh. "Poor Tom," he said, pulling the door outward. "This gold was supposed to pay for a new house. He was so happy. I was looking after it for him until it went to auction. He didn't want to keep it at home — he told me he was worried that other people had their eyes on it. He was going to let me keep ten-percent of the profits for keeping it safe, and arranging the sale."

"The people he was worried about," said Millie. "Did he say who they were?"

Pete retrieved a large leather pouch from the safe and placed it on his desk, the jangling sound of metal suggesting its contents. "He was over-reacting," said Pete. His eyes dropped. "Or so I thought. It was just the guys from the metal detecting club. Eric and the others. To be honest, I thought Tom was a little paranoid, but I wasn't going to turn down the offer of guarding his gold for him. Ten percent of the profits would have been a very nice nest egg. Very, very nice."

"How much gold did he find?" asked Judith.

Pete opened the drawstring holding the pouch closed, and poured the contents onto his desk. "That much," he said, as gold coins spilt from the neck of the bag and formed a pile. "A lot. That sort of haul is almost unheard of in the metal detecting community. He must have found a real hotspot."

Millie reached for the glittering pile, and picked up a coin. "Napoleon Empereur," she said, reading the letters which surrounded the head of a man, presumably Napoleon. She flipped the coin over. "Forty francs," she said.

"This pile is worth a fortune," said Pete.

"Isn't it classed as treasure?" said Judith. "Shouldn't it be reported?"

Pete licked his lips. "It *should* be," he said. "But the sales I arrange are attended by people who don't much care about little details like those."

"So, not only have you got stolen items on your premises, but you're also breaking the law by not reporting the discovery of treasure?" said Judith.

"No law has been broken yet," said Pete. "The finder has fourteen days in which to report any finds of importance. Tom only found this gold over the last few days."

"Forget about that for now," said Millie. "Keep the gold locked in your safe, Pete, and *don't* do anything with it."

"I won't," said Pete. "The gold is tarnished now anyway."

"I thought gold didn't rust," said Judith.

"Not tarnished in that way," said Pete, beginning to refill the pouch with coins. "Tarnished by violence. It happens with all precious metals and stones. The human race shouldn't be allowed pretty things — we don't know how to deal with them. That's what my mother says."

"She sounds very wise," said Millie. "We need to speak to the guys in the metal detecting club, Pete. Can you tell us where we can find them? Where their club-house is, or whatever it's called?"

"They don't have a club-house," said Pete, locking the safe. "Not what you're thinking of anyway. They meet in one of the sheds on the allotments at the end of Fish Row."

"Okay," said Millie. "And do you know when they meet there?"

"You'll find somebody there most days," said Pete. "Two of the guys are retired, and the other one is a part-time mechanic. They don't do much else with their time."

"Thank you for your help, Pete," said Judith, leaving the office and crossing the shop floor. "And don't you dare sell those computers you've got under your counter, I'm sure my dad will be interested in them after we get to the bottom of Tom's murder."

When the door had swung shut behind them, Judith smiled at Millie. "Fancy a visit to the allotments? If you're lucky, you'll find somebody kind enough to give you some nice fresh potatoes."

"What?" said Millie. "Why do I want potatoes?"

"For tonight!" said Judith. "George and I are coming for turkey, roast potatoes and cranberry sauce, remember?" She winked. "Unless for some reason you don't want George coming anymore? Unless he's done something that makes you mad? Jealous, even?"

Millie gritted her teeth, shrugged and walked in the direction of her car. "You're both still welcome to come," she said. "Like I said — I don't care what George does, *or* who he does *it* with. Dinner is still going ahead. As planned."

Chapter 10

With a fish processing factory at one end of the road, and allotment gardens at the other, the residents of Fish Row lived in terraced houses built on one side of the narrow road — sandwiched between the two suppliers of healthy eating staples. With the sea to the front, and the cliff with Spellbinder Hall atop it, away to the left, it seemed a pleasant place to live.

Millie parked the little two-seater car next to the open allotment gates, and gazed out to sea. A jet-ski bounced over waves close to the shoreline, its engine sound resembling the buzzing of an angry insect, and sun-worshipping holidaymakers were beginning to claim the areas of beach they would inhabit for the day.

The cafés, ice-cream parlours and tourist gift shops were already doing brisk business, and the aroma of frying onions emanated from the burger van parked alongside the small hut, from which people could rent old-fashioned wooden deck chairs for the day.

Seagulls squawked as they stood sentry on walls and roofs, waiting for the moment in which they would pounce on dropped food, and a group of elderly people, dressed in sporty clothing, hurried along the promenade.

"That's the pensioner's fitness club," said Judith. "And see the woman in the front? The one with white hair, wearing pink shorts?"

Millie nodded. "Yes. She looks very fit. I hope I can power walk like that when I reach her age."

Judith laughed. "That's Mrs Raymond," she said. "The lady who keeps asking Dad for a lift home from town with her shopping! Does she look like she needs any help to you?"

"Your father is a kind man," said Millie, smiling as Mrs Raymond dropped to the ground and began performing press-ups while the rest of the club caught up with her. "But I get your point. I think she's taking advantage of him."

"It's up to him, I suppose," said Judith. She sniffed at the salty air. "It's a shame we're investigating a murder. I wouldn't mind feeling the sand between my toes today."

Millie dragged her eyes from the seaside scene before her, and turned to face the allotments. "Speaking of which," she said, "let's get on with it. I want to find out who killed Tom. He was a nice guy. He didn't deserve a shovel in the skull."

"Which way?" said Judith. "There must be fifty sheds here, at least. It's not a small allotment, is it? Which shed do you think is the one the metal detectorists use?"

Millie gazed out over the carpet of crops. Several pathways led off into the allotments, one of them skirting the whole growing area, and others crisscrossing their way through the abundant plants. Sheds were dotted throughout the allotments, some painted in vivid colours, and others showing signs of age.

A few of the shed doors had been propped open, and a man nearby one of them gave a wave as he filled a watering can from one of the numerous wood shrouded taps, which rose from the ground.

Millie waved back. "Let's ask him," she said, heading along the nearest footpath, waving a honeybee from her face.

"Good morning!' said the man, as the girls approached. He put the watering can down at his feet and smiled. "It's nice to see some young folk here. The whole allotment lifestyle does seem to be catching on with the younger generation. I suspect it's the price of food in those supermarkets. I mean, who wants to pay a few quid for some mediocre spuds, when you can grow some real beauties for the price of some good old-fashioned digging and a few seeds? You can't beat potatoes dug fresh out of the ground, either!

They taste so much better. I haven't paid for a bag of spuds since nineteen-eighty-nine."

"As much as I agree with your sentiments," said Millie, dodging a wheelbarrow laden with dying weeds. "We're not here to do any gardening. We're looking for three men. One of them is named Eric. They're metal detectorists. Can you help us?"

"Everybody here knows Eric and the lads," said the man. "They've been a terrific help for lots of allotment owners — can you imagine how many rings fall off fingers when people are planting seeds, or digging weeds? You'd be surprised! Those chaps have found every single one! Necklaces and money, too." He pointed in the direction of a bright red shed in the centre of the gardens, its door standing open. "That's Eric's shed. The one with the lovely runner beans growing next to it. All three of the guys are inside — they arrived here early this morning, they seemed excited about something."

"Thank you," said Judith, glancing at Millie. "Oh, and the lovely fresh potatoes you spoke about... could you sell us a few? If you have any spare, of course."

"I've got plenty spare! Pop back here before you go," said the man. "I'll dig some up for you, but I won't take a penny from either of you. You'll enjoy eating them more if you don't pay — free food tastes so much nicer."

Following a footpath past a bed of courgettes on one side, and a bumper crop of rhubarb plants on the other, Millie heard men's voices drifting from the open doorway as she approached the shed.

"Are we rich?" said one voice.

"When it's been split three ways, we won't be *rich*," said another voice, which Millie recognised as the same man she'd witnessed threatening Tom in The Fur and Fangs. *Eric*. "But if we're sensible, none of us should ever be poor again. Especially you, Jack. You look like you've only got two years left in you!"

"Cheeky beggar," came a man's voice, almost drowned out by laughter. "There's plenty of life left in me! Just ask Pammy!"

"She'll spend all your gold finding a younger fella, Jack!" came the laughing retort.

Millie looked over her shoulder at Judith, and put a finger to her lips.

Nodding her understanding, Judith copied Millie's careful foot placement as she slowed her pace, and stopped next to the shed, hidden from its occupants by tall runner bean plants dotted with red flowers, around which several bees buzzed.

"She can have all my gold for all I care," said the man, who Millie presumed was Jack. "As long as Pamela is happy, I'm happy."

"You soft old sod," said another man, his voice sounding younger than the other two. "Use *some* of it to treat yourself."

"What will a young lad like you spend his on, Andy?" said Jack. "Flash cars and alcohol?"

"I don't know," said Andy. "I've never had much money before. Maybe a new car. We'll see."

The men went silent for a moment. Then Jack spoke again. "Do any of you feel guilty about Tom? I do. A little."

Millie's blood ran cold.

She stared at Judith, whose eyes widened. "They did it," she mouthed.

With a nod, Millie slipped her phone from her pocket and opened her voice recording app, aiming the microphone at the shed's open doorway.

"Don't feel guilty," said Eric. "I don't. Not in the slightest. He should have known better than to mess with the Spellbinder Sand Diggers."

"I don't know," said Jack. "I've always been an honest man. What we did last night, wasn't right. It wasn't honourable."

"Come on, Jack," said Eric. "Don't feel like that. Tom was devious. He crossed a line. He deserved it."

"It's alright for you two," said Andy. "I'm the one who did it. I'm the one who committed a crime. You three didn't *technically* break the law."

"We were all in a cordoned off area," said Jack. "There were signs stating that nobody was to go anywhere near that dinosaur skeleton that Tom found. That Sergeant Spencer bloke put them there himself. We were breaking the law just being there. You know how seriously illegal metal detecting is taken by the law."

"Wow," said Andy. "You sneaked past some police

tape. It was hardly the crime of the century. It's me who should be worried about the police, not you two. I can hardly believe I actually did it."

"Enough!" said Eric. "We were in it together, but as the founder of the Spellbinder Sand Diggers, and owner of this shed, I suggest we don't mention it again. Nobody will ever find out what happened, no evidence was left behind, and Tom's not going to report us, is he?"

"It *was* funny, though," said Jack. "When we left him there in the dunes like that!"

"That look on his face!" said Eric. "I'll never forget it! It was so funny! The look of absolute shock!"

For a brief moment, Millie wondered if one of the men was the possessed by the demon, but realised with a sinking hope for humanity, that all three of the men were in it together.

The evil emanating from the shed was of human origin. All forged by greed. *Gold fever*. She shuddered, and pointed at the open door. "After three," she mouthed at Judith. "One. Two. Three!"

Millie moved first, barging past the runner bean plants, angering the bees, which swarmed around her head. She swiped one away from the tip of her nose and burst into the shed, with Judith close behind her. "Nobody move!" she yelled, staring at the small gold-laden table standing in the centre of the semi-circle of men. "We know what you did last night!"

"Police!" shouted Judith, followed by a shriek. "Ow! I've been stung!"

Eric moved first. Grabbing the corner of the table, he hurled it in Millie's direction, the gold coins turning into painful projectiles which peppered Millie's face and neck.

"Ow!" shrieked Judith once more. "I'm getting stung all over!"

"Everybody leg it!" commanded Eric. "Good luck, fellas, it's each man for himself now! Godspeed, dear friends!"

"My Pammy's biscuits were on that table, Eric," said a balding man, placing a flat cap on his head. "Now they're all over the floor! Raisin and choc chip, they were, too! My favourites. She only makes them once a month!"

"Forget the biscuits, Jack," said Eric, kicking the toppled table towards Judith. "If this pair catches you, you'll be eating prison biscuits by next week, and *they* won't have raisins in them! I can assure you of that. And if they *do have*, I'd be dubious about their origin! Just run for it, Jack! *Both of you* run for it!"

A sharp pain erupted on Millie's neck, and she swiped at the attacking bee, knocking it to the floor. As another bee flew at her face, the three men in the shed made for the exit, barging past Millie and Judith as they made their escape.

Judith ran outside, her arms waving wildly as she swatted the stinging insects, and Millie followed her, fighting her own battle with the bees.

"They're escaping!" said Judith, a large red welt rising beneath her left eye.

Unhindered by bees, the three men each chose a different direction to run in. Eric made quick progress past a line of sheds, while Jack kept his head low as he limped through a cabbage patch, his biscuits seemingly forgotten, but it was Andy who Millie wanted most urgently to apprehend — the man who had confessed to having committed the crime.

Swatting a bee from her ear, she watched the young man preparing to vault a low fence on the opposite side of the allotments. He glanced over his shoulder as he placed a hand and a foot on top of the chain link metal, and began hoisting himself over.

"I can't chase them!" said Judith, swatting at the air. "I'm getting stung all over!"

Millie took a deep breath as instinct took control of her powers. The space behind her ribs burned as her magic grew, bubbling within her as it searched for a purpose. *A release.* Not sure of what spell she was about to cast, she raised a hand, purple sparks arcing between her fingertips, and pointed her fingers in Andy's direction.

A hand grasped her wrist, the fingers digging into her flesh, forcing it downwards. "No!" said Judith. "Look around you! There are too many witnesses. The concealment spell is good, but you shouldn't abuse its power by blatantly performing magic in front of so many non-paranormal people!"

Millie looked around the allotments. Judith was right. There were at least six people staring in her direction. She let the magic fizzle out, and the sparks vanished from her fingertips. "I'm sorry," she said. "It was the pain of the bee stings. I got angry. I wanted to catch Andy."

"Don't worry," said Judith, rubbing at the red marks on her face, and waving the last of the striped attackers from her arm. "He won't get far. We'll catch up with him. We'll catch up with all of them. That won't be hard, but we'll get Dad to do it. I think a uniformed police officer is required now. I don't know if anybody saw those sparks you created, but just in case — we need to make things appear as normal as they can be around here.

"We'll gather up the gold which Eric threw all over the place, and head back to your cottage. Then we'll use some magic to heal these stings. Dad can look for those three criminals while we keep an eye on the alien hunters and make sure they don't get near the demon skeleton."

"Excuse me," said a voice from behind them. "Will you still be wanting potatoes after that little fiasco? I dug some up for you."

"Oh, thank you," said Judith, taking the bag from the man's outstretched hand.

"That was quite the display you two put on," he said. "I couldn't help noticing what happened here. I think *everybody* in the allotments noticed what happened here."

"It was nothing," said Millie. "It's over now. Thank you for the potatoes."

The man smiled, his eyes briefly flashing vampire

black. "You used magic, young witch," he said. "I saw. Other people saw, too — non-paranormal people. You took a silly risk."

"You're a vampire?" said Millie.

The man bowed at the waist and gave a wide grin. "Indeed, I am. My name is Benjamin, but you may call me Ben. I know a little about what is going on in town — Henry has warned us all to be on the lookout for a demon, and has informed us that a man has been killed. Tom Temples, he said his name was. I didn't know of him, but no man deserves to have his life taken from him so cruelly. I hope the demon is caught soon."

"That's why we're here," said Millie. "We weren't sure if Tom had been murdered by the demon, or by a human. I think it's safe to say that after hearing the conversation we just listened to, *and* recorded, the demon is off the hook — for murder, at least. The men who just escaped are as evil as any demon."

"I'd be shocked to learn that any of the three men who were in that shed are capable of murder," said Ben. "But sometimes it transpires that people are not who we thought they were. Now, you two clear up that gold and get going. I'll lock Eric's shed and let Sergeant Spencer know if those three show their faces here again."

Chapter 11

Millie pressed the pause button on the screen of her phone, and the voice recording stopped.

"Okay," said Sergeant Spencer, nodding. "I'd class that as evidence. I'm leaving right away. I'm sure they'll all be in custody before teatime." He looked at Millie and Judith in turn. "Make sure you don't let those alien hunters near that skeleton, tell them that I'm still scouring the sand for forensic clues. I've sent off the campervan registration number, and I'm still waiting for it to go through the system. I've asked for the owner's identity and any criminal records he might have. It's taking longer than usual, but it shouldn't be too long."

Millie glanced through the patio window. The campervan remained where Mister Anon had parked it, and the two occupants were visible through the side window, seated at a table in the rear playing what looked like a board game.

"*Are* you still looking for evidence?" said Judith, applying some of the oily potion which Millie had made to the stings on her skin, her face relaxing as the magic began to work.

"No," said Sergeant Spencer. "There's nothing there to find. Soft sand doesn't hold footprints well, and I've found nothing else of interest. I've tested the shovel for fingerprints. There were two sets of prints on the handle, one was Tom's, and I can't find a match for the other person's prints in the system — they don't have a criminal record. I'm sure I'll find a match when I catch up with those metal detectorists, though."

"They killed him for gold," said Millie. "How awful."

Reuben gazed at the pile of gold on the kitchen table. "You think they killed Tom just to steal the gold he'd found?" he said. "Humans are so greedy."

"Some of them are," said Millie. "Not all. But yes, that's what I think. I can't think of any other reason why they'd have killed Tom, and the conversation I recorded at the shed seems to back up that theory."

"Money, love and jealousy," said Sergeant Spencer. "The three main motives for murder." He took a deep breath. "Okay. It's time I left. I doubt those detectorists will get very far, but I want them in custody sooner, rather than later."

"Be careful, Dad," said Judith. "There's three of them, and they're obviously willing to use violence."

"I'll be fine," said Sergeant Spencer, placing his hat on his head. He smiled at his daughter. "I promise."

Judith applied more of the potion to the back of her hand, the bee sting beginning to vanish almost immediately, and passed the little bottle to Millie. "I'll come with you, Dad," she said. "I don't want you to be on your own. I'd never forgive myself if something happened to you, and at least I can use magic if things do turn violent." She looked at Millie. "You'll be okay here on your own for a few hours, won't you? I'll be back in time for turkey and roast potatoes. Don't you worry about that. Or you could go with my dad, and I'll stay here? Somebody has to stay here, though — we don't want those alien hunters disturbing that skeleton."

Applying a small amount of the potion to her chin, the soothing scent of jasmine in her nostrils, Millie smiled. "I'll stay," she said. "Anyway, I won't be alone. I have Reuben."

Reuben flew to Millie's shoulder. "And I've got something I want to talk to you about," he said. "It's important."

Sergeant Spencer frowned. "I'm not sure it's a good idea. I think Judith should stay with you."

"Why?" said Millie. "The men from ASSHAT don't seem dangerous. I'll be fine. It will give me time to begin preparing the meal for tonight."

"And to listen to what I've got to tell you," said Reuben.

"And that," said Millie. "Don't worry."

"I'm more concerned about that other demon coming back, than I am about ASSHAT," said Sergeant Spencer.

Millie smiled. "I appreciate the concern, Dave, but I'm more than capable of looking after myself."

Sergeant Spencer's cheeks turned a rosy red, the cleft in his chin almost vanishing as he gave a wide grin. "Thank you, Millie," he said. "That meant a lot." He glanced at the door to the left of the fireplace. "If the worst did happen, and a manic demon broke into your cottage, then you've always got your cavern. Judith told me that when you lock it with magic from inside, nobody will be able to get in."

"The door becomes invisible if I lock it from inside," said Millie. "Like it was when I first arrived in Spellbinder Bay. Nobody will be able to see it, let alone get in." She pushed the cork stopper back into the potion bottle, and placed it on the table next to the gold coins. "You two get going. You've got a murderer to catch. I'll take this gold down to my cavern, where it'll be safe, and then keep a eye on the alien hunters while I prepare dinner. Reuben and I will be fine. Don't worry."

MILLIE PILED THE GOLD COINS IN AN EMPTY WOODEN

box, and placed it on one of the numerous shelves hewn into the rock wall of the cavern. The green glow from the cauldron — a waist high ring of stones containing magic captured from moonlight, cast a calming light over the cave walls, and Millie sighed as she stared into the swirling depths. "It's strange to think that my mother's energy is in there," she said. "She feels so close, yet she couldn't be further away from me."

Reuben flew from Millie's shoulder and landed on the rim of the cauldron, the green light reflected in his coal black eyes. He stared up at his witch. "Millie," he said. "You know I've been spending a lot of time down here recently?"

"Yes," said Millie, her eye catching movement below the surface of the liquid as a glowing white light flickered briefly, before darting away into the hidden depths.

"Well, I've been looking for something down here. Something in one of the books. A spell, to be exact," said Reuben. "A spell that I remember noticing when Esmeralda was creating potions down here one day. A spell which I think will help you." He averted his gaze. "A spell which I *hope* will help you."

Millie looked into the little birds eyes. "What spell, Reuben?" she said.

The cockatiel's little chest expanded as he took a deep breath. "It's... well, it's... it's a spell that... it's a spell that can..."

A loud hammering at the cottage's front door,

accompanied by shouting, drew Millie's attention. She glanced up the steps at the open cavern doorway which led to her living room. "Now what?" she said. "That sounds urgent!"

"The demon!" squawked Reuben, thrusting himself airborne and flying in erratic patterns around the cavern. "It's the demon! Trying to break the door down so it can devour me!"

"Calm down," said Millie. "That's not a demon. I know that voice, it's Mister Anon. I'll go and see what he wants, you can tell me all about that spell later."

Mister Anon's shouting grew louder, and the hammering on the door more urgent as Millie climbed the steps and approached the front door. "I'm coming!" she shouted. "Have some patience!"

The door opened to reveal the angry face of Mister Anon and the bewildered face of a man Millie had never seen before. Mister Anon removed his sunglasses and fixed Millie with an accusatory stare. "It's a good job one of us is watching the sand dunes, isn't it?" he said. "I just caught this man sniffing around!"

The tall man standing next to Mister Anon ripped his wrist from his captives hand, and took a step backwards. "How dare you!" he said. "You assaulted me!"

"I did not!" said Mister Anon. "I forcefully guided you away from an area of beach which is off limits to the general public. Didn't you see the police tape and the signs, or did you just choose to ignore them?" He looked at Millie. "Where is Sergeant Spencer? I saw him drive away almost an hour ago, and look what happened when he left — this man thought it was okay to trespass. He was digging around in the sand. He was taking photographs, too!"

"I wasn't digging!" said the man. "Or trespassing. I was checking that no damage was being done to the Sea-stock flowers. That's what I was taking photos of. They're a protected species, and when my department received an anonymous phone call, telling us that dinosaur hunters had been digging around in the area, we had to come and make sure the plants were safe. They only grow in a few sites in England, and this is one of them!"

"A likely story!" said Mister Anon. "Who are you? Are you trying to get your hands on *my* skeleton? Those bones are mine!"

"Forget about the bones for a moment," said Millie. "The area is off limits because it's the scene of a crime. The scene of a murder."

The man's eyes widened. "I had no idea there had been a murder! Our department was informed that fossil hunters were digging around in the dunes, but I haven't heard any reports about a murder. I certainly wouldn't have gone traipsing through a crime scene, had I known!"

"Okay," said Millie. "I can understand you not knowing about the murder. It hasn't been widely reported. Would you mind identifying yourself, though? You happen to be on my land."

The man nodded, and reached into the pocket of

his green jacket, withdrawing an identification card. "I'm Robin Price. I'm from DEFRA — the Department for Environment, food and Rural Affairs, and I didn't mean to trespass or sneak around." He pointed at the small white van parked near Millie's car. "I drove right up here, and nobody asked me any questions! It's not very well guarded for a murder scene, is it? I can't see one police officer, and I'd really like to speak with one about my mishandling at the hands of…" He looked Mister Anon up and down. "This… awful man in black."

"You're in luck," said Millie, pointing along the track as the sound of an engine drifted towards them on the wind. "Here comes the sergeant in charge."

"Wonderful timing," said Robin, slipping his identification back into his pocket as Mister Anon hurried away to intercept Sergeant Spencer's car.

"Yes," said Millie, with a puzzled frown. "He's back a lot sooner than I expected him to be."

"I'm not going to get that man in trouble," said Robin, watching as Mister Anon spoke to Sergeant Spencer through the car's open window. "He comes across as a little unhinged. I think he requires help, not criminal charges filed against him."

Millie nodded. " I agree," she said, looking out over the dunes. "So, are the flowers okay? I didn't know there were rare plants here. Not until yesterday, actually. A man I met told me. Perhaps it was him who phoned you?"

"Even if it was, and even if I knew — I couldn't

tell you," said Robin. "Everything's confidential these days. But I will tell you that are numerous members of several environmental organisations in this area, so you'd be surprised just how many people around here care for their surroundings."

"That's good to know," said Millie. "I've always tried not to stand on the flowers when I run through the dunes, but I'll take even more care not to damage them from now on."

"Don't worry too much. They're fine," said Robin. "The person who called the department yesterday exaggerated the extent of the problem. I didn't take the phone call, but the notes I was given say he was adamant that we came out immediately and stopped the fossil hunters from digging any more than they already had. He said the flowers were in imminent danger of being destroyed. We didn't have time to come out yesterday, but it seems it would have been a wasted journey anyway. The plants are fine, and as long as the police and fossil hunters are careful, there shouldn't be a problem. The storm damaged a few plants, but it's a healthy population."

Millie smiled as the crunch of gravel beneath boots indicated Sergeant Spencer's presence. The policeman gave her a quick nod, pointed at the campervan and spoke to Mister Anon, who shuffled alongside him. "I need to speak to the gentleman from DEFRA *without* your input. If he is, as you allege, about to make a false claim of assault against you, then I need to speak to him alone. I'll speak to you again later."

Mister Anon removed his sunglasses and glared at Robin. "Don't listen to anything he tells you, Sergeant Spencer. I hardly touched him."

Robin Price smiled at Mister Anon. "Don't worry, I'm not reporting you for assault. I'll put it down to over enthusiasm on your behalf."

"There we are!" said Sergeant Spencer. "Problem solved. Nice and simple! Nobody needs to get in trouble."

Mister Anon muttered something under his breath, and gave Robin a final glance laced with suspicion. He replaced his sunglasses, straightened his cap and made his way back to the campervan, his shoulders rolling as he walked. He paused as he opened the side door, and turned around to face the cottage. "I trust you'll hurry up and finish your forensic search of the sand dunes, Sergeant. I want access to that skeleton ASAP!" he shouted.

"Just get inside, would you?" yelled Sergeant Spencer. "I'll speak to you in due course."

When the van door had slammed shut behind the alien hunter, Sergeant Spencer smiled at Robin. "I just spoke to DEFRA on the telephone, after the gentleman who dragged you away from the sand dunes told me he thought you were using fake identification. Everything seems to be in order, but I would ask that you stay away from the dunes until my investigation is over," he said. "I *will* need to take a full statement from you, I'm afraid. It's standard procedure when somebody enters a crime scene without authorisation."

"In case I'm the murderer and I've returned to the scene of my heinous crime to spread my DNA everywhere, to put you off my scent?" smiled Robin.

Sergeant Spencer nodded. "That sort of thing," he said. "It's to protect you, too." He pointed towards his police car. "Would you mind taking a seat in my car for a moment, please? I'd like to have a quick word with this young lady."

"Of course," said Robin. He smiled at Millie. "It was nice meeting you. I'm not so sure about the man in black, though."

"You're back sooner than I expected," said Millie, as Robin headed for the car. "Where's Judith? Did you catch the detectorists already?"

"You could say that," said Sergeant Spencer. "Judith is in the hospital and —"

"The hospital?" said Millie, her stomach churning. "Oh no! What's happened?"

Sergeant Spencer placed a hand on Millie's arm. "Calm down," he urged. "It's not like that. Judith is fine. Honestly. It's not her who's been injured. It's one of those idiot metal detectorists — who, by the way, did *not* kill Tom."

"Really?" said Millie. "Are you sure?"

"Yes. With *total* certainty," said Sergeant Spencer. "That's why I rushed back here. I've spoken to Henry, and with a lack of other suspects, we're both in agreement that the demon probably killed Tom. Henry is still searching for it, but he says it's hiding well."

"And you think it might come back here. To the sand dunes. That's why you rushed back," said Millie.

Sergeant Spencer nodded. "Henry says that until the bones in the dunes are dust, the other demon may keep returning. I know you can look after yourself, Millie, but those two alien hunting clowns could be in danger."

"I could look after them, too," said Millie.

"Without magic?" said Sergeant Spencer. "You're tough, Millie, but what if the demon has possessed the body of a strong male? Without magic, I doubt you'd be able to fight him off, and to the alien hunters he'd appear to be a psychopathic human with anger issues — not a demon. Magic would need to be a last resort in their company."

"And you could use the magic you keep in that pouch on your belt," smiled Millie. "Without raising suspicion."

Sergeant Spencer patted the black nylon pouch on his hip. "Exactly," he said, with a wink. "A Taser would look a lot less dramatic than red sparks pouring from your fingertips! The demon has no supernatural powers while it's in a human body. A Taser should drop it like it would any other person."

"I understand," said Millie, smiling at the sergeant. "But I'll be happy when this is all over. I've got alien hunters camping in a rust-bucket next to my cottage, a murder scene and a decomposing demon in the sand dunes over there, a man from DEFRA sitting in a police car outside my home, and the worry that another demon might suddenly appear. Life is good."

"It will all be resolved soon enough," said Sergeant Spencer. "And life will get back to normal. In the meantime, Judith asked if you'd mind heading over to the hospital to help her. She's trying to take statements from the detectorists, but it's turned into a bit of a circus over there. I'll take a statement off the man from DEFRA, and then see if any information has come back about the owner of the campervan."

"Of course I'll help Judith," said Millie, closing the cottage door. She walked towards her car, pausing for a moment as Sergeant Spencer called her name. "Yes?" she answered.

"Do you call them biscuits or cookies?" said the sergeant. "You know, the things you dip in your tea."

"Erm, that was random," said Millie, opening the car door. "It depends. I call the thick ones cookies, and the thin ones biscuits. Why do you ask?"

Sergeant Spencer shrugged. "No reason," he said. "It was just a thought."

Chapter 12

"*B*iscuit, dear?" said the old lady in the seat alongside the hospital bed, thrusting a Tupperware box towards Millie. "There's a choice of chocolate chips or raisins. I *had* made a batch of raisins *and* chocolate chips, but these three fools dropped them all over the floor of that dusty shed when you two young ladies attempted to apprehend them." She pressed her lips together and glared at the man in the bed. "Isn't that right, Jack?"

"Yes, Pamela," said Jack, his striped pyjama jacket buttoned all the way up to his throat. "I'm sorry, but it was Eric who dropped them, not me."

"Whoa there, Jack," said Eric, from a seat near the window, the sunlight bouncing off the portion of his scalp not covered by his comb-over. "We don't tell tales on one another in The Spellbinder Sand Diggers! The youngsters call people like that *dirty grasses*."

"Sorry, Eric," said Jack, fiddling with the cannula inserted in the back of his hand. "It's the painkillers. They've given me loose lips."

"Stop saying sorry!" snapped Pamela, slapping Jack on the thigh, eliciting a grimace of pain from the injured man. "You're a daft old sod who has broken his hip because he should have known better. *Two* of you are daft old sods who should have known better, and the other one is a silly young man who is easily led." She fixed Andy with a fierce stare. "Isn't that right, young man?"

Andy passed his red baseball cap nervously from one hand to the other and gave a meek nod. "Yes, Mrs Hopkins," he said. "I'm sorry, Mrs Hopkins."

"What will your mother say, Andrew?" continued Pamela Hopkins. "When she finds out about this?"

Andy stared at the tiled floor, running a hand through his curly black hair. "She won't be happy?" he guessed.

"No! She won't!" said Pamela. "She'll be livid! I'm sure!" She smiled up at Millie and gave the box in her hand a seductive shake. "Go on, have one, my dear. You'll like them! The other policewoman did, didn't you, dear?"

"They were very nice," said Judith from her seat on the other side of the bed, wiping crumbs from the open file in her lap, giving Millie a nervous sideways glance.

Pamela's face blossomed with pride. "And the tubby sergeant really enjoyed them, didn't he? He had three, the greedy blighter! I don't mind, though. He could have had five if he'd liked. I do enjoy cooking for a man who tucks in!"

"Yes, he enjoyed them, too," said Judith.

"I didn't care much for his terminology, though," said Pamela. "He was a little disrespectful, but it transpired that it was ignorance on his behalf. Nothing more. There was no malice intended. Or so he says."

Plucking one of the biscuits from the box, Millie frowned. "Sergeant Spencer was disrespectful?" she said. "That doesn't sound like him at all. What did he do?"

Pamela placed the box on the bedside table, next to a plastic jug filled with water, and crossed her arms. She stared at Judith. "He's your father, my dear. You tell your colleague what he did."

Judith sighed. "He called them cookies," she said.

Pamela took a deep breath through her nose, and exhaled slowly. "Cookies!" she spat. "Cookies? Since when did we become so American? It's no good. What happened to traditional British standards?" She narrowed her eyes as she lectured Judith. "You keep an eye on him. I saw it happen during the war, when the young American soldiers were stationed here. My mother almost pulled her hair out when she invited a few of them for tea, and they called her homemade plum jam *fruit preserve.*" She tapped Jack on the leg again. "My mother told you that story when she was still alive, didn't she, Jack?"

Jack gave a soft moan. "Yes, Pamela. She did. The

memory of it never left her. She was very upset by the whole thing."

"Yes, she was," said Pamela, aiming a wagging finger at Judith. "She was very upset indeed! You watch that father of yours, my dear. It might just be calling biscuits *cookies* for the moment, but before you know it he'll be putting things in the *trunk* of his car, turning the *faucet* on when he wants to wash his hands and, God forbid, calling a nappy a *diaper*."

"I'm sure it won't get that far," said Judith. "I'll keep an eye on him. I promise."

"Good," said Pamela. She gazed around the room. "Now, where were we? Oh, yes! You were taking statements from these three idiots concerning the events surrounding the murder of Tom Temples! Then Sergeant Spencer *suddenly* remembered he had an appointment and needed to rush off. He promised he'd send another officer in his place, and *finally*, she's arrived." She selected a biscuit from the box and took a large bite. "Don't let me interfere with your questioning. Please, carry on. I've said my piece."

Millie grabbed a chair from the corner, and placed it next to Judith's. Taking a bite of her biscuit, she sat down, nodding in approval at Pamela as she discovered a spicy hit of cinnamon lurking below the juicy sweetness of a raisin.

Pamela gave a contented smile and nibbled at her own biscuit, tutting as Jack gave another groan of pain. "Count yourself lucky," she said. "It could have been both hips. Then you'd have had a reason to make those irritating sounds of discomfort."

Millie looked at the sheet of paper in Judith's lap. "Maybe you should update me?" she suggested.

"It's a sordid story," said Pamela. "Be warned."

Judith cleared her throat. "I'll start from when the three men attempted to escape from the allotments," she said. "They didn't get far. Jack almost covered a full three hundred metres before tripping on a kerb and breaking his hip. When he was brought to hospital he confessed he'd been running from the police, so one of the nurses called Sergeant Spencer."

"Called your father, my dear," said Pamela. "Don't be so formal. We're all friends, here."

Judith gave an almost imperceptible sigh, and looked at Millie. "The nurse phoned *my father* while he and I were searching for the suspects, so we came straight here and —"

"Good heavens!" said Pamela. "The wheels of justice really do spin slowly, don't they? Spit it out! Come on!" She took another bite of her biscuit. "In fact, allow me to tell your colleague what happened. When the hospital called me to inform me of my husband's mishap, I fed the cat, watered the plants, ironed some of Jack's pyjamas, waited for some oven-fresh biscuits to cool down, put them in a box and then rushed here in a blind panic. I was happy to find out that they'd put him in this lovely room on his own, and not some geriatric ward. That took the sting out of the shock of learning he'd hurt himself. I almost feel like I'm in a hotel room. I was even offered a coffee when I arrived. It's all a lot of fun, I must say."

"They knew the police would be coming to question him," said Judith. "That's why he's in this room. It's for his privacy."

"And they say crime doesn't pay," said Pamela. "Had Jack broken his hip while gardening, and not while on the run from the police, he'd have been thrown into a mixed ward — along with the other elderly losers. Drinking prune juice and gossiping about who takes the most medication."

"Shall we move this along?" suggested Millie. "What happened next?"

Judith wiped a biscuit crumb from the corner of her mouth. "Me and Dad found —"

"Dad and I," corrected Pamela. "Must we lose our beautiful language?"

Judith closed her eyes for a moment, her fingertips whitening on the pen in her hand. "*Dad and I* found Eric and Andy where Jack had suggested we would, in —"

Eric stood up, his seat rocking as he rammed it backwards. "Dirty grass, Jack!"

"Sit down, Eric," snapped Pamela. "I'd have told the police they could have found you and Andy in the snooker hall, if Jack hadn't! How dare you act like this. A man has been murdered, and it seems that you three idiots were the last people to see him alive, apart from the person who murdered him, of course. Show the police, and poor Tom Temples some respect!"

"Sorry, Pammy," said Eric, lowering himself into his seat. "I was forgetting myself. It must be the stress of the situation."

"Eric," hissed Jack, as his wife's eyes darkened.

"Pamela, I mean!" Eric said. "I'm sorry, Pamela. God forgive me."

"Never. Let. Me. Hear. You. Call. Me. That. Again, Eric," warned Pamela. "Only the milkman, my rheumatologist, the lovely Indian man in the corner shop and Jack – on the third Friday night of every month, may call me by my pet name!"

"Sorry," said Eric, lowering his gaze. "I won't do it again."

Pamela studied Eric for a moment, and then nodded in Judith's direction. "Carry on, young lady, but please hurry up and get to the meat and bones. I'm dying to find out whose idea it was, and when I do, that person had better watch out!"

Jack pulled the white bed-sheet up to his chin, and Eric made a squeaking sound as he bowed his head, his face losing colour as quickly as Millie was losing her patience. She shook her head in frustration, and snatched the piece of paper from Judith's lap, scanning the notes quickly. "Eric and Andy were brought here instead of the police station when they told Sergeant Spencer what had happened," she murmured. She read the next few lines and looked up. "The crime we heard Andy confessing to was not murder, it was… tampering with another man's metal detector?" She raised an eyebrow in Andy's direction.

"That's what you did? That's the crime you were talking about in the shed?"

Andy gave a worried nod. "Yes. And I'm sorry. I hope you'll be lenient with me. It's my first offence!"

"I have a recording on my phone of you three laughing about leaving Tom in the sand dunes," said Millie. "You said you'd never get caught because he couldn't possibly give evidence, and you even mentioned the look on his face when you left him there. If you hadn't hurt him, what was all that about? What exactly did you do, and what on earth happened in the sand dunes?"

Pamela reached across the bed and pointed at the sheet of paper. "That's all written on that paper, my dear. Your colleague wrote it down before you arrived. I'm only interested in whose idea it was."

Millie tossed the piece of paper onto the bed. "I'd like to hear it for myself, Pamela. If you don't mind, that is?" she said, staring the older woman in the eyes. "I happened to like Tom, and I'd like to know what these three men did to him. From their own mouths."

Pamela sat back in her seat and took another biscuit from the box. "Of course," she said. She pointed a bony finger at Andy. "Tell her what you did!"

Andy's face crumpled, and he made a soft sobbing sound. "I went in Tom's car and fiddled with his metal detector! I'm sorry. Eric made me do it! It was his idea!"

"I'm surrounded by grasses," muttered Eric.

"You'll be six-feet under the grass, by the time I've finished with you, Eric!" snapped Pamela.

"Eric found out which part of the beach Tom was finding the gold coins on," said Judith. "That's how it began."

"Mrs Jordan told me," said Eric. "She'd been walking her dog on the beach and had seen a lot of activity in the dunes. I saw her in town. She knows I'm a metal detectorist and assumed I'd like to know what another detectorist had been up to. She said Tom had found some bones in the dunes, and the area was being cordoned off."

"Go on," said Millie.

"Well, I assumed that Tom had found the bones in the same place he was looking for gold, so I went to have a look," said Eric, "but when I got to the nature reserve carpark, I found Tom in his car. He was about to leave, but when he saw me, he got out of his car to speak to me."

"What did he say?" asked Millie.

"I thought he wanted an argument," said Eric. "After what had happened in the pub the night before, you know? I even tried to roll my sleeves up – in case there were fisticuffs, but my forearms are too wide. It's all those years of swinging a detector. It really works the old muscles."

Massaging her temple with a finger, Millie took a breath. "Did he want an argument?"

"No," said Eric. "He wanted a truce. He told me that there was still gold in the dunes, but that the dinosaur bones he'd found were of an unknown species. They were of great importance, he told me. He said that the fossil hunters would keep on digging in the dunes, looking for more remains."

"And they'd find the gold," said Jack. "Instead of him."

"Quiet, Jack," snapped Pamela. "Speak when you're spoken to!"

"Jack is right," said Eric. "And not only that. Tom was only able to find those coins because that storm had shifted a lot of sand. The sand will soon shift back, though. Another week or two and a few gusts of heavy wind, and those coins would have been lost again – buried under too much sand. A detector can only find metal up to a certain depth, you see?"

"I see," said Millie. "Carry on, Eric. What sort of truce did Tom want?"

The seat creaked under Eric as he leaned forward. "He suggested that we sneak onto the dunes under the cover of darkness and find as many coins as we could. All of us. Him and The Spellbinder Sand Diggers working as a team. Four detectors would be better than one, he said, and rather than lose a lot of those coins, he suggested we find as many as we could between us, and then split them four ways."

"And you said yes?" asked Millie.

"Oh yes!" said Eric. "But I was angry at Tom. He'd dissed the Spellbinder Sand Diggers in front —"

"He did *what?*" said Pamela. "How old are you, Eric?"

"Sorry," said Eric. "He'd *disrespected* the club in front of all the other customers in The Fur and Fangs. You heard him! He embarrassed me!"

"You were both as bad as each other," said Millie, recalling the argument. "Anyway, what did you do?"

"I wanted to get him back," said Eric. "I wanted revenge."

"How petty," said Pamela. "You men and your pride."

"What sort of revenge?" said Millie.

"I didn't know," said Eric. "I couldn't think of anything. I've never had to wreak my revenge before, you see? I didn't know where to start, it was complicated if I'm honest, but then I had an idea! A good idea!"

"It wasn't a good idea," said Judith. She looked at Millie. "Wait until you hear this."

"It worked," said Eric. "That makes it a good idea. Before Tom left the carpark, he suggested we meet there again at eleven o'clock last night. When it would be *really* dark. We didn't want to get in trouble, you see. If we'd been caught using our detectors in an area we shouldn't have been in, the police would been entitled to confiscate our equipment, and none of us wanted that to happen. Especially Tom, with his fancy machine. Only a show off would need an expensive machine like that, anyway!"

"Don't speak ill of the dead, Eric," said Pamela. "It's rude."

"Sorry," said Eric. "Where was I? Oh yes. Before

Tom left the carpark, he told me he was taking his car to be fixed before he went home. To the garage that I knew Andy works in."

"I didn't want to do it!" said Andy. "Eric told me it was my duty as a member of The Spellbinder Sand Diggers!"

"What did he ask you to do, Andy?" said Millie.

"He wanted me to change the batteries in Tom's metal detector," said Andy. "It was easy. Tom left the keys with Shirley on reception, and I offered to do the work on his car. While I was doing it, I switched the batteries in his metal detector with the ones in mine. Most detectors use the same alkaline batteries, and the ones in my machine were on their last legs. They'd started giving up the last time I'd gone detecting. I'd been meaning to change them."

"You just happened to have your metal detector with you at work?" asked Judith.

"It's always in my car," said Andy. "You never know when the urge to swing a detector will strike."

"My plan worked," said Eric. "Tom was new to the hobby of metal detecting. He thought he was clever — finding all that gold, but he had a lot to learn. One of those things being to always carry spare batteries. When we met Tom last night, and went onto the dunes, his batteries only lasted for a few minutes before they gave out. He was devastated, and while we found all the gold coins, he could only watch with a look of disappointment on his face."

"I felt guilty," said Jack. "He asked if we were still

going to split the gold with him, but Eric just laughed in his face."

"Don't try and make Eric look worse than you are, Jack," said Pamela. "You're just as bad! And you lied to me — you told me you were going to Eric's house to play poker last night. Not infiltrating cordoned off areas looking for lost treasure! You're not Indiana Jones, Jack. You're a silly old man!"

"I'm sorry," said Jack. "I feel awful, about everything."

Eric looked at the floor. "Me, too. If I'd known he was going to die, I wouldn't have laughed at him, but how could I have known? The three of us stayed for an hour, until we couldn't find any more coins. We left Tom digging in the sand with his shovel, desperate to find gold. We had no idea what was going to happen to him. We wouldn't have left him there alone if we had."

"Why did you run?" said Millie. "When we came to your shed today?"

"Because we'd broken the law," said Eric. "We'd been nighthawking."

"And I'd have lost my job if the garage had found out what I'd done to a customer while his car was in our care," said Andy. "And what I did was stealing — I took the good batteries out of his detector and changed them for old ones. That's stealing! I've never broken the law in my life. That's why I ran!"

"I ran because Eric told us to," said Jack. "It was exciting, until I tripped and hurt myself."

"Would you jump off a cliff if Eric told you to, Jack?" said Pamela.

Jack shrugged. "I dunno," he muttered. "Maybe. How high is the cliff?"

"Okay. Let's get back on track," said Millie, wondering if the hospital room she'd wandered into was in a different dimension — a dimension populated by village idiots. "Did you see anybody else in the sand dunes before you left Tom behind? Or hear anything unusual?"

"No," said Eric. "Nothing."

"Were any of you shining a torch around?" asked Judith. "Torchlight was seen in the dunes just before Tom was killed. Was that one of you?"

"No chance," said Eric. "None of us brought a torch, neither us three or Tom. I brought a little headlamp along, but that uses red light which can't be seen from a distance. I hardly used it anyway — the moon gave us enough light to find the coins in the holes we'd dug. We wouldn't have been stupid enough to shine a torch around — we shouldn't have been there. We were nighthawking. We'd have been asking for trouble. That's what we meant when you heard us saying that Jack couldn't report us — he'd been nighthawking, too. He'd have dropped himself in trouble along with us."

Pamela cast a stern glance at each of the men. "You've been very silly," she said. "The three of you!" She bit into a biscuit and smiled at Millie. "Are they in trouble? Will they get criminal records? Or go to prison? I hope not, because I'm not sure I could wait for Jack if he had to do time. I'm not sure I could be married to an old lag."

"I doubt it," said Millie. "They've been foolish, but there are still bigger fish to fry."

"You mean finding the person who *did* kill Tom?" said Jack.

Or demon, thought Millie. "Yes," she said. "I mean finding the person who killed Tom."

Chapter 13

*P*lacing the turkey in an oven tray, and staring at the pile of unpeeled potatoes, Millie glanced at the wall clock. "I haven't got time," she said. "They'll be here soon. I meant to prepare it earlier, but I got side-tracked by Mister Anon and the man from DEFRA, and then all that nonsense in the hospital."

"You *know* you can do it, Millie," said Reuben, perched on the top-rail of a kitchen chair. "You could have it prepared in minutes — if you'd just give in to temptation."

Placing a whole head of cauliflower on a chopping board, Millie shook her head. "No. That's cheating. I promised George and Judith a home cooked meal."

Sergeant Spencer looked up from his notebook, and placed his empty mug on the table. "Don't worry about what Judith thinks," he said. "She uses magic in the kitchen all the time. She thinks I don't know, but I've seen her."

Millie rubbed butter into the turkey, the warm glow of magic rising in her chest as she considered utilising her powers for such a trivial task. She looked at Sergeant Spencer. "You won't tell them I cheated?" she said.

"You know me better than that, Millie," he said. "I hope so, anyway. Of course I won't... if you let me watch, that is. I enjoy watching magic being performed."

"I'll do better than that," said Millie. "Why don't you join us for dinner?"

"Oh no. I wouldn't do that to you," said Sergeant Spencer. "Judith told me you have a crush on George. I realise Judith will be eating with you and George, but that's a little different than a middle-aged policeman joining you. I'd cramp your style."

Heat burst from Millie's chest, wending a route over her shoulders, along her arms, and into her hands — where magic sparked at her fingertips. She focused on the turkey in the oven tray and allowed the magic to leave her in a frustrated burst of energy, the skin of the bird beginning to brown almost immediately as it was wrapped in coiling tendrils of purple light. She turned her head to face the policeman. "I do *not* have a crush on George," she said, magic still spewing from her fingertips. "How dare you!"

"Okay!" said Sergeant Spencer. "I got the wrong end of the stick! Judith told me you had a crush on him. I'm sorry. I spoke out of turn, but calm down, and save some of that energy for the roast potatoes. You're going to cremate that poor bird if you're not careful."

"Yeah. Calm the hell down, Millie," squawked Reuben. "Don't be so sensitive. We all know you like George, and we all know *he* is fond of *you*."

The salty aroma of crispy turkey skin rising to her nostrils, Millie took a calming breath and regained control of her powers, the sparks at her fingertips flickering as they died. "I'm sorry," she said. "I know I'm too sensitive when it comes to George."

"That's okay," said Sergeant Spencer. "We're all guilty of being a little sensitive when it comes to matters of the heart."

Her cheeks burning, Millie sat down next to the policeman. "I don't know what to do," she admitted. "I've only ever had one real boyfriend. I mean a boyfriend who I *actually* cared for, and he cheated on me. With my so-called best friend. I'm scared of that happening again, and I'm scared that maybe George *doesn't* like me. I don't want to make a fool of myself."

"He likes you," said Reuben. "Believe me. I've seen the way he looks at you."

"So how do you explain the fact that he's been seeing another girl?" said Millie. "A blonde bombshell, as Judith called her. A *nurse*. He went for a drink with her, and we saw him riding around on his motorbike with her this morning! Is that what George would do if he liked me?"

Sergeant Spencer reached into his pocket and withdrew a white handkerchief. "It's clean," he said. "I never use it. It's a habit my grandmother installed in me. 'Always carry a clean handkerchief, David,' she used to say. I put a clean one in my pocket every morning. It's about time one of them got some use."

Millie laughed as she wiped her eyes with soft cotton. "Thank you," she said. "It's nice to be able to let it out."

"Would you take some advice from a slightly overweight, middle-aged man, whose own dating history has not exactly been perfect?" asked Sergeant Spencer, his brow furrowed with concern.

Would she? Of course she would! The last time an older man had offered her advice, it had been her Uncle James. He cared about Millie, and her for him, but speaking to Millie about personal things — things a father would talk to a daughter about, had never come naturally to him. It had always been an uncomfortable experience for Millie, and she suspected it had been the same for her uncle, too.

Sergeant Spencer, on the other hand, seemed to be drawing on his experience of bringing up his adopted daughter as a single father. He offered a genuine smile, and his eyes showed a kind sparkle which put Millie at ease. She nodded. "Yes," she said. "I'd like some advice."

"Don't hold anything in, Millie. That's my advice," he said. "Be honest with George. Tell him how you feel." He gave a wide grin. "You know those butterflies you get in your stomach when you see him, and the lump which appears in your throat when you speak to him? The lump which makes it hard to get your words out properly?"

Millie nodded, giving the sergeant a smile. "Yes," she said. "I know all about those."

"Well, those aren't things which happen exclusively to women," said Sergeant Spencer. "I can almost guarantee that George is experiencing exactly the same emotions as you. Us men might try and pretend we're aloof when it comes to the opposite sex, but believe me, we turn to jelly inside when we see the person we like, too — just like you members of the fairer sex do."

"You think I should tell him?" asked Millie. "Just like that?"

"Wait for the right moment, of course," said Sergeant Spencer. "But yes. That would be my advice."

"What about the nurse, though?" said Millie. "I know we're not together or anything, so what he does is his business, but if he *does* like me, why is he going out for drinks and motorbike rides with another woman?"

Sergeant Spencer sat back in his seat. "I've known George Brown since I moved to this town. And I'm aware that he's lived here since the nineteen-fifties — never ageing, and with that annoyingly handsome head of his — easily able to attract women."

"That doesn't make me feel much better," said

Millie. "You telling me that he's had plenty of girl-friends."

"I didn't say that," said Sergeant Spencer, with a grin. "I said he was easily able to attract women. What I'm trying to say, is that in all the time I've been in Spellbinder Bay, I've never known him to be in a relationship with anyone, and as far as I know, he was never in one before I moved here." He leaned forward again. "What I'm saying, Millie. Is that I'd be very surprised if George has suddenly become interested in two women at the same time."

"You and the blonde bombshell nurse," added Reuben. "I feel that Sergeant Spencer could have been clearer about that."

"I understood what he meant, Reuben," said Millie. She looked at the policeman. "Then who is she? If not somebody he's romantically interested in? A friend?"

"I can't answer that," said Sergeant Spencer. "Only George can. You should ask him. He and Judith should be here soon."

Spinning in her seat, Millie looked up at the clock. "I didn't realise the time! Do you *both* promise that if I use magic to cook the rest of the meal, you won't tell them?"

"You can demand that *I* don't," said Reuben. "And I'd be forced to comply. I'm your familiar. That's the way it rolls. I hope you'll take my word instead, though." He bowed his head. "I promise I won't."

"I promise, too," said Sergeant Spencer. "I won't say a word."

"Thank you," said Millie, getting to her feet as two potatoes and a peeling knife rose gently into the air above the kitchen counter. "Are you sure you won't stay for some? There's plenty of turkey."

"No," said Sergeant Spencer. "Enjoy your meal with your friends, Millie. I'm going to have another look around in the sand dunes. To see if there's anything I missed. I may check on the demon's bones, too. To see how the rapid decomposition is coming along. I'll be glad when those bones are dust."

Millie frowned. "Thank you for that talk. It took my mind off other things. I'd almost forgotten about demons and murdered metal detectorists," she said. "Alien hunters in camping vans, too."

Sergeant Spencer stood up. "I'm glad I could help you," he said. "I once made the mistake of not telling a woman what I really thought of her. By the time I'd plucked up the courage to tell her, it was too late. She'd gone. And as for the other things — try and put them out of your mind for tonight. After hearing what those idiots from The Spellbinder Sand Diggers had to say, I'm now certain that Tom was killed by the second demon. Henry thinks he has a lead on it, so everything should be back to normal sooner, rather than later."

GEORGE CLOSED HIS EYES AS HE BIT INTO A ROAST potato. "Wow!" he said. "These are really good! They're so crunchy. Just how they should be."

Judith spooned a second blob of cranberry sauce onto her plate and reached for the gravy boat. "He's right, Millie. It's a wonderful meal, thank you."

Millie looked out into the darkness. "I wish your dad had eaten with us," she said. "I feel sorry for him, sitting out there in his car. Alone."

"You took a plate out to him," said Judith. "Anyway, he *wants* to be out there. He's worried that the other demon might come back, and he told me he's not taking his eyes off those two men in the campervan. He received an email from the FBI about Mister Anon."

"The FBI?" said Millie, loading her fork with gravy covered turkey meat. "Why do *they* have information about Mister Anon?"

Judith shrugged, and spooned some cauliflower onto the small plate in front of Reuben. "I'm not sure. Neither is Dad, yet. When he put the campervan registration through the system, the information he received informed him that the owner was of interest to American law enforcement agencies, particularly the FBI. Dad contacted them and they sent him a brief email telling him they'd compile all the information they had on whoever Mister Anon *really* is, and send it on to him. He's still waiting for that second email."

"Can we forget about all that stuff for tonight?"

said George. "Murders, demons and alien hunters, I mean. Maybe we should talk about other things?"

Reuben pecked at a slice of turkey. "Yeah, like who that blonde bimbo Millie and Judith saw you with on the back of your bike is, George. The one dressed like a cheap street hooker, and not a woman taking her safety as a pillion passenger very seriously."

"What did you say about her?" said George, his face hardening. "Watch your mouth, *birdbrain*, or I may be forced to do something I *might* regret."

"Calm it, bloodsucker!" squawked Reuben. "Don't threaten me at my own dinner table! I can't help it if you've got a liking for bimbos!"

The table shook as George's fist came down on it. "I mean it, Reuben!" he warned, his eyes flickering between black and hazel.

"George!" said Millie. "Don't speak to him like that. He was only repeating what he heard me and Judith saying." She stared at Reuben. "But I didn't use the word *bimbo*. I said *bombshell*. The difference is vast. But you must admit, George — when we saw you this morning, *whoever* she is, certainly wasn't dressed for motorbike riding."

George sighed. "I'm sorry," he said. "I'm very defensive about her, that's all."

"Oh, you are, are you?" said Millie, pouring herself some iced-water. "You're *very defensive* about her, are you?"

George chewed the food in his mouth slowly, and fixed Millie with a hard gaze. "Is there anything wrong with that?" he said. "Me being defensive about a young lady? Or is there something I should know about? Something which would make it wrong for me to care about her? Is there somebody else that I should be reserving my care for? Somebody who just can't tell me that that's the case?"

"You *care about her*, as well as being defensive about her?" said Millie, spearing a slice of turkey with her fork, the metal prongs screeching on her plate. "That's nice for you. And her. I suppose she's the nurse you spoke about, is she? The nurse you went for a *drink* with."

The vein above George's right eye throbbed, and he licked his lips. "Yes, she's the nurse. Are you trying to tell me something, Millie, or are you just being childish?"

"Oh," said Millie, mashing a chunk of cauliflower, the handle of her fork beginning to bend. "I'm being childish, am I?"

Judith gave a polite cough. "Did you use semolina on these potatoes to get them so crunchy, Millie?"

"No, Judith," said Millie. "Thank you for your interest, but I did not use semolina on the potatoes to get them so crispy. I used magic to cook the whole meal. And I'm glad I didn't waste time slaving over a hot stove. Some people don't deserve it!"

"Well, they're very nice potatoes, Millie," said Judith, pushing a garden pea around her plate. "Aren't they, George?"

George placed his knife and fork side by side on

his plate, and pushed the chair back as he got to his feet. "I've had better potatoes," he said. "*And* better company. I think I'll be leaving now. Thank you for the meal, Millie. It was adequate."

"You're welcome," said Millie. "Would you like me to put some in a doggy bag for you?"

"I don't have a —" began George. He nodded slowly, and sucked in a deep breath. "Oh. I see, Millie. *Very* clever. I won't be feeding her scraps from this table, though. She deserves far better than a mediocre meal cooked with magic, by a bitchy witch."

"Don't slam the door on your way out, George," said Millie, refusing to look the vampire in his eyes. "And I trust we won't be seeing you at the pub quiz next week? Judith and I are *The Dazzling Duo*. You cramped our style."

"Maybe I'll be there," said George stomping the full length of the open plan cottage, and grabbing his helmet and jacket from a hook near the front door. "And maybe I'll have a new pub quiz partner!"

"Maybe you'll get out of my cottage before I throw you out!" snapped Millie, her back to the front door, and a tear brimming in her eye.

"Maybe I will," said George, opening the door and allowing a fragrant gust of night air into the cottage. "Goodbye, Judith. I enjoyed your company. The other two, not so much."

"The feeling is mutual!" squawked Reuben. He lifted his head. "Are you really leaving, George? Can I have the potatoes you left on your plate, please?"

As the door slammed shut behind George, Millie looked at Judith. "I'm sorry I ruined the meal," she said, getting to her feet, warm tears on her cheeks. "I'm going to my bedroom. Please help yourself to pudding. It's a raspberry cheesecake. It's in the fridge."

"Millie," said Judith, getting to her feet. "Let me—"

"I'm sorry, Judith," said Millie, heading for the door to the right of the fireplace, which would take her to the bedrooms. "I know I'm being irrational, but I just need some time alone."

As George's motorbike engine burst into life outside. Millie curled up on her bed, the framed photograph of her mother laying on the pillow beside her. "I wish you were here, Mum," she said. "I need a cuddle, and I have nobody else to ask for one." She reached for the sealed envelope on the bedside table, and held it tight against her chest. "What does it say in this letter, Mum?" she said, closing her eyes. "What does it say?"

Chapter 14

"Millie? Millie? Wake up," said the small voice next to her ear.

"Reuben?" said Millie, blinking to clear her vision. "What time is it? How long have I been asleep? Is it morning? What time is it?"

The cockatiel hopped from the pillow, onto Millie's chest, and stared her in the eye. "You've only been asleep for twenty minutes. It's only nine o'clock at night. Judith said I should leave you to sleep when her father told her the news, but I disagreed. I told her you would want to know what was happening, too, after all, they're parked on your land."

"What are you talking about, Reuben?" said Millie, wiping a tear stain from the glass which protected the photograph of her mother.

"Sergeant Spencer had an email," said Reuben. "From the FBI. He's going to confront Mister Anon right away. I told him and Judith to wait for you. I told them you'd like to know what was happening."

"You're right, Reuben," said Millie, propping herself up on an elbow. "I would like to know what's happening."

"Well, let's get going," said Reuben. "Sergeant Spencer is chomping at the bit. He can't wait to knock on the campervan door and confront Mister Anon."

Millie rubbed her eyes and sat up. The envelope containing the letter from her mother lay on the mattress beneath her, and she picked it up, straightening a crease from it, and sighing as her fingertips brushed the damp spot on the corner which her tears had made. "I'm sorry about what happened at dinner," she said. "I don't know what came over me. I feel foolish. George must hate me."

"I'm sure he doesn't hate you, but I know what came over you," said Reuben. "It's that letter in your hand, Millie. I saw the way you acted earlier tonight, when Sergeant Spencer spoke to you about George. You looked at him in a way I've never seen you look at anyone before. You looked at him like a child would look at their parent. You soaked up every word he spoke to you."

Millie placed the letter on her bedside table, and swung her legs off the bed. "Don't be silly, Reuben," she said. "I didn't look at him like that, and *if* I did, it sounds a bit creepy. He must think I'm weird."

"He didn't notice. It wasn't *that* obvious," said Reuben. "I noticed because it's my duty as your familiar to make sure you're okay, Millie, and right now… I don't think you are. And in my opinion, it's all down to that letter. That letter holds the key to who you are, Millie. It contains your mother's last words to you, and it contains the identity of the man who is your father. It's affecting you. And not in a good way. Henry and I are the only other *people*, and I use that term loosely, who know about the letter. You don't really have anybody to talk to about it. No wonder you went off at George."

Letting out a long breath, Millie shook her head. "You're not my psychologist, okay, Reuben! I know why *I went off* at George, as you so eloquently put it!"

"Then, why did you?" said Reuben.

"Because he… because I," stammered Millie. "Because he made me mad, Reuben. Okay!"

"Because you think he's interested in another woman, and not you?" said Reuben. "Or because you hoped that you'd get the chance to tell him how you felt about him, and that would lead to you having somebody in your life who you could share your most personal emotions with. Somebody to cuddle, perhaps? I heard what you whispered when you spoke out loud to your mother, Millie. My hearing is better than a dog's, and when I heard what you said, I felt sad. That letter holds the answers to a lot of your problems, Millie. And it's also the cause of your problems."

Millie gritted her teeth. Grabbing the envelope, she took a corner between finger and thumb, and began to rip it along the upper seam. "Then I'll open it, if that will make you happy, Reuben!"

Reuben threw himself airborne and flew at Millie's hand. Pinching the envelope in his beak, he dragged it from her grasp and flew to the top of the wardrobe, where he landed, and gazed down at his witch. "No," he said. "That's not what I think the answer is. I think I have a better solution, but you'll need to trust me. Will you trust me, Millie?"

Confusion and anger threatening to spill over into words, aimed at Reuben, which she didn't mean, Millie took three deep breaths. She looked up at the cockatiel. "I trust you, Reuben. I know you want what's best for me."

"Then go with Sergeant Spencer and Judith to speak to Mister Anon. It will help you get yourself grounded again. When you've done that, come down to the coven cavern. There's something I want to show you," said Reuben.

"The spell you began telling me about this morning?" said Millie, with a frown.

Reuben nodded. "Yes, the spell."

"Tell me now," said Millie. "What spell is it, Reuben. What does it do?"

"You need to calm down a little first," said Reuben. "Please go with Sergeant Spencer and Judith. They're waiting for you. When you come back inside, you'll be calmer. Then we can talk, okay?"

Millie looked up at the bird, exasperation beginning to bore a hole in her sanity. She gave him a nod.

"Okay," she said, leaving the bedroom and making her way through the cottage, frowning as she passed the archway which divided the kitchen from the living room. Judith had tidied away the remnants of dinner, but the shame Millie felt about how she'd behaved in front of her guests still lingered in the air.

She headed outside into the cool night air, where Sergeant Spencer and Judith stood leaning against the police car, speaking in hushed tones. When Judith saw Millie approaching, she stepped towards her, pulling her into the shadows alongside the cottage. "Are you okay?" she said, her voice low. "I was worried about you. Reuben was, too."

Millie nodded. "I'm sorry," she said. "It was very childish of me. I feel better after a rest. I'm so sorry I ruined your meal. George and Reuben's, too."

"I wouldn't worry about Reuben," said Judith. "He tucked into the cheesecake after you'd gone to bed, and as for George — I think he deserved it. He's been flirting with you since you moved to this town. If he is involved with that blonde woman, then he should have been honest with you before now. He's been leading you along."

Millie glanced towards Sergeant Spencer. "Does your dad know what happened?"

Placing a comforting hand on Millie's arm, Judith shook her head. "No. He asked why George had left early, and I told him he had to be somewhere else. He didn't really take much notice. He was too busy watching ASSHAT in their campervan. They're playing Monopoly at the moment, and Dad can't wait to confront them with the information he got from the FBI. He says they'll be gone by tomorrow morning, and they won't be bothering us again, after he's spoken to them."

"What information does he have about them?" said Millie.

"I'm not sure," said Judith, walking towards her father. "Why don't we go and find out?"

Sergeant Spencer grinned as the girls approached. He put his hat on his head, and took his phone from his pocket. "Ready to learn the truth about Mister Anon, girls?" he said, gravel crunching under his boots as he stomped towards the campervan. With the two witches close behind him, the policeman paused at the campervan door, raised a fist and hammered on the thin metal. "Let me in," he shouted. "I want to speak to you about something, *Mister Anon*."

"What is it?" came the reply. "Have you come to tell me that you've finished your *painfully slow* forensic sweep of the sand dunes, and I'm now welcome to begin my investigation into the skeleton of the extra-terrestrial creature which awaits my expert scrutiny?"

"Not quite!" yelled Sergeant Spencer. "I'm here to ask you about some very interesting information I have about you."

Silence. Then the stomping of feet inside the vehicle. The door opened with a click, light flooding from the narrow doorway, and the smell of coffee following it. "Oh, you've brought your little fan club, I see,

Sergeant Spencer," said Mister Anon, peering at Millie and Judith. "What is it I can help you three fine people with?"

"You can let us in for a start," said Sergeant Spencer, stepping up into the van, brushing away Mister Anon's feeble attempt at blocking the entrance. "I've got a few things I'd like to speak with you about."

Mister Anon stood in the centre of the narrow aisle, the driver's cab to his left, and the small seating and sleeping area to his right, where Mister Incognito sat at a table with a monopoly board in front of him. "What sort of things?" he said.

"We could begin with deciding what we should call one another. I'm fine with you calling me Sergeant Spencer, but what should I call *you*? Should I call you Mister Anon?" said the policeman, glancing at his phone. "Or should I call you by your real name, Graham Spalding?"

Mister Incognito leapt to his feet, banging his head on a built-in overhead cupboard. "You shouldn't call him by his real name! It's against the rules of the Alien Search Syndicate and —"

"It's okay. Sit down," said Mister Anon, placing a hand on his companion's shoulder. He removed his cap, tossed it aside and sat down next to Mister Incognito, pushing a pile of monopoly money aside. "I assume it's not just my name you have?" he asked.

Sergeant Spencer smiled. "No, Graham. It's not

just your name I have. The email I received from the FBI is an eyeopener, to say the least."

"The FBI?" said Graham Spalding. "You have been busy, Sergeant Spencer."

"You've got a colourful history across the pond, haven't you?" said the sergeant. "And you've made quite an impact in our own country, too. I've never seen so many restraining orders filed against one person."

"Restraining orders?" said Millie.

"Used as political weapons against me!" said Graham. "The people on that list of yours are using those orders to keep their true identities a secret. Those people are the dangerous people, not me — as the FBI and NASA have falsely implied!"

Judith frowned. "NASA?" she said.

"Oh yes," said Sergeant Spencer. "Graham was sacked from his job as an electrical engineer at NASA last year."

"I didn't like Florida anyway. It was too hot," said Graham. "And the people at NASA didn't take their jobs seriously. They're too focused on outer space, when they should be concentrating on the dangers lurking on our own planet!"

"Why were you sacked from NASA?" asked Millie.

"Shall I tell her, or will you?" said Sergeant Spencer.

Graham sighed. "I was sacked because of a silly misunderstanding," he said.

"You tried to rip an astrophysicist's face off, Graham!" said Sergeant Spencer. "He was forced to take four weeks off from work, and he's not sure that he'll ever be able to regrow his beard. The medical report said you'd torn off two inches of flesh along with the goatee. How can you call that a silly misunderstanding?"

"I misunderstood the evidence I'd collated on him," said Graham. "I'd had my doubts about him from the day I'd infiltrated NASA. There was something about his eyes, *and* the way he walked. He looked uncomfortable in his own skin. Like it was a costume. I had to act. I followed him home from work on a few occasions, and on one Friday afternoon, I followed him to a shop specialising in exotic pets. Reptiles, mostly. When I saw what he'd bought — a box of frozen mice, I knew I had my man banged to rights! I thought I did, anyway. It turns out I was wrong on *that* occasion."

"Wrong about what?" asked Judith.

"Wrong in my assumption that he was one of the extraterrestrial Lizard Illuminati, of course!" said Graham. "He'd ticked so many boxes, too. The mice were the final piece of the puzzle. How was I to know he kept snakes? How was I to know the mice were food intended for his pets, and not for him? Like I said — a silly misunderstanding."

"You thought he was a lizard?" said Millie. "Really?"

"They're amongst us!" snapped Graham, bringing

his fist down on the table, making Mister Incognito jump. "They walk amongst us, but nobody takes the threat they pose seriously. And I won't rest until I've proved their existence to the world!"

"He wasn't the only person you accused of being a lizard person, was he, Graham?" said Sergeant Spencer. "I have a list of almost one hundred people you've accused, and those are just the ones who took out restraining orders against you. Who knows how many other people you've confronted with claims that they're aliens masquerading as humans."

"A hundred people?" said Judith. "That sounds serious."

"The problem of the Lizard Illuminati is serious!" said Graham. "The work I'm doing is serious! The lizard race must be exposed to humanity! I'm trying to save the human race! That *is* serious!"

Sergeant Spencer stared at the email displayed on his phone. "And that's what you thought you were doing when you harassed and stalked all those innocent people? Including seventy members of the public and several celebrities, such as Mark Zuckerberg, Jeff Bezos, William Shatner, Gordon Ramsay —"

"I'm still unsure about Chef Ramsay," said Graham. "That face of his looks very malleable. I'm certain it's a mask. I'm waiting to see if I've been accepted as a contestant on the next season of Hell's Kitchen. I want to be close to him. He'll slip up eventually. That temper of his will be the cause of his downfall. The lizard inside will make itself known during one of his outbursts. You wait and see!"

Sergeant Spencer continued reading from his phone, firing a stern glance at Graham. "The list doesn't end with Gordon. There's Lee Majors, Clint Eastwood, Dolly Parton, Chris de Burgh, David Blaine, Carol Thatcher *and* you were almost charged for assaulting Dame Edna Everage."

"I thought I'd finally caught one when her wig came off in my hand," said Graham, gazing at the table. "I had no idea. It was very good makeup. Luckily, Barry Humphries has his suspicions about the Chuckle Brothers being lizard people. He told the police he didn't want to press charges, and told me to keep up the good work."

"It says here that even David Icke has a restraining order out against you, Graham," said Sergeant Spencer. "If your search for lizard people is annoying David Icke, then I think it's high time you re-evaluated your life and your beliefs."

Graham Spalding smiled. "I won't need to keep looking for lizard people when I get that skeleton out of the dunes," he said. "That skeleton is my ticket to fame and recognition. I'm transporting it to America where I'll reveal it to the world!" He glanced at Millie. "Don't worry. I won't tell anybody where I found it. I'm a man of my word. Spellbinder Bay will be safe from intrusion by the press. Your quaint little town will carry on as normal, and I'll be the first man to have discovered the remains of an *actual* alien!"

"You're taking it to America?" said Sergeant Spencer. "I don't think so. It says in this email that you're banned from America, Brazil, Uzbekistan *and* Vatican City."

"They'll let me into America when I tell NASA I have an alien skeleton," said Graham. "I'll be forgiven for all the errors I made in my search for the Lizard Illuminati. They'll understand that the people with facial wounds and PTSD were collateral damage."

"What about Mister Incognito?" said Millie. "How does he fit into all of this?"

Mister Incognito leaned forward and peered at Millie over the rims of his glasses. "That's very convenient," he murmured. "Very congenial, indeed."

"Never mind, Mister Incognito," said Graham. "It *is* a difficult word."

"So, who is he, Graham?" said Judith. "He doesn't seem…. *all there*, if you ask me."

"He was a brilliant scientist, until a year ago," said Graham, opening the can of cola which Mister Incognito was struggling with. He poked a straw in the opening and handed it to his companion. "He had an accident while performing an experiment. His name is Peter Simmons, he was —"

"Not my real name!" said Mister Incognito, cola bubbling from his mouth. "You're not supposed to say it!"

"That doesn't matter anymore, Peter," said Graham. "It's okay, now."

"Oh," said Peter, wiping his chin with the back of

his hand. "So I can take my glasses off, now? It's hard to see inside the van with sunglasses on."

"Yes," said Graham. "You can take them off. Our identities are no longer a secret."

"You said he had an accident while performing an experiment?" said Millie. "What sort of experiment?"

"Peter was trying to prove that other dimensions existed," said Graham. "He was certain that our dimension is just one of thousands. Millions, even. He believed that creatures from the other dimensions sometimes slipped through from their world, into our reality. Whereas I was looking for aliens from outer space, Peter Simmons was focused on proving that creatures from other dimensions inhabited our world."

"That's mad," said Judith, raising an eyebrow at Millie. "Other dimensions! I've heard it all, now!"

"Whether I believed him or not," said Graham. "He was a great ally to me. He had access to the Large Hadron Collider, near Geneva. Everybody wants access to that!"

"That's where they search for new particles and types of matter, isn't it?" said Millie. "I've read about it. There was a concern that they might accidentally open a black-hole and destroy the planet."

"That was a concern to *some* people, but I hoped it *would* happen," said Graham. "I have a theory that aliens travel across the vast distances of space using black-holes, and not worm-holes, as portrayed by science fiction. I hoped Peter Simmons could help me prove I was correct."

"Is that what happened to him?" said Judith. "He accidentally opened a black-hole and had a terrible accident? Is that why he's so... different? The poor man."

"Gosh, no," said Graham. "Nobody managed to accidentally open a black-hole. Peter was electrocuted."

"By the Hadron Collider?" said Millie, watching Peter Simmons slip a wad of monopoly money into his Batman wallet, while Graham was facing the other way. "The poor man."

"No," said Graham. "It was a toaster."

"A toaster?" said Sergeant Spencer. "From another dimension?"

Graham shook his head. "Nothing so extravagant. He'd finished the first phase of an experiment, and had taken half an hour for lunch," he said. "It was a toaster in the cafeteria which broke Peter's brilliant mind. Everybody knows you shouldn't dislodge stuck toast from a toaster with a metal knife, yet people *still* insist on doing it, and they get away with it for the most part, without injury. It wasn't Peter's lucky day, though — it was a thick wholemeal crust which had become stuck in the machine. Peter *really* had to wiggle the knife around in the bowels of that toaster. The electric shock stopped his heart, and it was the lack of oxygen supply to his brain before the paramedics managed to revive him, which damaged his great mind."

"So, it was nothing to do with the Large Hadron Collider, black-holes or other dimensions?" said Sergeant Spencer.

"Not directly," said Graham.

"Not at all," said Millie. "It was a kitchen accident."

"Cafeteria," said Graham.

"Why is Peter here with you, Graham?" asked Sergeant Spencer. "If his mind is no longer as brilliant as it once was, then what help is he to you?"

"I make Pop-Tarts in the microwave, don't I, Mister Anon?" said Peter. "I help out, don't I?"

"You do, Peter," said Graham. "*And* you have an extraordinary collection of scientific equipment in the lab you built in the basement beneath your house, before the toaster incident rendered you incapable of being able to use it."

"That's my stuff!" snapped Peter. "You be careful with it! I like my stuff!"

Graham put a hand on Peter's arm. "It is your stuff, yes, and I've promised you lots of times that it will be looked after. There's no need to worry." He looked at Sergeant Spencer. "He's very protective about his equipment and his lab — which is where we'll be taking the skeleton when you allow us to excavate it. I'll put Peter's equipment to good use, and when I've proved, using science, that it is of extraterrestrial origin, we'll transport it to America —

where I'll finally be recognised as the man who proved we are not alone in the vastness of space!"

"What makes you think you'll be getting anywhere near that skeleton?" said Sergeant Spencer.

"I have to!" said Graham. "I must have that skeleton, and if you don't allow me access to it, I'll do as I threatened when I first arrived here. I'll tell the whole world what lays in the sand! I'll bring the world's media giants down on Spellbinder Bay! I'll ruin your town!"

"Two things," said Sergeant Spencer. "One — nobody will believe a word you say. Your reputation is ruined in the alien hunting world. Even David Icke thinks you're a fish short of a shoal. Nobody will take you seriously. Especially when you don't have a skeleton to back up your claims."

Graham's eyes narrowed, and he formed a fist. "I'll get that skeleton," he said. "Even if I have to force my way past you."

"Which brings me to the second point, Graham," said Sergeant Spencer. "You're on bail. You were released from police custody two weeks ago. You were arrested in London on charges of interfering with an archaeological dig alongside the River Thames. One of the stipulations of your bail was that you do not go near any protected sites in the United Kingdom, and the sand dunes, thanks to the rare flowers which flourish within them, *are* a protected site." He smiled at Graham. "I'm giving you a choice. You can either disappear tonight, and never come back. Or I can arrest you for breach of bail, and hand you over to the Metropolitan Police. You'll be in jail by the weekend if you choose the second option."

Graham stared at the big policeman, his face etched with anger. He opened and closed his hands a few times, took a steadying breath, and stood up. "Very well," he said. "We shall leave immediately."

"Just like that?" said Millie. "Without an argument?"

Graham sighed. "How *can* I argue? The sergeant is right. He can arrest me if he wants to. I'm in breach of my bail, and I do not wish to go to jail. I have important things to do. Important work to finish, and being incarcerated will not help me complete that work. One must choose his battles wisely, and this is a battle I cannot win. If you'd all be so kind as to step out of my campervan, Peter and I will be on our way. We shall not trouble you again."

Sergeant Spencer nodded. "You chose wisely," he said, pushing the narrow door open. "Come on, girls. We'll wave them off."

As the three of them stepped outside and Graham pulled the campervan door closed, displaying a forced smile, Judith looked at her Father, his face illuminated by the full moon. "Do you think that's the last we'll see of them?" she asked.

"I think so," said Sergeant Spencer, raising his voice as the campervan's engine rattled into life, forcing a plume of exhaust fumes into the night sky. "And even if it's not, those bones will be dust soon enough. There will be nothing here for them to see, and any photos they took will be worthless without physical evidence to back them up. Especially photos taken by a man with Graham's reputation."

As the van trundled along the track, it's rear lights becoming dimmer by the second, Millie smiled at Sergeant Spencer. "What now?" she asked. "The alien hunters may no longer be a concern, but somebody, or something, needs to be punished for killing Tom Temples."

"We wait," said Sergeant Spencer. "We wait until Henry catches up with the demon, and then we wait to find out if it *was* the demon that killed Tom. My money is on it being the demon. The fingerprints on the shovel don't match any of those idiot detectorists I met at the hospital, and we have no other leads. I'll wager that when the demon is found, and forced from the human it's possessing, that the fingerprints of that unfortunate soul will match the ones on the murder weapon."

"Wow, imagine that," said Judith. "Discovering not only that you've been possessed by a demon, but that you murdered a man while you were under its control."

'That's not something I'd like to imagine," said Sergeant Spencer. "I'm sure it would devastate the person who'd been possessed. I doubt they'd ever be the same again. Until the possessed person is caught, though, we have to stay alert. The demon may still come back here, searching for its partner." He smiled at Millie. "And I'm not sure I trust Graham Spalding completely. He might return. I'd like to stay here tonight. If that's okay? I'll sleep in my car, of course. With one eye and one ear open, naturally."

Millie stared out over the sand dunes, wondering if a human possessed by an evil entity lurked in the shadows. She smiled at the sergeant. "Of course you can stay here, but not in your car. You can have the sofa, and Judith can have the spare bedroom. You'll be able to hear any sound through the roof window, and Reuben has great hearing, too. If anything *does* happen, he'll hear it first. I'm sure nothing will happen, though. I'm sure we'll have a peaceful night."

Chapter 15

Millie closed the door behind herself and descended the rock steps which led to the secret cavern below her cottage. Reuben looked up from his perching position on the handle of an old-fashioned broomstick, and gave a low whistle. "Do you feel better, now?" he asked.

Millie gazed into the cauldron, the swirling greens and bright flashes of light having a soothing effect on her. She smiled at her familiar. "I'm fine now, Reuben," she said, feeling shame rising. "I've apologised to Judith, and now I want to apologise to you. I'm sorry about what happened at dinner. It was silly of me."

Reuben fluttered to the rim of the cauldron, and cocked his head. He looked up at Millie. "You don't need to apologise to me. Everybody's entitled to a catastrophic neurotic breakdown at some point in their life."

"I'm not sure I had a catastrophic neurotic breakdown, Reuben," said Millie. "I think I was just venting my emotions."

"Six of one, half a dozen of the other," said Reuben. "But I'll go with the term *emotional venting*, if that will help you feel less foolish about the whole episode."

"It would, actually," said Millie.

"Emotional venting it is, then," said Reuben. He looked up the stairs at the closed door. "Are Judith and Sergeant Spencer still up there? Are we likely to be disturbed?"

"Yes, they're still here," said Millie. "They're staying for the night. They won't disturb us, though. I told them I needed some time with you, alone. What is it you wanted to show me?"

Reuben looked away, his eyelids briefly hiding his coal black eyes. He hopped from foot to foot and shook out his feathers. "What I'm going to show you is quite sensitive," he said. "And if it's offensive to you in any way, I hope you know I'm only thinking of your well-being."

"This is beginning to sound more serious than I thought it would be, Reuben," said Millie. "When you said you had a spell to show me — which would help me, I thought you were going to show me how to make a potion which would shrink my bum, or something as equally insulting."

Reuben shook his small head. "Do you remember what you said to me before you went to The Fur and

Fangs for the pub quiz?" he asked. "You told me that you speak out loud sometimes, to your mother. You told me that you wished she could answer you. You told me you had questions which you wanted her to answer. Questions that the letter she left for you could never answer."

A creeping tendril of dread probed Millie's insides. "Yes," she said, stepping closer to the cockatiel and placing a hand on one of the cool stones which the waist-high cauldron was built of. "I remember saying that."

Reuben remained quiet for a few seconds. He lowered his head, and rearranged his wings. "After you'd said that, and you'd gone to the pub," he said. "I remembered something. A spell I'd seen in one of the books down here in the cavern — while Esmeralda was creating potions. I remember Esmeralda saying it was a spell which she'd never seen being cast, and wasn't certain if it *ever had* been cast by *any* witch." Reuben cocked his head. "It took me a while, but I found it again. I found the spell, and I think it's feasible that it will work for you. If you have the courage to cast it."

"What is the spell?" whispered Millie, the small hairs on her arms standing rigid. "What does it do, Reuben?"

"Loosely translated, it's called the *spell of unheard last words*," said Reuben. "And as for what it does — it can... it's supposed to... it's for..."

"What is it for?" said Millie. "Just say it!"

Reuben's tiny chest expanded as he took a deep breath. "I think it will allow you to speak with your mother," he said, his voice quiet. "It will allow your mother to appear before you, and she'll be able to communicate with you."

Millie placed her other hand on the rim of the cauldron, and steadied herself, her legs suddenly unstable beneath her. "How?" she said, a tremble in her voice. "How does it work?"

Reuben's eyes brightened. "Good," he said. "You're interested. I'd hoped you would be."

Millie shook her head, pressing her feet hard onto the rock floor. Grounding herself. "Just tell me how it works," she said. "Then I'll tell you if I'm interested, or not."

"The spell requires three ingredients, two of which you have, and the third ingredient being available to you… with a little effort on your behalf," said Reuben. He spread his wings and flew from the cauldron to the rickety oak table placed alongside an umbrella stand stuffed with ornate walking canes.

He hopped onto the large leather-bound book which lay open on the tabletop, and lowered his head as he read from the page. "The first ingredient is the last words that the person you wish to bring back spoke to you, the important factor being that those words must remain unheard by the intended recipient."

"The letter," murmured Millie. "The letter from my mother."

"Yes!" said Reuben. "Those are technically her last words to you, and you are yet to hear them — or read them, in your circumstances."

"What's the next ingredient?" said Millie, her legs beginning to feel stronger, and her heart beating faster.

"A tear shed for the person you wish to bring back," said Reuben, excitement in his words. He nodded in the direction of the envelope placed next to the book. "I hope you don't mind, but I brought the letter down here with me. It has your tears on it, the envelope was still damp when I brought it with me, but it doesn't matter if the tear is wet or dry. It's the sentiment behind it which will power the magic."

The speed of her breathing matching her heart rate, Millie stepped towards the table and gazed down at the book, the words within it written in ink which was fading with time. "And the last ingredient?" she said. "The one which will require a little effort on my behalf?"

"A pearl of wisdom," said Reuben, with a look that Millie assumed was an avian version of a frown.

"What is that?" said Millie. "That's just a thing people say, isn't it? A pearl of wisdom is a wise piece of advice."

"It *has* become a phrase which people use," said Reuben. "But it's a phrase based on reality. Pearls of wisdom exist, Millie, and you just need to get one."

"What are they?" said Millie. "Are they pearls? Like the name suggests?"

"They are, and I did some research on them," said Reuben, nodding towards the rows of books which populated three shelves hewn into the rock wall of the cavern. "Pearls of wisdom grow in oysters which can only be found in the deepest parts of an ocean directly influenced by a magical beacon." He looked up at Millie. "Places like that are rare, but we happen to live in one. Spellbinder Hall is a magical beacon which transmits the concealment spell over the town, and you only need to look out of a window upstairs to see the ocean."

Using her tongue to moisten her dry lips, Millie ran a finger below a line of writing on the page before her. "It says they can only be harvested under a full moon, from the depths of the ocean," she said.

"It's a full moon tonight, Millie," said Reuben, a twinkle in his eye.

"Do the words *depths of the ocean* mean anything to you?" said Millie, her heart sinking. "How am I supposed to get to the depths of the ocean, Reuben? In a submarine? Have you got a submarine stashed away which you're not telling me about? A little yellow one, perhaps?"

"Very funny," said Reuben. "No, I don't have a submarine, but I *do* have a plan."

"Let me hear it," said Millie, anxiety tightening its hand around her throat.

"I *had* thought of the obvious thing," said Reuben. "I thought we could ask Lillieth. A mermaid would have no problem in retrieving a pearl of wisdom for us."

"But Lillieth isn't here, Reuben!" said Millie. "She's travelling the oceans, and mermaids are rare. I can't just run down to the seashore and ask the next passing mermaid to fetch me a pearl of wisdom!"

"You're right. Lillieth isn't here," said Reuben, swivelling his head, and staring at a spot behind Millie. "But there is something of hers here. Something that will help you."

Millie turned around, following the cockatiel's gaze. "That won't work," she said, stepping towards the shimmering white dress, and running a finger over the soft silk. "The magic in the dress gives mermaids legs, it doesn't give humans fins."

"I wouldn't have suggested any of this to you," said Reuben, "if I hadn't done my research. You're right, that dress won't work on humans — they have no magic within them, but according to everything I can find in the old books, the magic in that dress should be reversible, when worn by somebody of a paranormal persuasion." He flew to Millie's shoulder. "You think you've fixed that dress, Millie, and if you have, and you put it on — I'm ninety-seven percent certain that you'll gain all the powers of a mermaid. You'll be able to harvest a pearl of wisdom, and you'll be able to speak to your mother."

"I don't believe it," said Millie, shaking her head. "I *can't* believe it."

""You *won't* believe it. But you could try to," said

Reuben. "You could step into the sea, and put the dress on. It's a full moon tonight, and the sea is calm. The books say that the oysters which contain pearls of wisdom will glow blue beneath a full moon, and will be highly visible. If the dress works, you'll be able to swim in the sea as confidently as Lillieth can walk on land, when she's wearing it."

"And if it doesn't work?" said Millie.

"Then you either wait for Lillieth to return, *and* wait for another full moon. Or you read the letter your mother left for you, but then her words will no longer be unheard, and the spell will be lost to you," said Reuben. "You'll never speak with her."

"And if I get the pearl?" said Millie. "How does the spell work?"

"That's the part that's worrying me more than thinking about you travelling into the depths of the ocean," said Reuben.

"Why?" said Millie. "What's so scary?"

"Because to cast the spell, the letter must be burned. That's why this spell has rarely been cast by anybody in the past," said Reuben. "Unheard last words are normally spoken, and spoken words can't be captured and burned. The last words to you from your mother are in that envelope, but if we burn that letter, and the spell doesn't work…"

Millie closed her eyes. Henry Pinkerton had informed her that *he* knew who her father was, but receiving the information from him would not be the same as receiving it from her mother. And anyway,

Millie was sure the envelope didn't just contain a name — it would contain more than that.

She hoped it would contain an explanation as to why her mother had lied to her about her father, and about the fact that she'd been a witch. She opened her eyes. "If the spell doesn't work," she said. "My mother's last words will be lost to me forever."

"Yes," whispered Reuben.

Millie pressed the soft fabric of Lillieth's dress between a finger and thumb. "Then let's hope that *when* I get that pearl, the spell will work," she said, unhooking the dress from its hanging place.

Chapter 16

Having told Judith and Sergeant Spencer that she wanted to go for a walk alone along the beach, Millie took tentative steps towards the sea's edge, the full moon casting her shadow over the gentle surf.

With Lillieth's dress in one hand, and her slip-on shoes in the other, she wiggled her toes in the sand and gazed out at the horizon wondering whether, if the spell *did* work, she'd have the courage to swim out into the darkness and the unknown.

She took a sharp intake of breath as a rogue wave rode higher up the beach than the others, enveloping her feet and ankles in cold water. Reuben had surmised that the magic of the dress would give Millie all the qualities of a mermaid, including the ability to regulate her body temperature in even the coldest of water, and Millie hoped that her familiar was correct.

Glancing along the beach in both directions, and checking behind her, Millie took a few steps back from the edge of the sea, slipped her T-shirt over her head and allowed her shorts to drop to the sand, enjoying the sensation of the warm breeze on her naked body.

Tracing her steps back towards the sand dunes, she placed her clothing in a pile, with her shoes on top — a safe distance from the sea, and gathered as much courage as she could muster from within herself.

With an image of her mother's smiling face firmly imprinted on her mind, Millie stepped towards the water's edge once more, Lillieth's dress still in her hand, and cold sea spray chilling her legs.

She stepped slowly into the sea, wishing that Spellbinder Bay was situated on the coast of the warm Adriatic, and not alongside the chilly English Channel. Bracing herself against the cold rolling waves, she ventured further into the surf until only her torso and head remained above water, her body trembling as the cold took hold.

She ran through the three possible scenarios. Scenario one — she'd put the dress on and nothing would happen. Either she hadn't fixed the magic in the dress, or the magic wouldn't work in reverse. A disappointing outcome, but probably the safest. Scenario two — she'd put the dress on, transform into a beautiful mermaid, and swim away confidently in search of a pearl of wisdom.

And the third scenario, the one which troubled

Millie the most — she'd put the dress on, turn into a beautiful mermaid and sink in the surf, unable to control her new body, becoming tangled in the dress — unable to remove it before she drowned.

A ball of anxiety swelling in her stomach, Millie looked at the moon and spoke in a whisper. "Wish me luck, Mum," she said.

Holding the dress above her in both hands, she drew the garment over her head, and allowed the soft silk to rest on her shoulders for a moment or two. Wondering at which point during the process of adorning the garment, the magic within the dress would be activated, she inserted her arms through the thin straps and allowed the material to slide down her body.

As the hem of the dress touched the water, Millie got her answer, and she got it faster than she had expected — with hardly a chance of sucking in, and holding, a lungful of air.

As if her legs had vanished from beneath her, Millie tumbled into the surf, her arms flailing as she attempted to keep itself afloat, but aware that the heavy weight where her legs had been was dragging her beneath the surface.

Panic rising in her throat, she attempted to remove the dress, but realised with horror that the worst scenario she'd envisioned had come true — instead of calmly lifting the dress over her head, as she was commanding them to, her arms refused to cooperate, and flailed helplessly in the surf as she tried to get her head above the surface.

Tangled in the garment, and with her lungs desperate for air, Millie realised with a calming acceptance which frightened her, that she needed to breathe. That she *had* to breathe. That she was *going* to breathe. That she was about to give in to the pain in her chest, and allow the sea to claim her. She searched for the ball of magic in her chest, hoping her powers would give her a last minute reprieve, but she felt nothing there, only a chunk of heavy despair which seemed to be adding to the weight which kept her from surfacing.

Unable to bear the pain in her chest any longer, Millie closed her eyes, stopped struggling and allowed the seawater into her mouth, hoping she wouldn't suffer for too long. Expecting the salt water to flood her lungs quickly, she kept her eyes closed tight, waiting for the inevitable.

The light-headedness which the lack of oxygen had caused beginning to leave her, Millie realised with growing hope that her body was becoming oxygenated, her lungs no longer hurting, and her arms gaining strength. Assuming she'd made it to the surface at the last moment, she opened her eyes and prepared to swim to shore.

Instead of the white-tipped waves and full moon which she'd expected to see, Millie gazed around at the subsurface seascape and realised with both fear and delight that she was breathing — underwater.

Not only was she breathing, but she felt at home in the water — everything seemed natural, and even her eyesight had adapted. Instead of the blurred shadows and hazy horizons which usually accompanied an underwater swim, her vision was sharp, the moonlight which filtered through the surface offering ample light, and casting the sand below her in a silvery glow.

She concentrated on what was happening in her mouth and lungs, and realised that her chest was not rising and falling, and no water was in her lungs. In fact, no water had penetrated past her mouth — as if a force field was preventing seawater from entering her throat. Somehow, her body was extracting oxygen from the water in her mouth and nostrils, and she realised with delight that she was in full control of her body.

Her hair floating gently around her face, and the dress moulded tightly to her body as if fused with her skin, Millie drew the appendage which had once been her legs towards her chest, and smiled as she examined her fin.

Speckled in purples and greens, the scales shimmering under the curtain of moonlight which lit the underwater scene, her fin merged almost seamlessly with Lillieth's dress, which had become a second skin — fitted tightly over her breasts and midriff, offering her a dignity she knew was wasted so far away from other people.

Instinctively, she flicked her fin, the muscles in her

stomach tightening, and her body slicing effortlessly through the water as she propelled herself forward.

With a bubbling giggle, she flicked her fin again, this time with more power, and directed herself towards the surface — from which she burst in a shower of sea spray, and with a shout of delight.

Mimicking the dolphins she'd seen playing in the bay, she twisted her body in the air and allowed herself to fall to the water, flicking her fin as she landed, and holding her arms tight against her body as she headed for deeper water.

As the depth of water increased, the silvery sand below her gave way to coral — the purples, yellows and greens illuminated by beams of moonlight which shimmered, and seemed almost to move with the sea as the tide pushed towards the shore.

Fish peered out of hiding holes in the coral, and a lobster scuttled across a bare patch of sand, heading for a refuge into which it vanished as Millie swam deeper to take a closer look. Spinning in the water, her shouts of joy lost to all but herself and the marine life which populated the depths, she sped through the sea, her body arching with every powerful flick of her fin.

Not sure how far she'd swam, and not sure she cared, she noticed the coral had once more given way to sand, and the full moon — a blurred orb of blue and silver, had become smaller. Coming to a gentle halt, water currents making her hair dance, and the thin membrane which made up the V of her fin, sway

— she hovered in the water, getting her emotions under control. Remembering she was there for a reason other than feeling freer than she'd ever felt before.

Her vision as perfect underwater as it had been on land, Millie studied her surroundings. Moonlight still penetrated to the depth she was at, but the gloom below her had begun to dominate. She remembered what Reuben had said — the oysters she was looking for lived in deep water. Bending almost double, her fin grazing her chest, she performed a graceful tumble-toss, and with a few powerful flicks of her fin, slid from the silvery moonlit water she'd been floating in, and deep down into the inky blues in which even her newly adapted vision struggled to perform properly.

Slicing effortlessly through the water, Millie headed deeper, veering left as a large eye loomed from the shadows, its pupil reflecting the last slivers of moonlight. Surprisingly unnerved by the sudden appearance of the creature, she placed a hand on the animal's large flank, the basking shark's skin rough against her fingers as it glided peacefully past her, and was swallowed by shadows.

Her eyes adjusting to the gloom, Millie studied the seabed below her. Not under enough water to blot out sunlight entirely, the sand was home to large beds of kelp, whose tendrils danced in the currents, reaching high above their anchor points among rocks and seashell littered sand.

Swimming through the nearest bed of kelp, the

rubbery fronds tickling her fin as she navigated the underwater forest, she found what she'd been searching for. Packed tight together, seemingly growing atop one another, with seaweed covered tips of rocks visible where the shells were less abundant, the oyster bed spread out before her, the oval shells a mix of porcelain white which glowed softly under the dim light, and dark blacks which blended with the shadows.

Her fin grazing the rough surfaces of oyster shells, Millie meandered through the kelp forest, searching for the blue glow which would indicate the presence of the magical pearls she was searching for.

The oyster bed spread for as far as she could see in all directions, and a startled crab reared up and threatened her with large pincers as Millie pushed into a thicker growth of kelp, the thick fronds creating a cold rubbery curtain. As she pushed the seaweed aside, and gave a flick of her fin, a faint blue glow in the distance stood out like a single lit window in a city shrouded in darkness.

Her fin slicing easily through the water, Millie covered the distance quickly, and gazed down at the source of the neon blue glow. Unlike the other oysters, whose shells were clamped tightly shut, the dinner plate sized oyster below her had opened wide, its magical prize proudly displayed, as if on offer to the first person who found it.

Millie swam closer, the blue glow of the pearl so bright it formed a circle of light two metres wide around its oyster. Her fin making gentle movements which held her steady in the tide, Millie reached for the pearl, and plucked it from its bed of vivid white flesh, holding it between a finger and thumb.

As its prize was removed, the oyster slowly closed, becoming just another of the countless shells which covered the seabed.

With the pearl making her finger and thumb tingle with magical energy, Millie gazed at it in wonder. The bright blues shifting and shimmering, the marble-sized pearl reminded her of the crystal balls portrayed in the books of fairy tales she'd loved to read as a child.

Tightening her hand around the jewel of the sea, Millie turned in the water and prepared for the peaceful swim back to shore. No sooner had her hand formed a fist — she knew something was wrong. Very wrong. There was too much magic.

She didn't know *how* she knew, but even as cold water flooded her throat, and her fin transformed into kicking legs, she knew that between her own magical powers, the magic contained in the dress, and the paranormal properties of the pearl — there was too much variance in the magic which coursed through, and over, her body.

The weakest of the three magical elements, Lillieth's dress, had been overcome by more powerful magic, and the spell interwoven with the silk had temporarily collapsed.

Realising that this time there would be no

reprieve, Millie closed her eyes as a fresh surge of salt water forced its way into her lungs. She stopped kicking her legs, pictured her mother's face, and prepared to be taken by the sea.

Chapter 17

*W*ondering if the clamping fingers which gripped her wrist belonged to the hand of death himself, and whether the sensation of being dragged upwards was her soul leaving her body, Millie kept her eyes closed, her lungs burning as she travelled at speed to whatever afterlife was waiting for her.

The fact that she was travelling upwards gave her some hope that she'd lived her life relatively sin free. The pressure of the water around her becoming weaker, and a gust of cold wind on her face, Millie spluttered as a voice shouted in her ear.

"Breathe, Millie! Breathe!"

Gasping for breath, and with her legs kicking aimlessly below the surface, Millie clung tightly to the source of the voice, opening her eyes as her body expelled a torrent of seawater in a coughing fountain. "Lillieth?" she managed. "It's you."

"Yes," said Lillieth, her face moving closer to

Millie's, her golden hair glimmering in the moonlight. "Don't speak. I will make you better."

Lillieth's soft lips closed over Millie's mouth, and a warming glow spread throughout her body as Lillieth blew a gentle breath between her lips. The pain leaving her lungs, and the cold water no longer affecting her, Millie smiled at the mermaid. "What was that?" she said. "Was it magic?"

Lillieth nodded, her face etched with concern. "Yes," she said, her accent a soft mix of different dialects. "It is mermaid magic. It is the magic which has saved many human sailors over the centuries." She gazed into Millie's eyes. "You are lucky. I heard you struggling for air. We mer-people can hear somebody in distress from a long way away. You took a risk, putting on my dress."

Kicking her legs, Millie clung to Lillieth's arm, both of them bobbing up and down in the rolling sea. "I know," said Millie. "I thought I had it all under control. Until I picked that pearl from the shell." Aware the pearl was in neither of her hands, she gave a sigh. "Which I've lost."

Lillieth smiled, and opened her hand, the small round orb glowing in her palm. "I have your magical pearl," she said. "I caught it as you dropped it."

Millie took the pearl from Lillieth, and clenched it tightly in her fist. "Thank you," she said. "And I'm sorry for using your dress. It was important that I got this pearl, and there was no other way to get it."

"You could have asked me," said Lillieth. "I would have brought your pearl to you."

Millie turned her body so she was facing the shore. "I didn't know you were back in Spellbinder Bay, Lillieth," she said, wondering what the two lights in the sand dunes were.

"I have been back for one moon and one sun," said Lillieth. "My travels across the oceans took me to the same woman who made that very dress you are wearing. I told her of the damage that had been done to it, and she was of great help."

Lillieth lifted her hand, the large green ring on her index finger reflecting the moonlight. "She made me this ring. It has the same powers as the dress, but as well as giving me legs, it also clothes me as a land person when I wish to come ashore. All I need to do is kiss the ring, and I may leave the sea." She smiled at Millie. "You have fixed my dress, as you promised. I no longer need it. You may keep it. It is a gift from me to you. You must promise to never wear it if you are planning to harvest magical pearls. That is the only condition."

Millie clenched her fist tighter around the pearl, the small ball warming her palm. "Thank you, Lillieth," she said. "I'll treasure it."

Dragging Millie alongside her, Lillieth propelled them both towards the shore, water blurring Millie's vision. "You land people. You have a lot of arguments, don't you?"

"Pardon?" said Millie, spitting water from her

mouth and wondering if the two powerful beams of light illuminating a portion of the sand dunes were being created by torches. "Why do you say that?"

"Before I heard you struggling," said Lillieth, holding Millie close to her side. "I was listening to the land people fighting in the hills of sand. They are so angry."

"In the sand dunes?" said Millie, kicking her legs behind her. "What's happening in the dunes, Lillieth?"

"I do not know," said Lillieth. "I watched as one of the land people's metal chariots sped towards the hills of sand — into which it crashed. Then I watched as two men emerged from the chariot, both of them shouting. Then the kind policeman and his daughter emerged from the home in which you dwell, Millie. There was a bright flash of light in the hills of sand, and then more shouting."

Millie kicked harder, her legs still weak after her ordeal. "Did you hear what was being said?" asked Millie, pleased to feel sand brushing her toes as they neared the beach.

"No," said Lillieth. "They are too far away. And I do not like anger. We people of the sea try to keep our emotions under control. I did not try to listen to them. It made me sad."

The water now shallow enough, Millie clambered to her feet, her wet hair stuck to her face and the dress cold on her skin. "Thank you, Lillieth," she said, stepping from the sea as the mermaid watched her from the surf. "You saved my life. I won't forget that. Will you come ashore with me?"

Lillieth shook her head, her wet golden hair framing the gentle features of her face. "No. Being ashore still makes me nervous. I will gain courage and join you on shore in the future."

Millie span to face the sand dunes as a shout carried on the wind. Lillieth was right. The voice sounded angry. "I have to go!" she said, scanning the beach for the pile of clothes she'd left behind.

"Farewell, Millie," came the soft reply.

Hearing the powerful slap of a fin in the surf behind her, Millie knew the mermaid was gone. Spotting her clothes fifty metres to her left, she ran as quickly as her sore legs would allow, stripping the wet dress from her body and slipping the pearl of wisdom into the pocket of her shorts as she hurriedly got dressed.

Another shout carrying towards her from the dunes, Millie hurried towards her cottage, realising that the beams of light in the dunes were the headlights of a vehicle. The *metal chariot* which Lillieth had said she'd seen.

The box shape of the vehicle breaking the skyline, she recognised it as the campervan which she'd witnessed the alien hunters leave in. They must have come back, and judging by another angry yell which reached her on the breeze, Millie surmised they weren't happy.

Moving with as much speed as her legs would

allow, Millie struggled through the soft sand at the top of the beach as she neared the edge of the dunes, slowing her approach as yet more voices penetrated the night.

Two voices — *or was it three*, carried on the wind, and the twin beams of light emitted by the campervan's headlights flickered briefly as people moved across their path. Millie stood still as she heard another shout. A female voice, and it sounded panicked. *Judith.*

Peering into the shadows, Millie gave a shout. "What's happening?" she yelled.

Her answer came in the form of a man's shout. No. Not a shout. A scream. A scream which sent icy chills along her spine.

Then a familiar voice, urgent. "He's heading in your direction, Millie!" shouted Sergeant Spencer. "Run, Millie! He's dangerous!"

Who was coming? Who was dangerous? Millie gazed into the long shadows created by the sand dunes, certain she had seen movement. Quick movement. Movement which suggested that somebody was coming toward her with speed.

She took a step backwards, her legs still unsteady beneath her, and let out a short scream of shock as the shadows appeared to part like curtains, and a man lunged at her from the darkness, a gurgling shout beginning to form on his snarling lips as he sped at Millie.

"Watch out, Millie!" came Sergeant Spencer's

voice from the darkness. "He's possessed by a demon! He's strong!"

Millie recognised the lumbering man as Peter Simmons — or Mister Incognito, as she'd become accustomed to referring to him as. His face a mask of anger — made more hideous by the moonlight which glinted in his eyes, the wild man emitted a blood-curdling scream, his appearance a world away from the gentle demeanour he'd displayed over the last few days.

Attempting to step out of his way, her legs stiff, Millie faltered, stumbling as Peter Simmons threw himself at her, his eyes wide and his teeth bared. Putting a hand out to cushion her fall, Millie rolled to the side, a second too late to avoid the bone-crunching collision of the possessed man's attack.

Winded, and with Peter's hands clawing at her face and neck, Millie could do little to help herself as she gasped for breath, aware of a shouting voice carrying on the wind. "Millie!" yelled Sergeant Spencer. "Are you okay? I'm coming!"

Scrambling in the sand, her legs kicking at empty air, Millie put a hand on Peter's face as he straddled her midriff and found her neck with both of his hands, tightening his grip as Millie searched for his eyes with her fingers, struggling to breathe as Peter strangled her.

Her panic rising, Millie moved her attack from Peter's face, to his hands, digging her nails deep into his flesh, her attempts to inflict pain having no effect on her deranged attacker. She concentrated on the space behind her breastbone, searching within herself for her magic, knowing she needed to be calmer if she was to access it, but acutely aware that she could barely breathe.

Pain searing through her throat, and Peter's weight crushing her chest, Millie wondered for the third time that night if she was about to die. Her heartbeat thudding in her ears, and Peter's enraged scream adding to her fear, she dug her nails deeper into the backs of his hands, silently urging Sergeant Spencer to hurry, aware that time was passing more slowly than it seemed to be, and knowing that she couldn't rely on help reaching her before she lost consciousness.

Her neck muscles straining, Millie closed her eyes, ignoring the pain and the rabid scream of the man who was attempting to kill her. Hearing those words in her mind, Millie's rage rose. *Nobody was going to kill her.* Not like this. She would not die in the sand — with the ingredient she needed to cast the spell which might enable her to speak to her mother in her pocket. Not today. *Not on any day*.

"I'm coming!" yelled Sergeant Spencer, his voice closer, but not near enough.

Her throat burning, Millie searched for the ball of magic within her, willing it to appear. Forcing it to blossom. Dragging it forcefully into her chest, where it simmered, gaining strength as she concentrated on being calm.

She opened her eyes, anger boiling in her veins, the burning ball behind her ribs urging her to release it, like an attack dog straining at a leash. As her vision blurred, and dizziness threatened to render her helpless, Millie released her magic, not knowing what form it would take, but aware that the spell she'd cast would be vengeful.

The beach vibrated beneath Millie's back, as if an earthquake was in progress, and she released her grip on Peter's hands as sand erupted around her in a violent explosion which rattled through her body. Peter's hands relaxed on her throat, and his scream ended abruptly as a thick tentacle, formed from sand, snaked across his body and wrapped itself around his throat.

No longer concerned with strangling Millie, Peter clawed at the tentacle, his eyes bulging and his breathing ragged. His body tensed, and he wriggled from side to side as another tentacle joined the first, wrapping Peter in strong loops of sand which dragged him from on top of Millie and pinned him to the beach. Staring at the night sky, Peter kicked at more tendrils which grew from the sand, forming writhing coils which slid over the man's body and held him still.

Millie got to her feet, her hands on her throat as she gasped for air, spitting sand from her mouth. Her legs trembling, she concentrated on the spell she'd cast, willing whatever monster she'd created to spare Peter's life. The tentacles of sand responded quickly to her commands, loosening their grasp on Peter, allowing him to breathe, but holding him captive. Millie gazed down at the man, her throat sore as she spoke. "Don't worry, Peter," she said. "I know you didn't do this to me. I'll get the demon out of you, I promise."

Millie looked up as Sergeant Spencer approached, limping as he hurried towards her. "Are you alright?" he said, ignoring the monster Millie's magic had created, and placing a hand on each of her shoulders, staring at her with concern. "What did he do to you?"

"I'll be okay," said Millie. "I'm just a little bruised. It's nothing that a magic potion won't be able to help."

Sergeant Spencer nodded. "I'm sorry I couldn't get here quicker. The demon — Peter, I mean, took us by surprise. Judith's hurt and —"

"Judith?" said Millie. "What did he do to her? Is she okay?"

"She'll be fine," said Sergeant Spencer. "She's had the wind knocked out of her. She didn't have time to use magic. It all happened so fast." He glanced at the struggling man, imprisoned by sand. "It seems you managed to use your magic."

With little time to spare. "Yes," said Millie. "I'm not sure how long the spell will hold, though."

Sergeant Spencer slipped his handcuffs from his belt. "These will hold him. He doesn't have super-human strength, he's just very, very angry. I'll get him cuffed, and we'll lock him in the cottage. I'll get in touch with Henry. He'll know what to do with him."

Millie nodded, her throat aching. "What happened?" she said. "Why does Mister Incognito have a demon inside him?"

Sergeant Spencer crouched beside Peter. "Let's get him safely locked away in your cottage, and then we'll discuss what happened."

Chapter 18

After Sergeant Spencer had secured Peter to the cast-iron rail which ran along the base of Millie's stone fireplace, he checked the handcuffs were tight, took the piece of thick sticky tape Millie offered him, and placed it over Peter's mouth. "There," he said. "He's still subdued after his struggle with the spell you cast, Millie. It won't be long until he's regained his energy, though."

"What's happening, Sergeant?" said Graham Spalding, his hands trembling as he lowered himself onto the sofa.

Sergeant Spencer ignored him, taking his phone from his pocket and typing out a quick message. "There," he said. "I've just told Henry what's happened. He shouldn't be long."

A whip crack echoed through the cottage, and Henry appeared next to the fireplace in a brief explosion of light, dressed impeccably in a tartan three-piece suit. He gazed around the room, his spectacles reflecting Graham's startled face. "I came as soon as I received Sergeant Spencer's message," he said.

"We noticed," said Judith, her hands on her ribs.

"Are you sure I can't get you something for that?" said Millie. "I can make a potion which will take the pain away."

Judith shook her head. "No. I told you. I'm fine — it's my pride that hurts the most. I couldn't use my magic in time. I couldn't do anything to stop him, and then he attacked my father."

Sergeant Spencer put an arm around his daughter. "It's only my leg. I twisted my knee when I fell. I'll be as right as rain by tomorrow."

"It was only because Millie shouted that the demon's attention was drawn away from you, Dad," said Judith. "It could have been so much worse. I'm sorry."

"Nobody's got anything to be sorry for," said Millie.

Graham Spalding looked up from the sofa. "A man just appeared out of thin air. Will somebody please tell me what's happening. Have I gone mad?"

"Why don't you tell us what happened, Graham?" said Sergeant Spencer. "We saw you leave. Why did you decide to come back?"

His face white, Graham shook his head. "It wasn't my decision," he said. "It was Peters. I had no control over him. He's normally very calm and collected, but since his accident, he's become infatuated with the scientific equipment he owns. He's very protective of it. We were almost back at his house when he realised we'd left his forensic tent behind — covering the skeleton in the dunes. I told him we'd come back for it another day, but he lost his temper. He almost caused us to crash when he grabbed the steering wheel from my hands. He made me pull over and forced me to let him drive, and then he sped all the way back here."

"Where he crashed into the sand dunes," said Sergeant Spencer. "And touched the skeleton. Judith and I saw the flash of light from inside the tent when we rushed out of the cottage to see what was happening."

"Yes," said Graham. "And him crashing into the dunes was a good thing, as far as I'm concerned. I don't think I could have taken another ten seconds of his driving. It was terrifying. As soon as he'd crashed, he leapt out of the van and headed for his tent. I followed him, trying to calm him down. He was having none of it, though, but when he saw his tent, he cheered up, and went inside. I could hear the Sergeant shouting by then, and realised he was probably going to arrest me — as he'd promised he would. I thought that if I was going to be arrested anyway, I may as well try and take away some evidence of the alien skeleton with me, I took my phone out and used it as a torch, but I couldn't believe what I was seeing when I looked in the hole where the skeleton *had* been. Most of it had gone! Like it had crumbled to dust."

"But there was some left, wasn't there?" said Henry.

"Yes," said Graham. "But I didn't see it, Peter did. He got to his knees and picked it up — a single tooth, and then it happened — there was a bright flash of light, and Peter turned into…" He pointed at the struggling man chained to the fireplace. "Into that. What happened? Was it the alien? Is the alien inside him, controlling him? With space energy? His eyes look a bit mad! Will his skin turn blue?"

"Your friend is possessed," said Henry. "But not by an alien. By a demon."

"A demon?" said Graham. "Demons don't exist!"

"Not in this dimension," said Henry. He looked at Peter. "Or at least they *shouldn't*. The demon inside your friend sneaked into our dimension, along with a second one, and the other one is responsible for the death of a man."

"Demons?" said Graham. "Other dimensions?" He shook his head. "Then Peter was right. Other dimensions do exist."

"At least one other. And the creatures that live in it are worse than anything your imagination could possibly conjure up," said Reuben.

Graham's draw dropped open. "The bird spoke. The bird spoke," he muttered.

"I can see why you'd think a demon was responsible for Tom's murder, Henry," said Millie. "Look at his eyes."

Peter shook his arms violently, the handcuffs

clanking against the iron rail. His bloodshot eyes opened wide as he struggled, and the sticky tape across his mouth transformed his attempts at shouting into muffled grunts.

"He's in the early stages of possession," said Henry. "It won't take long until the demon has full control of the unfortunate gentleman, and at that stage of the process, it becomes very hard to know when a person is possessed, from outward appearances alone."

Graham made a grunting sound, his face white. "What will happen to Peter?" he said. "Is it possible to get the... demon out of him?"

Henry nodded. "Oh yes," he said. "I can get the demon out of him. That's simple."

Graham frowned. "Well?" he said. "Would you mind getting it out of him? As soon as possible?"

Henry approached Peter, and stared down at him. "Not yet," he said. "I'll remove the demon from him after I've used him as bait to catch the second demon. The one which killed Tom Temples."

"Bait?" said Judith, rubbing her ribs. "How will that work?"

Reuben flew from the sofa and landed on Millie's shoulder. "Because demons belong in pairs," he said. "Isn't that right, Henry?"

"Yes," said Henry. "It is. And when the other demon becomes aware that its partner is still alive, and not lying dead in the sand, it will come for it. And then we can remove the evil entities from both Peter and whoever the poor person is who was forced to kill Tom Temples by their unwelcome parasite."

Graham frowned. "Bait?" he said. "Is that safe? For Peter?"

"It's perfectly safe," said Henry. "We'll wait for dawn — so we have light, and then take Peter outside, make sure he's firmly secured, and remove the tape from his mouth. The sounds he'll make will attract the other demon, and then we just have to wait for it to arrive. And catch it. We'll have to be careful, though. The other demon has already killed Tom Temples, we don't want another death in Spellbinder Bay."

Chapter 19

It felt strange to be making coffee as a man possessed by a demon struggled at the handcuffs that held him captive in her living room, but everybody appreciated Millie's gesture, and even Graham Spalding's face regained some of its colour as he sipped his drink.

As Millie stared out of the patio doors at the ocean, the sun beginning to peek over the horizon and paint the waves in soft orange, Reuben landed gently on her shoulder. "Did you get it?" he whispered.

Millie smiled. "I got the pearl, Reuben."

"There!" he said, quietly. "I knew it would be easy!"

"Yes," said Millie, shuddering as she recalled cold seawater flooding her throat. "It was easy."

"Okay everybody!" said Henry, from behind her. "Dawn has arrived. It's time to catch the creature which killed Tom Temples, and return normality to

Spellbinder Bay." He winked in Millie's direction. "As much normality as we're used to, anyway."

Peter Simmons struggled as Sergeant Spencer wrapped his wrists in tape and removing the handcuffs, replacing them on his wrists when he was free of the fireplace. "If you can hear me in there, Peter," he said. "Try and remain calm. We'll get the creature out of you as soon as possible."

"I doubt he can hear you," said Henry. "It would take great strength to remain aware of oneself while possessed by such a malevolent entity."

"Poor Peter," said Millie.

Henry opened the cottage door. "Well, come on them, all of you. The sooner we catch the other one, the sooner Peter may have his body returned to him."

As Sergeant Spencer struggled to control Peter, Graham came to his aid. "Let me help you," he said, grabbing his friend under his arm, and helping the policeman guide him towards the open door. "I can't help feeling that some of this is my fault."

"Oh, really?" said Sergeant Spencer. "Just some of it?"

"To be fair, Dad," said Judith, "it's not really his fault, is it? The two demons which came into our world must take the blame for everything that's happened."

"This world, though?" said Graham, helping Sergeant Spencer push Peter through the door and into the cool morning air. "What is it? I mean *this* world. *Your* world — with speaking birds, short men dressed like Scottish lawyers appearing from nowhere and young ladies talking about making potions which can cure injuries? What have I walked into?"

"Not now," said Sergeant Spencer. "I'm sure Henry will want to speak with you when all of this is over, but until then, why don't you just focus on what's important right now — which is catching a killer demon."

"Of course," said Graham, stumbling as Peter grunted and attempted to shake off his two escorts. "There'll be plenty of time for answers."

"Put him over there," said Henry, pointing towards the sand dunes. "Handcuff him to the campervan and take the tape off his mouth. If events unfold as I expect them to, we shouldn't have to wait long for the other demon to make an appearance. Their senses are highly attuned to one another, even when in a human body. The other demon will hear the screams of the creature inside Peter from a long way off, and be drawn to it like a moth to a flame."

With Reuben still on her shoulder, Millie watched Sergeant Spencer and Graham attach Peter's handcuffs to the front tow ring of the campervan, and remove the tape from his mouth. As soon as the makeshift gag had been removed, Peter Simmons looked at the sky and gave a long, strangled howl, his body tense as he strained to free himself from the cuffs, the rattling of metal on metal adding a chilling backdrop to his eerie vocals.

"He'll be sore when the demon is cast from his

body," said Henry, raising his voice to compete with Peter's continued screams. "But a few cuts and bruises are a small price to pay to be relieved of a parasite which would cause its host to perform all manner of evil deeds."

"How *will* you remove the demons from Peter and whoever the other possessed person is?" said Millie.

Straightening his dicky bow, Henry pointed at the cliff on the far side of the bay, where Spellbinder Hall stood, its many windows reflecting the orange glow of the dawn sun. "I'll take them beneath the hall," he said. "To the gate which separates this dimension from The Chaos. We will force them to step into the gateway, and as it is impossible for a human to pass between dimensions, the demons will be ripped from within them and cast back into the dimension from which they crawled. With no harm being done to the humans they violated."

Sitting in the sand dunes, the sun rising higher by the minute, Millie stared off into the distance, the pearl of wisdom digging into her leg as the pocket it was contained in stretched tight over her thigh. "Which way do you think it will come from?" she said. "If it comes?"

"I do not know," said Henry, retrieving his timepiece from his breast pocket and glancing at the dial.

"I'm more interested in discovering who it is that the demon dwells within."

"Somebody strong," said Judith. "That shovel went deep into Tom Temples's skull."

"So not somebody like that?" said Graham Spalding, pointing along the track which led from Millie's cottage to the country lanes beyond.

"Why does she walk in such a queer fashion?" asked Henry, shielding his eyes from the sun. "She wobbles from side to side."

Mille stared at the figure approaching them at speed. The white hair, swept back by a pink headband, and the matching shorts and training shoes gave the woman's identity away almost immediately. "It's Mrs Raymond," she said. "She's power walking, Henry. It's a form of exercise."

"But she can't be possessed by the demon," said Judith. "Surely?"

"She *does* exercise on the beach," said Millie. "And Henry surmised that because the other demon was found dormant in the sand dunes, then the other one would have been nearby. It could have happened upon poor Mrs Raymond as she exercised, and possessed her."

"We'll know soon enough," said Henry. "She's almost upon us. She moves with great speed for such a frail old lady."

Millie got to her feet, wiping sand from her legs, and smiled at Mrs Raymond as she crested a sand dune and headed for the crashed campervan. "Good morning, Mrs Raymond!" she called.

"Oh!" chirped Mrs Raymond, coming to an abrupt halt. "I didn't see you all, hiding there in the dunes! Good morning, everybody! And what a lovely morning it is, too! It's a shame that man next to the campervan is making such a racket. I heard him from the other side of town and rushed here immediately to see what all the fuss was about! He seems to have quietened down a little in the past few minutes. How kind of him!"

"The demon has full control of her," whispered Reuben in Millie's ear. "Don't trust her. She may look sweet and fragile, but she killed Tom Temples. The thing within her is evil."

Henry Pinkerton studied Mrs Raymond over the rims of his glasses. "Are you certain you only hurried across town, with a vigour normally displayed by women sixty years your junior, because you heard some shouting? And just how good are your ears, anyway, Mrs Raymond? I happen to know your home is at least two miles away. Are you sure there isn't something you'd like to tell us? Something we should be aware of? Something within you, perhaps?"

Mrs Raymond stood on tiptoes and pointed her fingers at the sky, arching her back a little as she stretched. "Are you sure there's not anything *you'd* like to tell *me*, Henry Pinkerton? After all, it's you and your little *community* who have been keeping secrets from the rest of the town for longer than I've been alive!"

"What secrets are you referring to?" asked Henry.

"Oh," said Mrs Raymond, bending easily at the waist and touching the toes of her bright pink training shoes. "Just the fact that the town is full of people of a… paranormal nature, shall we say?" She stood upright, and stared Henry in the eyes. "And you're the ringleader! I know everything. The things I've learned in the last week about this town are shocking."

Sergeant Spencer's hand closed on the handle of the Taser protruding from the pouch on his belt. He leaned closer to Millie, and spoke in hushed tones. "When it turns violent, don't use magic unless you have to. Let me use the Taser. I didn't have time to use it on Peter — it all happened so fast. I think the Taser will be kinder to Mrs Raymond than magical tentacles of sand strangling her."

"I heard that, Sergeant Spencer," said Mrs Raymond, stepping closer to the policeman. "You're thinking of using your Taser on me? And you're normally so kind — giving me lifts home from the shops with my groceries."

Henry stepped between Mrs Raymond and Sergeant Spencer. "Don't come any closer, Mrs Raymond. And let's stop this little game, shall we? We know your true nature. Reveal yourself to us!"

Mrs Raymond's face seemed to crumple, and she gave a soft sigh, her hands forming tiny fists. "Help me," she whimpered. "Help me."

Henry stepped forward. "Mrs Raymond?" he said. "You can hear us! That's good news! Keep fighting the demon within you! We're going to help you. You're going to be okay, but you must remain strong!"

"I'll try," whispered Mrs Raymond, her voice becoming husky, "but can we hurry? I want to be home in time for my morning TV programmes."

"Pardon?" said Henry.

Mrs Raymond's face broke into a wide smile, and she shook as she laughed. "Oh, ignore him," she smiled. "He's got such a great sense of humour for a creature that came from such a dark place, haven't you, Baskillazarataman?"

"What's happening?" said Judith.

"I'd like to know that, too," said Graham Spalding. "I don't mind admitting I'm scared. It was all fun and games when I thought I was hunting for lizard people, but this town is something else. Something else altogether."

Her voice deepening slightly, Mrs Raymond spoke again. "I have indeed got a great sense of humour, Hilda. Although a sense of humour is a concept I've only just begun to understand. Thanks to you."

"What's happening?" repeated Judith.

"I'm just having some fun with you all!" laughed Mrs Raymond. "Baskillaza – *Basil*, and I are having some fun with you!"

"Basil?" said Millie.

"My new best friend," said Mrs Raymond. "From the other dimension! He's a wonderful companion! We got off to a rocky start when he tried to possess me as I was enjoying a walk along the beach last week, but I soon put him in his place! I went through rationing during the war. Preventing a demon from possessing my mind was child's play in comparison. Anyway — it transpires that he's a very nice… being. And he's explained everything about the paranormal nature of this town to me."

"Are you trying to tell us that you have control of the demon within you, Mrs Raymond?" said Henry.

"Call me Hilda, please," smiled Mrs Raymond. "And yes, I do — although control is not the word I'd use. Basil and I cohabit — we share my body. Since he's been inside me, I've developed such vigour! I'm far fitter than the other members of the pensioner's fitness club, and I'm going abseiling next week! From a cliff! Wearing a helmet! I'm having such fun!"

"I'm not sure I believe you… Hilda," said Henry. "How do I know I'm not speaking to the demon? How do I know that Mrs Raymond is still in there?"

"Because it's the truth," said Hilda, her voice deep again. "I attempted to take control of Hilda, but she was too strong. I had no chance, and I'm glad I didn't. I'd always wondered if the whole thing about sneaking into this dimension, and taking control of a human, was morally justified, and it seems it wasn't. It's quite an evil idea, if I'm being honest, and I'm not evil. I was led astray by a demon who *is* evil. That one over there! In the body of the man who was screaming! He's evil, not me."

"Not evil?" said Sergeant Spencer. "You're a demon! You've possessed a woman!"

Reuben gave a little cough. "Excuse me, Sergeant Spencer. I'm a demon, and I'm not evil. Not all demons are innately evil. And I've *technically* been possessing the body of this bird since Esmeralda brought me from the other dimension and placed my energy within it. It's very possible that Baskill — Basil, and Mrs Raymond *are* sharing a body. Peacefully."

"It's *entirely* possible," said Mrs Raymond, her voice her own again. "And I'm having a wonderful time with Basil inside me. I've never felt healthier, and I have the senses of a superhero! Basil and I could hear the cries of his rowdy companion all the way from my garden, where we were doing early morning yoga. We were in extended puppy pose when we heard the screams. We rushed here straight away."

"Why did you rush here?" said Henry, narrowing his eyes, his pupils magnified by his spectacles. "To come to the aid of your fellow demon, perhaps? To set him free? Or to revisit the scene of your heinous crime?"

"Crime?" said Hilda, confusion furrowing her brow. "What crime, Henry Pinkerton?"

"The murder of Tom Temples!" snapped Henry. "You can't fool me, demon. I'm not stupid! This is an act. Hilda is not speaking to us! We are listening to the false utterings of a demon."

"It's me," said Hilda. "Really. It's me."

"I don't believe you, demon," said Henry. "And

this isn't the first time you've been back to this spot since the two of you *malevolent entities* arrived from The Chaos. Is it? You came back looking for your partner on Tuesday night, didn't you? Under the cover of darkness. And when you discovered his skeletal remains, you couldn't control your rage! When you stumbled upon poor Tom Temples digging for gold in the dunes, you took your anger out on him, and bludgeoned him to death with his own shovel! And when I've cast you from Hilda's body, demon, the poor woman will have to live with the memory of what you forced her to do to a fellow human being, for the rest of her days. You've taken Tom's life, and you've ruined Hilda's!"

"Of course I didn't kill Tom Temples!" said Hilda. "I wasn't even aware that the poor man was dead! I've been very busy this week, becoming accustomed to Basil's presence in my mind. I haven't had the time to keep abreast of town affairs. Poor, poor, Tom. I liked him. You must believe me, Henry! You're talking to Hilda — Basil *does not* control me, and we certainly did not kill a man!"

Henry turned to Sergeant Spencer. "If she moves, use that Taser. I shall return momentarily."

"Where are you going?" said Millie.

"To get the stone of integrity," said Henry. "The same one I used on you, Millie. It doesn't work on humans, but Hilda has a demon within her. She is, at the moment, a paranormal person. The stone will work on her and allow us to get to the truth. It will tell us if she speaks honestly, or lies to our faces."

"Go and get your silly stone, Henry," said Hilda, adjusting her headband. "Basil and I have nothing to hide!"

A whip crack marking his departure, Henry was gone, leaving Hilda staring at the space he'd been standing in. She glanced around at the rest of the people watching her, her eyes travelling to the pouch on Sergeant Spencer's belt. "I did not kill Tom," she said. "And you won't need that weapon today, Sergeant Spencer. Not to use on me."

"Why *did* you come here today, Hilda?" said Judith.

"Because we heard the screams," said Hilda. "I told you. The demon in that man's body over there is emitting high pitched sounds, along with the shouts and screams that you could hear. He was calling to Basil."

"And you came to help him?" said Sergeant Spencer.

"No!" said Hilda. "We came here to make sure he didn't do any harm to anybody. Basil had hoped that his bones would have been dust by now! We were shocked to hear his screams — it could mean only one thing — that he had possessed a human host! We rushed here when we realised! Basil wants to send him back to the dimension he came from, don't you, Basil?"

Hilda's voice deepened once more. "I do indeed," she said. She moved towards Peter Simmons, and raised her voice. "Did you hear that, Krackanagromit? I'm going to make sure you return to where you belong. You've always led me astray! I've tried to be a good demon, but you wouldn't let me be good. Well, now I've found a new companion. A kind and caring companion, and I won't be needing you any longer! You can go back to the dark and find another idiot to manipulate!"

Peter Simmons's face darkened, and he opened his mouth wide, struggling against the handcuffs and emitting an angry screech which hurt Millie's ears.

"He's not happy," said the demon within Hilda. "He's promising vengeance."

Another whip crack echoed across the dunes, and Henry appeared with a pouch in his hand. "I can assure you that he won't be getting his vengeance," he said, opening the leather pouch and retrieving an orb from inside. "Hold out your hand, please, Hilda," he ordered.

Hilda did as Henry asked, the stone glowing amber as it touched her palm. "I can feel it vibrating," she said.

"That's because it's working," said Henry. "And soon, it will give us the truth." He pushed his glasses along his nose, and stared into Hilda's eyes. "Are you in control of Hilda's body, demon?" he asked.

Hilda frowned, and answered in a deep voice. "No, and neither do I wish to be. She is my friend and can speak for herself. I have no control over her."

Reflected in the thick glass of Henry's spectacles, the stone glowed a bright blue, shimmering and flickering as Henry asked a second question. "Did you kill Tom Temples?" he said.

"No," said the voice of Basil. "Hilda and I did not kill Tom. We killed nobody, and we have no intention of ever harming anybody. You need not fear our relationship. You need not fear *me*."

Emitting a gentle hum as it throbbed an even brighter blue, Henry plucked the stone from Hilda's outstretched hand, and placed it back in the pouch. "You speak the truth. The stone is never wrong. I am sorry I doubted you," he said.

"And Basil can stay? In this world? In my body?" said Hilda.

"I see no reason why not, Hilda," said Henry. "It is with your consent that he dwells within you. It is nobody else's right to tell you what you may do with your life, and as Basil seems benign, I believe he poses no risk to this world or its occupants. The stone was quite adamant that you spoke the truth." He looked at Peter Simmons, as the captive man gave another angry shout. "The demon within *him*, on the other hand," he said, "must be banished from this dimension. I will arrange to have him transported to Spellbinder Hall, where I will free Peter from his unwelcome guest, and send the demon back into The Chaos."

"Do you think he killed Tom?" said Hilda. "The other demon, I mean?"

"No," said Millie. "That would be impossible. The demon had already begun to decompose before Tom was killed, and it would have been dust by now if Peter Simmons hadn't touched it and become possessed by it. The demon didn't kill Tom."

"Then who did?" said Hilda. "Do you have a suspect, Sergeant Spencer?"

"No," said Sergeant Spencer. "We don't. We have no suspects, and no leads. It's still a mystery. A mystery I want to solve as soon as possible, but until we do, life must go on as normal."

Chapter 20

Reuben woke Millie from a deep sleep, his beak cold on her ear. "Time to get up," he said. "Judith is here, and she needs your help."

"Help with what?" Millie said. "It's Saturday, and Sergeant Spencer said that until he had any further leads on the Tom Temples's murder, he was focusing on routine police work. What does Judith want?"

"You're supposed to be the mind reader, not me," said the bird. "You tell me."

"I can pick up on *some* thoughts, Reuben," said Millie. "I'm *not* a mind-reader, and anyway, it's not a gift I like to use. It can be upsetting, sometimes."

"I didn't want a speech, Millie," said Reuben. "I was saying it in jest. I just want you to get out of bed so you can make me breakfast. Everything's back to normal — I'd like to revert to normal meal times again, if that's not too much trouble?"

"Everything's not back to normal, really,

Reuben," said Millie, swinging her legs from the bed. "We don't know who killed Tom."

"Apart from that little detail," said Reuben. "Everything else is, though. There's not a campervan in sight. There are no skeletons in the sand dunes. Mrs Raymond and Basil seem very happy together, Henry removed the demon from Peter and sent it scurrying back to The Chaos, you and George still haven't spoken since that ridiculous argument, and I have a belly which is going to rumble its way out of my ears if it's not fed soon. That's normality enough for me."

Millie smiled. "Me too. Come on then, let's go and see what Judith wants, and then I'll make some bacon."

"And eggs?"

"And eggs," said Millie.

Reuben fluffed up his plumage. "And tonight? Are we going to do… our thing?"

"Pizza and wine?" said Millie.

"No," said Reuben. "You know what I mean. The pearl of wisdom. I think we should use it tonight. You said we'd use it last night, but then you said you were too tired. I really think you need to do it, Millie. I think it will change your life. For the better."

"Maybe," said Millie, glancing at the envelope propped up against her bedside lamp. "*Just*, maybe."

Throwing her dressing gown on over her favourite sleeping shirt, Millie entered the living room to find Judith standing next to the fireplace, dressed in a white hoodie and shorts, with an apology in her eyes, and a police file in her hands.

"What's that look for?" said Millie. "What are you going to ask me?"

"I'm sorry to wake you so early at, erm…" She glanced at her phone. "Half-past seven, but I need a favour? If you'd be so kind?"

"What sort of favour?" said Millie.

"Dad updated the missing person file for Jill Harris yesterday," she said.

"The missing mother," said Millie, switching the kettle on. "And how can I help you with that?"

"I phoned Jill yesterday to tell her, and she asked if I could take it to her today. At eleven o'clock. On a Saturday," said Judith. "She's expecting me."

"And you can't, so you'd like me to do it for you," said Millie, smiling. "Of course I will. I had nothing else planned."

"Thank you," said Judith. "It's for Dad, more than me. I just go along with it, to make him happy."

"Go along with what?" said Millie.

Judith smiled. "It's this thing we do together — every year. It's like an anniversary, but I sometimes forget, like I did this year — hence me phoning Jill Harris and arranging an appointment on a Saturday of all days. When Dad came down for breakfast this morning dressed in his shorts and his Bexington Zoo t-shirt, I pretended I'd remembered. I went upstairs and changed into my zoo shirt, then I told him I was just nipping out to get some sun-cream as it's going to be so hot today, and rushed over here on my bike. I didn't want to cancel with Jill, the poor woman, and I think Dad would be gutted if he thought I'd forgotten our thing again."

"Okay," said Millie. "I definitely don't mind helping you, Judith, but I will be needing help with something myself."

"Anything!" said Judith.

Millie frowned. "I need to know why your father came down to breakfast dressed in a Bexington Zoo t-shirt. Then I need to know why you put a zoo shirt on, and then I need to know why zoo t-shirts are an important factor in the story you just told me."

Judith smiled. "It's nice, really," she said. "When Dad adopted me as a two-year-old, and brought me to Spellbinder Bay when I was three…after the accident… you know."

Millie approached Judith and put a hand on her arm. "You don't need to talk about it," she said. "I'm sorry for asking, I didn't think it would dredge up bad memories."

"Don't be silly," said Judith. "The bad memories were from a time before Dad adopted me and brought me here. Those memories are locked in one box, and the memories I have of my time in Spellbinder Bay are locked in a different box. I'm rummaging through the second box today."

"I understand," said Millie. *She did understand.* The two boxes in her own head may not have contained the awful memories that one of the boxes in Judith's head contained — the memory of accidentally killing her own parents with magic, but her two boxes each held memories of a different part of her own life — one box brimming with ten years worth of memories of the time before her mother died, and the other box containing the memories of the fourteen years afterwards.

Judith placed her hand over Millie's. "So, when we moved here, lots of people in town were very supportive of me and Dad, especially the paranormal community — who knew of my history. There was always somebody at our house. I was only three, but I still remember all the cakes people brought for us, and all the meals they cooked. I don't remember who they all were. I was young — all their faces have blurred into one over time, but they were kind people."

"A real community," said Millie.

"It was… *is*," said Judith. "And they arranged things, you know? Community picnics on the beach, day trips — that sort of thing. Things that would help take a three-year old's mind off her past. As I grew older, the visits to our house became less frequent, and the picnics and day trips stopped, but Dad and I still took our trips together. Especially to Bexington zoo. I used to love it there! Dad would take me once a month until I was six or seven, then once every six months or so, and now it's once a year — on the same day — or the closest Saturday to it."

"Today," said Millie.

"Yes," said Judith with a grin. "Dad has turned it

into *our* day. He's very big on it — he never forgets. We've only missed it twice, and that was because of Dad's work, but he always took me as soon after the day we'd missed as he could."

"It sounds like a lovely tradition," said Millie.

"It is," said Judith. "If you like zoos."

"But the t-shirts?" said Millie. "What's that all about?"

Judith laughed. "There's a gift shop at the zoo, and Dad buys us both a t-shirt from it every time we go — it's the last place we visit before leaving the zoo. Then we wear the shirts he's bought the next time we go. So the shirts we're wearing today, are the shirts he bought us last year. It's silly, really, but Dad loves it."

"And is your shirt under that hoodie?" said Millie, raising an eyebrow.

"It is," said Judith. "Would you like to see it?"

"Naturally," said Millie, taking a step backwards, and smiling as Judith unzipped her jacket.

"The arrow on Dad's shirt is pointing the other way," said Judith, rolling her eyes as she revealed the grinning face of a chimpanzee, with an arrow below it, and the words, *I'm with that cheeky monkey*.

"That's so funny!" said Millie. "You're lucky to have a father like that, Judith. I hope you both have a lovely day at the zoo, and don't worry about your appointment with Jill Harris. I'll be there on time."

Chester Harris opened the door. Dressed in scruffy clothing, his eyes bloodshot and his hair dishevelled, he looked ill. "Hello?" he said.

"Hello, Mister Harris," said Millie. "I've come to bring your wife the updated files concerning her missing mother. My colleague spoke on the phone with her yesterday. She made an appointment for eleven. My colleague couldn't come, so I'm here instead."

"Oh, yes, right. Come in, I suppose," said Chester. "She's in the kitchen. Would you mind showing yourself through? You remember where it is from the last time you were here? I was just going upstairs for a lie-down."

"Yes, I remember. Thank you," said Millie, stepping into the hallway and closing the door behind her as Chester began climbing the stairs to her left.

"You're welcome," said Chester, his back to Millie as he reached the top of the stairs and vanished into one of the rooms.

Giving a gentle knock first, Millie pushed the kitchen door open. "Hello, Mrs Harris," she said, speaking to the lady sitting at the table, a mess of pieces of paper and envelopes in front of her.

"Oh, hello!" she said, getting to her feet. "Please, come on in, and call me Jill. Would you like a cup of tea or coffee?"

"A coffee would be lovely," said Millie. "Black, no sugar, please."

"I was expecting the other young lady," said Jill. "Not that it matters, of course."

"She sends her apologies," said Millie. "She couldn't make it."

"That's fine. I hope that husband of mine was polite when he let you in," said Jill, grabbing two mugs from a cupboard. "He's been like a bear with a sore head this last week."

"He was fine," said Millie. "He *did* look a little tired, though."

"He's not sleeping, you see," said Jill. "He's got something on his mind, but he refuses to tell me what. He's adamant that he's okay." She winked. "Men, hey?"

Millie sighed. "Indeed," she said. "Men."

"You've got a man problem, yourself?" said Jill.

"Sort of," said Millie. "An unresolved argument. It will work itself out, though."

"Don't let it simmer, is my advice," said Jill. "Because if you let it simmer and don't turn the heat down, it will get hotter and hotter, until it's boiling. And then it will be too late. The pan will boil dry."

"I'll bear that in mind," said Millie.

Jill smiled. "Please, sit down, sorry about the mess on the table top. When your colleague phoned me yesterday, I got to thinking about Mum again, and fetched the box I keep her letters in. It's all love letters, from her Canadian fella, but it gives me a glimpse at a part of her that I never really knew."

Lowering herself into a chair, Millie placed her

file on the table, and glanced at the nearest letter. "Do you mind?" she said. "If I have a look?"

"Please feel free," said Jill, adding milk to one of the mugs. "The police looked at them all those years ago, but they were of no help. The address on the letters is where the man used to live at the time my mother was writing to him, a town in Quebec but when Mum went missing he'd moved on. The Canadian police found his wife living there, but with no husband, and with no forwarding address. He'd already left her."

"For your mother?" said Millie.

"Who knows?" said Jill, placing a mug in front of Millie. "His ex-wife said he'd moved out a month before Mum went missing. They never traced him. The assumption is that Mum went to Canada to join him. They're probably living the good life in some remote peaceful corner of Canada. On the coast. That's how I like to picture her, anyway. She loved the sea. I like to think that she'll spend the rest of her days with a sea-view."

"I'm sorry," said Millie. "It must have been so hard for you."

"It was," said Jill. "It was very —" She leapt to her feet and hurried towards the open back door. "Harry!" she shouted. "Get that dirty thing out of the kitchen! Go on, take it back in the garden — shoo!" She sat down next to Millie. "Sorry about that," she said. "He's been digging in the vegetable patch all morning. He must have picked up on a scent, he keeps wandering in here with dirty feet. I've only just mopped the floor."

"That's why I have a cockatiel, and not a dog," said Millie. "Although he doesn't come without his own problems and habits." She picked up a piece of paper from the table, and scanned the neatly written letter. "He seemed to love her," she murmured, reading the affectionate outpourings.

"Oh yes," said Jill. "The letters are lovely, aren't they? They could be *just* words, though — he left his wife, remember. Who's to say he never did the same to my mother?" She jumped to her feet. "Harry! What on earth is that? Get it outside immediately! It's disgusting!"

Millie turned the letter over, and stared at the single sentence at the bottom of the page. The sentence preceding three kisses. Her blood ran cold. "Jill," she said. "What does this mean? At the bottom of the letter?"

"Oh," said Jill, pushing Harry through the door with gentle persuasion from her foot. "The French part you mean? He was from Quebec, as I've said, and French is the main language spoken in that part of Canada. I looked that phrase up in an old French dictionary — as far as I can tell, it means *I will love you forever*. He signed off like that on all the letters he sent to Mum. I think it's lovely."

Millie silently re-read the sentence at the bottom of the page. *Je t'aimerai pour toujours.* "Jill," she said.

"Did your mother have any jewellery with that phrase engraved on it?"

"Yes," said Jill, wrestling something from the little dog's mouth. Something long and white. Something which fell to the floor and bounced a few times before coming to rest at Jill's slipper-clad feet. "She had a ring. He bought it for her while he was working over here, when they first met. A gold ring, with a heart on the band. She would never take it off." She bent at the waist and peered at the saliva covered item which Harry had dropped. "What is that, Harry? It looks like a bone."

Footsteps on the stairs drew Millie's attention, and she stood up as the front door clicked open and then slammed shut. "Jill," she said, rushing for the kitchen door. "Don't touch that bone. And keep Harry away from the garden. Don't let him dig anymore. Stay here and wait for one of my colleagues to arrive."

"You've gone white, dear," said Jill. "What's wrong? Where are you going?"

"I'm sorry," said Millie, hurrying along the hallway and opening the front door as a car engine burst into life. "I think something terrible may have happened."

"Where's he going?" said Jill, joining Millie on the pavement, and watching as a blue car sped off down the road, turning left at the end. "He said he was going to lie down."

"I think he heard us talking," said Millie, staring at

her car wheels. "And he didn't like what we had to say. So much so that he's slashed my tyres."

"What do you mean?" said Jill. "What's going on? Where is Chester going? Who slashed your tyres?"

Millie placed her phone to her ear, and cursed silently as she reached Sergeant Spencer's answering service. Of course — he and Judith were at the zoo. She was on her own. She dialled the only other number she could think of. "I need you. Urgently. In Sandy-hill Terrace. And bring a spare helmet," she said.

Chapter 21

Jill Harris watched on with shock scrawled across her face as George brought his motorbike to a screeching halt outside her house. "What's happening?" she shouted, as the rumbling tones of the bike's engine made normal conversation impossible.

Millie slid the open-faced helmet, which George had handed her, over her head, Jill's anxious face begging her for answers — answers Millie didn't have — yet. She took a long breath, and decided to share her honest suspicions with the woman. "Jill," she yelled. "I think Chester may have done something to your mother. Is there a neighbour you can wait with? Somebody to give you support?"

As Millie climbed onto the bike, Jill gave a slow nod.

"I'm sorry, Jill. We have to go!" she yelled, as she

nudged George in the small of his back. "Left at the end of the road. We're looking for a blue hatchback."

The engine screamed as the bike moved away, the rear tyre screeching on tarmac. "The car must be heading out of town," shouted George. "There's only one road. It shouldn't be hard to catch it. Why *are* we trying to catch it? Who is it?"

Holding tightly to George's leather jacket as he leaned the bike low to the left, Millie shouted over his shoulder. "I think he killed his mother-in-law. And buried her... somewhere."

If Chester *had* killed her, and buried her body in his garden thirty years ago — why was it only now that Harry had discovered her remains — *if* the bone the dog had brought into the kitchen *did* belong to the missing woman, and why was her ring discovered in the sand dunes by Tom Temples, the man who was murdered in the same spot? If it even *was* her ring.

Millie shook such complicated thoughts from her head. *One task at a time.* The first one being to catch Chester Harris.

George opened the throttle as the road widened, and lines of houses became thick hedgerows. "So, does this mean we're friends, or are you just using me for the ride?" he yelled, his voice competing with the whoosh of wind.

"Not now, George!" shouted Millie, shutting her eyes as the bike roared around a blind corner.

"That woman, Millie," shouted George. "The nurse. She's —"

"Not now!" yelled Millie. "I don't care!"

George responded by giving the engine more fuel, the bike lurching forward as he dropped a gear and lowered his chest closer to the fuel tank, allowing a wall of wind to push hard into Millie's face.

Bending with him, Millie watched the road ahead, a sudden reflection of sunlight on metal visible at the crest of the hill, where the road began to head inland. "There!" shouted Millie. "I saw a car!"

Expertly manoeuvring the bike, George opened the throttle wider, the hedges zipping past in a blur of green. "I see him," he yelled, as the bike reached the top of the hill. "Now we have to stop him!"

"Ride alongside him," said Millie. "Maybe when he sees us he'll pull over!" Lurching backwards as the bike powered forward, her training shoes pressed firmly on the foot grips, she held on tightly to George as he neared the tail end of the hatchback, its driver glancing nervously in the rear-view mirror as the car swerved to the left.

"He's not going to stop!" shouted George. "He's seen us! He knows we're here, but he's speeding up!"

"Be careful!" yelled Millie, as George matched the speed of the car and drew alongside it, a distance of a few feet between the two fast-moving vehicles. She pointed at Chester Harris, whose panicked face peered at her. "Pull over, Chester!" she shouted, jabbing her finger in his direction. "Pull over!"

The car's engine gave a loud roar, and the vehicle gained a small advantage over the motorbike, easily matched by George as he twisted the throttle grip. He turned his head to look at the driver. "Stop!" he ordered. "Stop the car!"

Millie saw what was about to happen a millisecond before it did. "Watch out!" she screamed. "He's going to —"

Her words abruptly cut off by the heavy thud of the car's side panelling striking the motorbike, and her hands losing their grip on George's jacket as the violent collision launched her from the pillion seat, time seemed to slow for Millie as she twisted in the air, gaining height as she watched Chester beginning to lose control of his car, the front-end heading for the closely spaced trees which lined the side of the road.

"Millie!" she heard George shout, his voice distant as the front wheel of the motorbike swivelled too far to the right, the bike's rear end travelling upwards as if the front brakes had been slammed on, ejecting the vampire from his seat.

Hearing the sickening thump of the car colliding with a tree, and watching the front end begin to crumple, Millie closed her eyes, awaiting her own collision. Awaiting the crumpling of her body. She wondered if it would be painful, or quick, and gritted her teeth as she felt herself losing height, plummeting at speed towards her fate.

THE COLLISION CAME QUICKLY, AND NOT AS VIOLENTLY

as Millie had expected. She waited for the pain, wondering if her adrenaline was acting as natural morphine, and held her breath, becoming aware that she was still moving. The clamping of strong hands, one on the back of her neck, and one on the curve at the top of her calf muscle, persuaded her to breathe again, her breath leaving her in a gasp of shock.

She opened her eyes, and looked up at George, his open-faced helmet framing his expression of rage, and his eyes an ebony black, in stark contrast to the long white fangs protruding from beneath his top lip.

George landed with a soft thud, and lowered Millie onto the grass verge, kneeling next to her, his eyes becoming hazel again, and his fangs retreating. He ripped his helmet from his head, and moved his face close to Millie's. "Are you alright?" he said. "Millie? Please be alright!"

Blinking twice, Millie gave a gentle nod. "You saved me," she said.

"Are you okay?" demanded George, his hands sliding gently along Millie's legs, feeling for injuries.

"I'm fine," said Millie. "You leapt through the air and saved me. That was some move."

"Never mind that," said George, the smell of his leather jacket and aftershave in Millie's nostrils. "That nurse," he said. "It's not like that. I promise. It's you I —"

Millie put a finger to his lips, his breath warm on her hand. "Just kiss me, George," she said. "We don't have time. We can talk later."

Colour rising in his cheeks, George lowered his face to Millie's, his hands on her shoulders and his knees against her thigh. As his lips brushed Millie's, she closed her eyes and returned his kiss, wondering what the acrid smell was that was beginning to mask the spicy scent of the vampire's aftershave.

Millie opened her eyes as a loud thumping bang shook the ground beneath her, and the crackling sound of fire reached her ears. "What the —" she said, pushing George away.

George leapt to his feet. "It's the car," he said, turning to face the billowing black smoke cloud which was rising from the opposite side of the road.

"We were kissing while a man was trapped in a burning car!" said Millie, allowing George to help her up.

"We were in shock!" said George, rushing towards the crashed car, slowing as he neared it, and shielding his face with both arms. "It's hot!" he said, his eyes blackening and long fangs sliding into position.

A panicked shout came from the burning car, the flames enveloping the bonnet and beginning to climb the thick trunk of the tree which the vehicle had collided with. The windows blackened by smoke, it was impossible to see Chester, but his shouts of fear increased in intensity as Millie reached George's side.

"Can a vampire walk through fire?" shouted Millie, as George approached the car, his arms still shielding his face.

"No!" he said, inching nearer to the inferno. "But it's okay. I'll take the pain. I'm not leaving him to die!"

"I'm not going to let him die, either," said Millie, the heat of the flames pricking her cheeks. "But let me deal with the fire! We'll need your strength when the flames are out. The car's mangled, there's no way the door will open!"

George nodded. "Be careful, Millie! If you can't do it, step away. I'll fight my way through the flames. I'll heal quickly if I'm burnt. Don't worry!"

"I *can* do it!" said Millie, lifting her hands as she took slow steps towards the car, the flames spreading to the doors, and the windscreen succumbing to the heat — a tortured creaking sound rising above the vicious crackling of hungry flames, as it began to crack.

"Help me!" came the fearful pleading of Chester Harris, the car rocking as he struggled.

Finding the ball of energy in her chest, Millie reached deep within herself, her arms becoming cold as her magic rushed towards her hands, bursting from her quivering fingertips in a bright flash of blue light, which arched through the space between her and the car, the flames hissing in protest as tendrils of magic wrestled with them, wrapping each tongue of hot orange in an icy cold death grip.

George leapt into action as Millie's magic held the flames at bay, more bursting into life as others gave in to the cold energy which danced between them. Grasping the top edge of the driver's door in his fingertips, George winced and gave a short cry of pain, ignoring the heat, and wrenching the door from its fittings, a loud groaning of bending metal joining Chester's cries for help.

Tossing the crumpled door aside, George reached into the car and dragged Chester Harris from what had almost become his funeral pyre. He carried him a safe distance from the vehicle, and placed him on the ground, the groaning man's hair singed, and his face and arms black with a thick layer of soot.

Chester Harris looked up at Millie, his eyes frightened. "I'm sorry," he said, his voice hoarse. "I never meant to do it. Any of it. It was an accident."

Grabbing her phone from her pocket, Millie dialled nine-nine-nine. "Try and stay calm, Chester," she said. "You're injured. An ambulance will be here soon. There'll be plenty of time for talking, later."

Chapter 22

Sergeant Spencer hurried along the hospital corridor, with Judith close behind him, both still dressed in their Bexington Zoo t-shirts. "Are you okay, Millie?" he said, his stomach straining at his t-shirt. "Judith and I have been so worried."

"I'm fine," said Millie. "I'm sorry I had to contact the zoo, but both of your phones were off."

"Don't be silly," said Judith, gripping Millie in a fierce hug. "The man who came looking for us, found us in the gift shop. We were just about to leave."

"Were you getting your t-shirts for next year?" smiled Millie.

Judith rolled her eyes and zipped up her hoodie. "It's going to be so embarrassing next year," she said, lowering her voice. "They have a new machine in the gift shop. You can add a photo from your phone to your t-shirt — they print them out while you wait. When we were told by the staff member that we had to come straight to the hospital, the lady in the shop promised she'd forward them on to the police station for us when they'd finished being printed. I was kind of hoping we would never see them."

"What's that?" said Sergeant Spencer. "What were you hoping for, Judith?"

"I was just telling Millie about the t-shirts," said Judith. "I was telling her that I'm happy that they're being forwarded on to us."

Sergeant Spencer smiled. "Oh yes," he said. "It was very kind of the lady to offer. I'd have been gutted if we'd missed out on them. They're brilliant t-shirts!"

"Yes," said Judith. "Brilliant." She took a seat next to the coffee machine. "Did they say when we'd be allowed in to see him?" she asked.

"Soon," said Millie. "They've begun treatment on his burns and they're moving him to a private room. It shouldn't be too long."

"And you and George are both fine?" said Judith.

"We're both okay," said Millie, sitting next to her friend. "George was burned, but he healed within five minutes. It was amazing." She smiled. "He was a great help. And now he's gone to Chester and Jill's house to stop Harry from disturbing what I think might be Jill's mother's remains. He's had a look in the garden, and he's found a large bag in the spot the dog was digging in." She paused for a moment. "He saved my life, you know? He caught me in mid-air when I was thrown from the bike. He was like… Superman."

"I suppose that makes up for his... whatever it is he has going on with his blonde bombshell," said Judith.

"It's not like that," said Millie. "I don't know who she is, yet, but George promised me it wasn't what I thought it was, and I believe him. He'll tell me when he's ready, but I get the impression that she's important to him in a different way than we thought."

"So, you two are friends again?" said Judith.

"You could say that," said Millie, heat in her cheeks.

"Wait!" said Judith. "Something happened! Did you kiss him, Millie Thorn?"

"Hold on," said Millie, getting to her feet. "There's a doctor coming. The doctor who treated Chester."

"Saved by the bell," said Judith. "I know you kissed him!"

"You can go in, now," said the doctor, snaking a stethoscope around her neck. "But please don't excite him. He's still very poorly. He was badly burned, and he suffered smoke inhalation. Oh, and his wife is in the family waiting room. I told her she's not allowed in to see him unless the police agree to it."

"Thank you, Doctor," said Sergeant Spencer, approaching from the vending machine he'd been standing next to, a half-eaten bar of chocolate in his hand. "I'll speak with the wife myself."

The doctor looked Sergeant Spencer up and

down. "Undercover, are you?" she said, attempting to hide a smile.

"It's my zoo visiting outfit," said Sergeant Spencer. He patted the pocket of his shorts. "But I always carry my police notebook, so you could *technically* say I'm undercover."

"Well, it's a very nice outfit, Sergeant," said the doctor, turning her back. "Chester Harris is in room eighty-seven. Next door to the last suspect you came here to question. The poor man who's married to a biscuit baking machine."

Only Chester's eyes and a small portion of his mouth and nose were visible beneath the swathes of bandages which covered his head, chest and arms. The machine next to his bed beeped every few seconds, and a drip supplied antibiotics to the back of his hand.

Millie smiled at him. "How are you?" she asked, taking a seat next to the bed.

"Alive," said Chester, his voice cracking. "Thanks to you. I don't know what you and that young man did, or how you got me out of that car, but you saved my life."

"After you tried to run us off the road," said Millie.

"I'm sorry," said Chester. "I was panicking. Are you both okay?"

"You're lucky we're both alive," said Millie. "The motorbike is ruined, but we're okay."

"And my wife?" said Chester. "Is she okay?"

"She's in the waiting room, Mister Harris," said Sergeant Spencer. "You can't see her until we've spoken to her, and if you're going to tell us what Miss Thorn thinks you're going to tell us, then I don't think she'll want to see you ever again. Only in court, on the day you get sent down for a very long time."

"I'm not saying a word to anybody until my wife is here," said Chester, a harsh rasp to his voice.

"We can wait," said Sergeant Spencer. "You'll speak to us eventually, whether it's tomorrow, next week or next year."

Chester attempted to prop himself up on his elbows but sank back down to the mattress with a groan of pain. "Miss Thorn couldn't see my face properly when I was laying on the side of the road, or while she was in the ambulance with me, due to all the soot that was covering me," he said. "But what's beneath these bandages is not pretty. One ear is going to be removed when I'm strong enough to have surgery, the other one resembles pork crackling, my nose has no flesh on the bridge and my throat and lungs are scorched.

"My fingers have no feeling in them, and my scalp requires a skin graft, taken from my buttock. The painkillers are helping, but I realise that my life as I know it, is over. I know I'm going to prison, and I know I've lost the only person who means anything to me… my wife. If you think I'm going to speak to the police before I speak to my wife, who my confession concerns the most, then you are sadly mistaken. I don't care about living, Sergeant. I certainly don't care about providing you with a statement."

Sergeant Spencer blew out a long sigh. "Okay, Chester," he said. "I'll go and speak with her. I'll ask her if she wants to hear your confession."

Chester groaned, and his head slumped to the side, blood beginning to seep through the portion of bandages covering his nose. "Thank you," he grunted.

Sergeant Spencer wasn't gone long, and when he returned, Jill Harris shuffled ahead of him, her head bowed, and a handkerchief clutched in her fist. She looked at the man in the bed, her eyes red and her cheeks wet with tears. "Did. You. Kill. My. Mother?" she said, standing at the foot of the bed.

"Jill," said Chester. "I want to tell —"

The bed shook as Jill slammed her fist into the space between Chester's feet. "Did you kill my mother?" she screamed.

Chester groaned. "I'm sorry, Jill. I'm so, so sorry. It was an accident. I couldn't take her mood swings anymore, and she refused to get medical help for them. You thought she had bipolar, but I think it was something worse. She was awful to me, Jill. She wasn't nice to me, not at all — she was only nice to me when you were around. When she had to pretend. She hated me, and one day I snapped. We had no money, we were both stressed — living in that tiny house with your mother, and she wouldn't stop! She wouldn't stop telling me how terrible I was! I'm sorry!"

"How did you kill my mother?" said Jill, her voice flat.

"It was an accident, it —"

Jill's face reddened, and she slammed her fist into the bed again. "How did you kill my mother?" she shouted, spittle flying from her mouth.

"I drowned her," murmured Chester. "While she was taking a bath. You were out with your friends, and when you came home I pretended I didn't know where she was. I packed her suitcase and burned it along with her passport on the waste ground near the marshes."

"And you buried my mother's body in our garden?" said Jill, both hands forming tight fists.

"No," said Chester. "Of course not. I wouldn't do something so terrible! I buried her on the beach. In the sand dunes."

"A metal detectorist found her ring, Mrs Harris," explained Millie. "And when I saw the messages in French at the bottom of her letters from the Canadian gentleman, I put two and two together."

"Don't call me Mrs Harris, please," said Jill. "I no longer want a murderer's surname. Call me Jill. Jill Richards, the same surname my mother carried when she was murdered by this pig."

"Okay, Mrs Richards," said Millie.

"*Miss* Richards," said Jill. She stood up straight and stared at the bandaged man in the bed. "No wonder the police couldn't find my mother in Canada," she said. "But how did you know the Canadian police wouldn't be able to find the gentleman she loved?"

"I didn't, Jill!" said Chester. "I didn't plan it! It was an accident! It was a coincidence that the man she loved had left his wife! Maybe he didn't love your mother at all, and maybe she didn't love him. We surmised all the stuff about them being together because you and the police thought she was in Canada! She never was, Jill. She never was. She was always here, at the beach."

"You cold, cold bastard," said Jill. "I wish those flames had given you a lingering death and dragged you to hell with them."

"You don't mean that, Jill," said Chester. "You don't know what she did to me! She was horrible, always telling me I wasn't good enough for you, and always telling me that you'd leave me when you realised it!"

"And she was right, wasn't she, Chester?" said Jill. "On both points."

"I love you, Jill," said Chester. "I'm sorry! Please don't leave me!"

"Are the bones that Harry dug up today in the garden, my mother's bones?" said Jill, her legs giving way beneath her momentarily. "Was the bone that my little dog dragged into the kitchen a part of my own mother's skeleton?"

Sergeant Spencer's pen danced across his notebook as the conversation unfolded, his eyes flicking between Millie and Judith, and his face locked in an expression of sadness. "Is this too much for you, Jill?" he said. "Do you need a break? A cup of tea, maybe?"

"No thank you, Sergeant," said Jill. "I don't want a cup of tea." She stared at her husband. "What I do want to know is if that bone on my kitchen floor belonged to my poor mother."

Chester shifted his weight, giving a gasp of pain as he moved his arms. "I didn't see what Harry brought into the kitchen, Jill," he said. "But yes. It was probably one of your mother's bones. I'm sorry. I transferred them from the sand dunes late on Tuesday night. When I told you I couldn't sleep and was going for a long drive."

"And you told me you couldn't sleep because the curry I'd made you was too spicy!" said Jill, "You told me it had given you acid. I felt awful, thinking of you driving the streets because of my cooking. I didn't get to sleep for almost an hour! And while I was feeling guilty, you were digging up my poor mother's remains and dragging them across town so you could bury them in our garden!"

"The garden was a temporary measure!" said Chester. "I wasn't thinking straight! I was going to move them again. I promise. I'm not such a terrible man, Jill!"

Jill steadied herself with a hand on the foot-rail of the bed. "You're removed from reality, Chester," she said. "I don't know what to say to you." She sighed. "Why did you dig my mother up, Chester? Why did you move her from the sand dunes to our garden?"

Millie knew the answer, but she stayed quiet, wanting nothing more than to stand up and give Jill a hug, but aware that the poor woman needed to hear what her husband had to say. She gave her a reassuring smile instead, knowing that when Chester revealed the true extent of the crimes he'd committed, her life was going to be irrevocably altered.

Chester gave a rasping cough and reached for the glass of water next to his bed. Judith picked it up for him, and placed the straw between the small gap in the bandages around his mouth as he took slow sips. "Thank you," he said. He looked at his wife. "I moved her remains because of that dinosaur skeleton that was found," he said. "I knew they'd start digging around, and I knew the storm had shifted a lot of sand. I was worried that her remains would be revealed. I didn't want to get found out, Jill! I didn't want to go to jail! I wanted to spend the rest of my life with you."

"That's why you were so concerned about those stupid rare flowers," said Jill. "That's why you were on the phone to those DEFRA people! You hoped they'd stop people from digging in the dunes!"

"Only until I could remove your mother's remains," said Chester. "But they didn't seem very concerned. I telephoned them twice, but nobody came out straight away, like I hoped they would. I had to move your mother that night, Jill. I thought the whole place would be dug up by fossil hunters the next day, and my secret would be out."

Jill nodded. "But the fossil hunters couldn't dig, could they? Because that poor man was murdered —" Her face whitened, and she stumbled backwards, into the arms of Sergeant Spencer, who helped her to a seat. She took long ragged breaths, her sobs loud in the small room. "You killed him, too, didn't you, Chester? You murdered that man!"

"I had to!" said Chester, gasping for breath. "He saw me with your mother's bones! It was an accident!"

Jill placed her head in both hands and let out an anguished cry, her body shaking as she sobbed. "Another accident. I can't listen to any more of this," she wept. "I want to leave."

Judith leapt to her feet. "Let me help you," she said, offering Jill her hand. "Come on. We'll get a cup of tea."

"Jill, wait!" said Chester, as his wife was led from the room, her body shaking and her head low. "Please come back."

Sergeant Spencer approached the bed, his notebook in hand. "You may as well finish telling us what happened, Chester. Jill would want you to be honest."

The machine next to the bed beeped a little faster, and Chester nodded. "I didn't mean for it to happen," he said, his voice devoid of emotion. "Any of it. I thought I'd got away with killing Jill's mother, and I'd even begun to come to terms with what I'd done — to forgive myself, even. I thought she'd stay hidden in those dunes forever, or at least until I was dead. I knew those dunes were a good place to hide her body. Even all those years ago, those dunes were a protected area, because of those flowers. I knew it wouldn't be long until she'd decomposed in that environment. I thought she'd never be disturbed."

"You make it sound so clinical," said Millie, a sadness in her throat.

Chester nodded. "It has to be," he said. "If you don't want to be caught."

"Tell us about Tom," said Millie. "I was there when you killed him. I heard the shovel hit his head."

"You weren't the only person who was there that night," said Chester. "I couldn't believe my misfortune. I arrived at the dunes as soon as it got dark and began searching for Jill's mother. It took a while, but I knew where I'd buried her, and that storm had taken a lot of sand away. I soon found her."

"Yes," said Millie. "The shallower sand made it possible for Tom to find Jill's mother's ring. It must have slid off her finger over time, as she... decomposed. Tom could never have realised how close he was to discovering the poor woman's remains."

"What did you do when you'd found her bones?" said Sergeant Spencer.

"I put them in the big bag I'd brought with me," said Chester. "Along with my shovel and torch. I was going to bury her somewhere else. Everything was going perfectly to plan."

"Until some men with metal detectors arrived," said Millie.

"Yes," said Chester. "I thought the game was up! I hid in a dip in the sand. I couldn't see them, and they couldn't see me, but luckily for me, the closest anybody got to me was a few feet away. It was dark, and they didn't have torches. Nobody saw me. They were there for an hour… the longest hour of my life. I couldn't hear what was being said — they were being quiet, but I could tell there was an argument going on by the tones in their voices, and then there was laughter."

Millie looked at Sergeant Spencer. "They were laughing at Tom," she said. "Because they'd changed the batteries in his detector so he couldn't find any gold."

Sergeant Spencer nodded. "Poor Tom had an awful night," he said. "Tell us what you did to him, Chester."

"I waited for them to leave," said Chester. "And when they were far enough away, I began making my way back through the dunes. I'd parked my car on the main road and crossed the fields to get to the dunes, so I was going in the opposite direction to them. They must have parked in the nature reserve. But then I had an awful feeling. One of those feelings that you can't ignore."

"A feeling about what?" said Millie.

"I panicked. I had the awful feeling that perhaps I'd left a bone behind. Maybe just a small one, but one that might be found. I *had* to go back to check," said Chester.

"But you didn't know that Tom had stayed behind in the dunes," said Millie.

"No," said Chester. "And he was being very quiet. I was, too. Even though the cottage you live in is a couple of hundred metres from where I was, I could still hear you talking. You were on your patio, and I figured that if I could hear you, you could hear me."

"I saw torchlight," said Millie. "Was that you?"

"I was being as careful as I could to hide the light," said Chester. "But I needed to be sure there were no bones left. I just moved the top layer of the sand I'd put back in the hole I'd dug to retrieve Jill's remains, and had a good look around. And then I heard breathing, behind me. I looked up and saw him, and then he said something. He sounded shocked."

"Tom," said Millie.

"Yes," said Chester. "I was on my hands and knees in the sand, with the bag next to me. It was unzipped, and Jill's mother's skull was on full display. I'd switched my torch off, but the moon was bright enough to give Tom enough light to see what was in my bag. He looked terrified."

"Go on," said Sergeant Spencer.

Chester gave a groan of pain. "He shouted something. I don't know what. So I stood up."

"I heard," said Millie. "Me and Judith were already in the dunes, looking for whoever was using a torch."

"He had a shovel in his hand," said Chester. "It was easier to grab his, than to turn around and pick mine up."

"And you hit him with it," said Sergeant Spencer.

Chester nodded, blood seeping through several parts of his bandages. "I did," he said. "Then I panicked and threw the shovel aside, grabbed my bag and shovel, and ran."

"Straight home," said Millie. "And you buried the remains of Jill's mother in your garden."

"Yes, I wasn't thinking straight, and it was all downhill from there," said Chester. "I'd murdered a man, and buried the remains of my mother-in-law in my garden. My mind stopped working. I couldn't sleep. I couldn't eat, and every time I heard a car outside I thought it would be the police." He looked at Millie, his eyes barely visible through the slit in his bandages. "And when you came today, I listened to what you were saying. I realised the game was up, and panicked."

"So you slashed my tyres, and ran," said Millie.

"Yes," said Chester. "I'm sorry. For everything."

Sergeant Spencer closed his notebook. "Two murders, the attempted murder of George and Millie, and criminal damage. You'll be going away for a very long time, Chester Harris," he said.

Chapter 23

Millie answered her phone. "Hi, Judith," she said.

"Hey, detective of the year, twenty-eighteen," said Judith. "The bones have been positively identified as Jill's mother's remains, and the fingerprints on Tom Temples's shovel belong to Chester. How does it feel to have solved two murders at the same time? Well, one murder and one missing person's case which turned out to *be* a murder. I bet it feels like a great excuse for a bottle or two of fine wine — which I just happen to have in my possession! What do you say? Shall I come round straight away?"

"I'd love to, Judith, but —"

"Seriously?" said Judith. "You're turning me down?" She paused. "Oh, wait. I see… somebody's got a certain hot vampire coming over, hasn't she? For wine, food and nibbles on the neck. Make sure you don't let him nibble you too hard, Millie — those teeth could really hurt, and not the nice pain which makes you beg for more — I mean the bad pain, which makes you cry."

"You paint a… weird picture, Judith," said Millie. "But no. George isn't coming. There's no nibbling of necks happening in my cottage tonight."

"Then what are you doing that's more important than a bottle or two of wine?" asked Judith. "You solved two mysteries, Millie. That deserves a celebration."

Millie gazed at her familiar. "I've still got one more mystery to solve, Judith. A mystery Reuben is helping me with. We need some time alone."

"Oh," said Judith. "Well, you make sure you tell me when you solve it. I'm intrigued."

"I will," said Millie, ending the call. She smiled at Reuben. "What's wrong?" she asked, staring at the little cockatiel. His head bowed low, and his normally vivid red cheeks appearing duller than usual, he looked nervous as he perched on the table next to the spell book.

"I'm scared," he said. "I'm scared of what will happen if the spell doesn't work. I'm scared of what will happen to you."

Millie approached the table, and offered Reuben her hand. The little bird leapt onto her index finger and looked up at her face as she spoke in soft tones. "If the spell doesn't work, Reuben, I'll be disappointed. I'll be very disappointed, but I'll get over it with time — like everybody gets over disappointments in time. There's nothing to fear."

"And you won't be... angry, with me?" said Reuben.

Millie brought her finger close to her face, and gave the bird a gentle kiss on the crown of his head. "Reuben, you can be the most annoying... bird, in the world. You're sometimes rude, you're sometimes brash, but I could never be angry with you. Not really angry, anyway." Millie placed her hand on the spell book, and Reuben hopped off her finger. "Come on. Let's cast the spell — it will either work, or it won't work."

Reuben puffed out his chest, his eyes gaining brightness. "Okay," he said. "I'll read from the book and you do as I say, how does that sound?"

"It sounds like a plan," said Millie. She glanced down at the clothes she'd chosen to wear. A knee length burgundy skirt with a little gold detailing around the hem, a flower print button up blouse, and her smart black heels over a pair of tights. She looked at her familiar. "How do I look?" she said.

"You look amazing, Millie," said Reuben. "If your mother does appear when we cast the spell, she'll be proud of her daughter."

Millie turned away as she wiped a tear from beneath her eye. "What's first?" she said.

Reuben studied the book. "As with every spell, you must introduce some of your own magic to the cauldron before you begin."

Approaching the cauldron, and peering into the green fluid which swirled and shimmered within it, Millie nodded. She gazed into the stone-rimmed pool as she inserted a hand in the warm liquid, her fingers tingling as she focused on allowing a little of her magic to trickle from her fingertips. "There," she said, removing her hand, her fingers already dry. "That part's done."

"Okay," said Reuben. "Now we need the unspoken words and a tear shed for the person who said them."

Millie reached for the table, butterflies in her stomach as she picked up the envelope. "Are you sure the dry tear on the envelope counts?" she asked.

"As sure as I can be," said Reuben. "As long as the ingredients are there, it shouldn't matter in what form they are presented to the cauldron." He looked up at Millie. "This is the hard part," he said. "You must burn the envelope, and allow the ashes to fall into the cauldron, being sure to picture your mother's face in your mind's eye as you do it. Remember, when the letter has been burned — there's no going back. If the spell doesn't work, you'll never know what was written by your mother."

"And the pearl of wisdom," said Millie, moistening her lips with her tongue, and taking a lit candle from one of the shelves set in the cavern wall. "When do I use that?"

"That goes in last," said Reuben, reading from the page before him. "You should hold it over your heart while the letter burns, and when the last of the ashes from the envelope fall into the cauldron, you should drop the pearl in and say the words '*I choose to not hear your last words. I demand that you come forth and speak them from your mouth.*'"

"And then?" said Millie.

"We'll see," said Reuben.

Taking a deep breath, and fighting the rising anxiety in her throat, Millie stared at the envelope. Placing one of the worn corners against the edge of the candle's flame, she swallowed hard as a curling finger of smoke rose to the rough rock of the cavern ceiling.

As the envelope began to burn, Millie placed the candleholder on the edge of the cauldron and placed her left hand flat against her chest, the pearl of wisdom pressing into the flesh of her breast.

As black ash fluttered from the envelope and spiralled into the glowing contents of the cauldron, Millie pictured the smiling face of her mother. She pictured her gentle brown eyes and her long dark hair. She pictured the small mole on her forehead above her left eye, and she pictured the slight bend in her nose — not as prominent as Millie's, but a family feature all the same.

As the flames ate the final piece of the envelope, beginning to burn Millie's fingers, she began to imagine she could even smell her mother. The sweet cinnamon scent of her favourite shampoo, and the fruity tang on her breath from the pear drops she'd always seemed to have a bag of in her handbag.

No longer able to bear the pain of the flames on her flesh, Millie released the tiny portion of blackened paper which remained between her finger and thumb, watching as it landed gently in the cauldron, and was sucked beneath the surface.

"The pearl," whispered Reuben. "Drop the pearl in, and say the words."

Moving her hand from her chest, Millie gazed at the tiny blue pearl which shone in her hand. Her fingers trembling, she held it above the cauldron, and said the words slowly and clearly as she allowed the pearl to drop from her hand, watching it land with a gentle splash in the magical fluid. "I choose not to hear your last words. I demand that you come forth and speak them from your mouth."

Her mouth as dry as the stone which her right hand gripped, Millie steadied herself against the edge of the cauldron, her heartbeat filling her head, and her legs no longer hers.

The green liquid in the cauldron shimmered and shone, and a bright light darted from left to right in the very depths of the magic. She bit her lip, and looked at Reuben for support.

"I don't know, Millie," said the little bird. "I don't know how long it should take. The book doesn't say."

Taking a step back from the cauldron, Millie spun slowly on the spot, searching the shadows of the cavern for the familiar shape of her mother. There was nothing there. There was *nobody* there — only she and Reuben, and the lingering stench of the smoke caused by the fire which had destroyed her mother's final letter to her.

She closed her eyes, and waited. She waited for longer than she knew was sensible. *If the magic was going to work, it would have worked by now.* She closed her eyes tighter, and waited some more, the warm trickle of tears on her cheeks. She flinched as something touched her shoulder, but took a deep breath when she realised it was Reuben, landing.

"I'm sorry," said the cockatiel. "I'm really sorry, Millie. I don't think it worked."

Millie opened her eyes, and nodded. "Not to worry," she said, turning her back on the cauldron and climbing the stairs, a sickness rolling in her stomach. "Come on, Reuben. I'm tired. I want to go to bed. And tomorrow morning I'm going to go and see Henry. He knows who my father is. He can tell me. I need to know."

Halfway up the steps, Millie stalled for a moment, lifting a hand to her face and touching her cheek.

"What's wrong?" said Reuben.

Looking to the left, Millie gave her head a gentle shake. "Nothing," she said. "I thought I felt something on my cheek. That's all."

Chapter 24

The entrance hall of Spellbinder Hall was the busiest Millie had ever seen it. A crowd of young children laughed and jostled with one another as they were ushered up the stairs by Florence – the first ghost Millie had met when she'd moved to the bay, and Timothy, the short man who Millie had seen turn into a giant of a werewolf, during a fight on the beach, hurried across the floor, carrying a pile of thick books.

He gave Millie a smile. "Hello," he said. "I'm sorry I can't stop to chat. It's lesson change over time, and if the kids see the teachers talking in the hallway…"

"It sets a bad example," finished Millie.

"It does, indeed," said Timothy, heading for an open doorway next to a suit of armour.

Millie jumped as a hand brushed her shoulder.

"Miss Thorn?" said a soft voice from behind her. "May I speak with you?"

"Peter? Graham?" said Millie, turning to find the two men standing behind her.

"Erm, hello," said Graham Spalding. "I'm sorry about all that Mister Anon stuff, and the way in which I spoke to you on several occasions."

"I'm also sorry," said Peter Simmons, dressed in a long white lab coat. "And I'm absolutely horrified about what I did to you while under the influence of that demon. I tried to stop myself, but I had no control. I can remember everything that terrible creature forced me to do, though. Including attempting to murder you. How is your poor throat, Miss Thorn?"

"Oh, it's fine," said Millie. "A little blob of a special balm, and it soon stopped hurting." She looked Peter up and down. "You seem… different than the last time I saw you, Peter — before you were possessed, I mean."

"You mean I no longer give people the impression that Graham had recruited a village simpleton to be his sidekick?" said Peter, glancing at Graham, who looked away. "The demon may have been evil, Miss Thorn, but its presence amongst the neurons of my brain seems to have fixed the damage done to me by a simple kitchen accessory used to transform bread into toast."

"A toaster," said Millie.

"Quite," said Peter. "It was an unfortunate accident to which I succumbed, however, it was extremely *convenient* for Graham, who took advantage of my decreased intellect and sought to turn me into his alien hunting lackey." He looked down his nose at Graham. "You used me for my lab and my equipment. I remember everything, Graham. Everything."

Graham's cheeks reddened. "I'm sorry, Peter, but everything has turned out for the best, hasn't it?"

Peter straightened his back and smiled at Millie. "It has indeed," he said. "Henry Pinkerton has informed Graham and I of all the intricacies of your wonderful paranormal community, and he's given both Graham and I jobs. The most wonderful jobs!"

"Oh?" said Millie. "What sort of jobs?"

"We've been tasked with attempting to work out ways of strengthening the gateway into The Chaos," said Peter. "We're fully aware that it is your magic which provides the gate's stability, Miss Thorn, but Henry was open to exploring the concept of combining science with magic, to see if we can prevent any future incidents of creatures passing through the gate into this world. It's my dream job! I've always been convinced that other dimensions exist, and now I get the chance to study a gateway to one of them!"

"And we're science teachers," said Graham, shuffling from foot to foot. "Here in Spellbinder Hall."

"Teaching a wonderful group of paranormal children," said Peter. "I've never been happier."

Millie gave the two men a sincere smile. "I'm

happy for you both," she said. "But I must be going, I have an appointment with Henry."

"He's a remarkable person, Miss Thorn," said Peter. "And the children in this equally remarkable school are lucky to have him as an influence. He's a great help to them."

"He is," said Millie, heading for the staircase. "And now I need him to be a great help to me, too."

"Millie, welcome," said Henry Pinkerton, standing up behind the long desk as Millie stepped into his office. The pleasant aromas of leather, old books and furniture polish hung in the air, and the floorboards creaked as Millie made her way to the armchair which Henry offered her, next to the fireplace.

"Thanks for seeing me," said Millie. "I know you're busy."

"I'm never too busy to offer you my time. You've done more for this town in your short time here, than many people do in a lifetime," said Henry, sitting in the armchair opposite her, the cracked leather upholstery creaking as he crossed his legs and made himself comfortable. "That's three murders you've solved now! You deserve all the time I can possibly offer you. How may I be of help to you?"

Millie took a deep breath. "It's about the letter

from my mother," she said. "The one she gave to you."

Henry removed his glasses and polished the lenses with a crisp white handkerchief he took from the breast pocket of his suit jacket. "What about it? I trust you've read it?"

"Not quite," said Millie.

"You're still not aware who your father is?" said Henry, replacing his glasses and fiddling with his cufflinks. "I thought as much."

Millie shook her head. "No," she said. "And something happened to the letter… I… well, I burnt it."

"It was hard to come to terms with what may have been inside?" said Henry. "I can understand that."

"It wasn't like that," said Millie. "I didn't burn it to destroy it. I burnt it to cast a spell. A spell which was supposed to make it possible for me to speak to my mother."

Henry frowned. "It sounds like it was a powerful spell you tried to cast, Millie. Powerful spells are impressive when they work, but tend to fail more often than their simpler counterparts," he said.

"Yes, well, this one failed," said Millie. She dropped her eyes. "And now I have no letter from my mother."

Henry gave a gentle smile. "I'm sorry, Millie," he said, "but you're aware that I know who your father is. I can't tell you every word your mother wrote in that letter, but I can help you discover where you came from. Would you like to know who your father is, Millie? Is that why you're here?"

"Yes, and no," said Millie. "I was hoping there would be other ways of speaking to my mother."

Henry raised an eyebrow. "Such as?"

"Is there no way at all that my mother could become a ghost?" said Millie.

Henry sighed. "You know that's not possible, Millie. Witches can never become ghosts; their energy works in different ways than a human's energy does. Not all humans become ghosts either, Millie. Tom Temples didn't, or Jill Harris's mother -- at least they haven't yet. Some ghosts take their time before they make an appearance." He smiled at Millie. "But your mother won't become a ghost, Millie, although her energy will always be tied to the cottage you live in. The cottage that she once lived in."

"I knew that," said Millie, her heart heavy. "But I just wanted to make absolutely sure before I asked you to tell me who my father is, Henry. I wanted to hear it from my mother, but that's not going to happen."

Henry leaned forward in his seat. "Would you like me to tell you, Millie? Do you want to know who your father is?"

Millie shifted her weight. "When you told me you knew who he was, you told me he lived in Spellbinder Bay. Is that still the case? Is he still here?"

"Very much so," said Henry.

"Do you think he'd be happy to discover he has a daughter he didn't know about?" said Millie.

"I can't answer that, Millie," said Henry. "It wouldn't be fair on him, or you."

Millie closed her eyes, and wrapped her fingers around the seat's armrests. "Okay, Henry," she said. "I'm ready. Tell me who my father is. Please."

Henry remained silent for a few moments, and Millie kept her eyes shut, hoping the words would be more easily digestible if she couldn't see Henry's mouth moving. When he finally spoke, his voice was calm. "Millie Thorn," he said. "Your father is —"

"Don't you dare, Henry Pinkerton!"

Hearing Henry gasp, Millie held her breath, a heaviness building behind her eyes as tears threatened to spill. *That voice. It couldn't be.*

"Hello, Millie," said the soft female voice. "Hello, my darling. Open your eyes."

Tears ran freely as Millie tentatively opened her eyes. With her vision blurred, she stared at the woman standing alongside her. Taking long ragged gasps of air, Millie sobbed as she attempted to smile. "Is it you?" she gasped. "Is it really you?"

The woman smiled, her brown eyes as warm as Millie had remembered them. "Yes," she said. "It's really me."

Chapter 25

Henry stood up. "Josephine! How wonderful to see you, but how did you—"

The woman raised a hand. "Would you leave us alone, Henry?" she said. "Please?"

With a wide smile, Henry hurried towards the door. "Of course! My office is yours for as long as you need it."

When the door had closed behind Henry, Millie gazed up at the smiling woman, her cheeks wet with tears and her breathing beginning to steady. "Mum?" she said. "Mum?"

"Oh, Millie," said her mother, her face appearing to shift in and out of focus. "Your spell worked! I've been trying for so long to reach you. Ever since you moved into Windy-dune Cottage! I've heard every word you've spoken to me, and I've seen every tear you've cried for me. I tried so hard to touch you, to speak to you, but I couldn't reach across the divide between my world and yours."

Millie stood up, her legs struggling to take her weight, and reached for her mother with a trembling hand. "I can't feel you, Mum," she said, as her hand passed through her mother's shoulder. "You look so young."

Her mother smiled, her cheeks radiant, and the hem of the long loose dress she wore, blowing in an invisible breeze. "I'm as the cottage remembers me, Millie," she said. "I'm at the age I was at when I lived in the cottage."

"When you were pregnant with me?" said Millie, instantly regretting the accusatory tone she'd used.

"Yes, Millie," said her mother. "And I'm so sorry I never told you about your past. Henry did a good job of explaining why when he gave you the letter I wrote. I was there when you spoke to him in the cavern. I could hear you, but I couldn't reach you."

"Henry told me that when Sergeant Spencer and Judith moved to town you helped them adjust," said Millie, "but when you became pregnant you also became terrified of me growing up around magic, because of what Judith had done to her real parents."

"There was more to it than that, sweetheart," said her mother. "But, yes. Judith had accidentally killed her parents with magic, and when I discovered I was pregnant, I worried that my own child would one day make the same terrible mistake and suffer the awful guilt that Judith was destined to suffer with. So, I left the bay, and I never told you that you were the daughter of a witch. I'm sorry, Millie."

Millie wiped her eyes. "You look so beautiful, Mum. So healthy. Not like the last time I saw you."

"I was very ill, sweetheart. I'm sorry you had to see me like that while you were still at such a young age. It broke my heart every time I saw you cry when you looked at me," said her mother, her dress shimmering with a golden light.

"I'm sorry you got ill, Mum," said Millie. "Aunty Hannah and Uncle James acted as perfect parents to me, but I missed you so much, Mum." More tears spilt over her cheeks. "So much."

"I know, sweetie," said her mother. "But I'm here now, aren't I?"

Millie looked around the room. "Why are you here, Mum? I mean *here* — in Spellbinder Hall. I cast the spell in the cavern under the cottage."

Her mother's eyes twinkled as she spoke. "There wasn't enough magic in the cottage cauldron, Millie. You haven't lived in the cottage long enough, nor used the cauldron often enough to provide it with the energy it requires to perform the sort of magic you asked it to last night. I almost broke through to you, but there just wasn't enough magic to make myself visible — I blew on your cheek, but I don't think you felt it."

Millie put her fingers to her face. "I did feel it, Mum."

Her mother smiled. "When you left the cavern, Esmeralda had an idea."

"Esmeralda?" said Millie. "I don't understand."

"We're all there, Millie," said her mother, with a smile. "All the witches who've ever lived above the coven cavern, be it when the building above it was a bronze-age roundhouse, or the cottage you live in now. There are lots of us, Millie. Our energies manifested as the way we were in life, all of us living together in a world of sunshine, nature and happiness."

"Heaven?" said Millie.

"As good as," said her mother. "Anyway — Esmeralda's idea. As she pointed out, the spell you cast is linked to you — to your heart, not to the place you cast it in, and when we heard you telling Reuben that you were coming here today, to see Henry, Esmeralda suggested I try and break through to you here — where the magic is stronger.

"The moon-pool beneath Spellbinder Hall is infinitely more powerful than your cauldron, Millie, it was easier than I thought it would be to break through to this world, and with time, I'll be able to break through to you in Windy-dune cottage, too."

"With time?" whispered Millie. "You mean the spell I cast can bring you here again? It doesn't work only once?"

"You've built a bridge," said her mother, placing a hand on her chest. "Between our hearts. An unbreakable bridge. I may not be able to cross the bridge as often as I'd like to, but yes, I can come back again. Over, and over again."

Millie moved close to her mother, and placed her arms around her shape, not able to feel her form, but able to smell the faint tang of pear drops.

"I don't have long, Millie," murmured her mother. "Not on this first trip. I'll be able to stay longer each time I cross our bridge."

Her mother's cheek next to hers, and the tingling of soft energy against her earlobe, Millie whispered the question burning a hole in her heart. "Did you love him, Mum? Did you love my father?"

"Oh, yes, Millie," said her mother. "I loved him with everything I had. We only knew each other for a short time, but in that short time he proved what a wonderfully good man he is."

"You told me I was the result of a meaningless fling," said Millie. "You told me you couldn't find my father to tell him about me."

"I'm sorry, Millie," said her mother, her voice trembling. "I was a coward. I was too afraid to tell you what I'd done to your father. That I'd left him without saying goodbye."

"Why did you leave without telling him you were pregnant?" said Millie, her words heavy in her mouth.

"He had responsibilities, Millie," she whispered in her daughter's ear. "Huge responsibilities. Too many responsibilities for one person. I feared that another responsibility would break him, Millie, and I worried about how magic would affect you in the future, I left Spellbinder Bay without telling him. I left magic behind, and I left him behind — for his sake, and yours. Or so I thought, but really, it was for my sake. I see that now. I saw that a long time ago, before I died, but it was too late. I was selfish, Millie. I wanted you and me to be safe, and I didn't consider how you or your father would feel. I'm sorry. So, so sorry."

Millie licked her lips, the final question trapped in her throat, unwilling to be born into reality. She forced it from herself, pulling away from her mother and staring into her eyes. "Who is it, Mum? Who's my father?"

HER MOTHER'S EYES LIT UP, AND SHE REACHED FOR her daughter, her hand dissolving in a shower of dim sparks as it slid over Millie's arm. "A good man, Millie. A man you're already very close to."

"Just say his name, Mum," said Millie. "Please, just say his name."

"Okay," said her mother. "Your father is David Spencer, and I loved him when we created you, and I believe he loved me, too."

Millie stepped backwards and dropped into the armchair, her veins fizzing with adrenaline. "Sergeant Spencer is my father?" said Millie.

"He is," said her mother.

"I have so many questions," said Millie, her

fingernails digging deep into her thighs. "I don't know what to ask."

Bending slowly, her mother got to her knees in front of Millie, placing her formless hands over her daughter's. "Then let me try and answer the questions I'd have if I was in your position," she said. "Beginning with why I didn't tell him. I couldn't, Millie. He was a young man who'd fostered a toddler. A toddler who'd killed her parents. David was thrown into a world of magic he knew nothing about, and despite what he may think he remembers, he struggled to cope. I mean *really* struggled to cope. I couldn't add to his responsibilities, Millie. I couldn't tell him I was pregnant."

"*You* decided he couldn't cope," said Millie. "*You* made the decision for him."

"I know," said her mother. "I'm sorry, but I can't turn back the clock. I was young. We were *both* young. I was frightened about bringing you into a world of magic. I did the wrong thing. I know that."

"You met him when he moved to town," said Millie. "Henry told me you'd met Sergeant Spencer and Judith — he said you'd helped them settle in, but it never occurred to me... that... that..."

"That we fell in love?" said her mother. "That I was there for him, and he was there for me, too? That sometimes life can reach inside your head and make you forget about being sensible? That we didn't use precautions? That I cried every day for weeks after leaving Spellbinder Bay? That I sneaked back here on numerous occasions and watched David from afar? That when you were born, I wanted nothing more than to place you in his safe hands and hear him tell me how happy I'd made him — to hear him tell me how much he loved you, and me? That I never loved another man again? That I want nothing more than to live my life over, and change every mistake I ever made?" She looked at the floor. "There are a lot of *that's*, Millie? Some I regret, and some... I wouldn't change for the world, my beautiful girl."

The salty taste of tears on her lips, Millie looked at her Mother. "I love you, Mum."

"I love you, too, sweetheart," said her mother. "And when I've seen you and David together in your cottage, watching you from a place I couldn't reach you from, I've seen him look at you sometimes, like he knows."

Millie wiped her eyes with the back of her hand. "Do you think he does know? Or suspect? I do look like you."

"Our noses may be similar, but we don't look that alike," said her mother. "Not to him. Not after twenty-four years."

"It's a good job I kept the photograph of you in my bedroom," said Millie. "That would have freaked him out — seeing a picture of you in my living room!"

Her mother laughed, the same high pitched sing-song laughter that Millie remembered so well. "I've been watching David for years," said her mother. "He took his job as a community policeman very seriously, and would visit people regularly — especially those who lived off the beaten track. When I died, and found my energy back in the cottage, I'd look forward to the days he'd visit Esmeralda, watching him age gracefully, and wondering what he'd say if he knew he had a daughter."

A coldness gripped Millie's insides. "But he has a daughter! A daughter he loves! I can't tell him that he's my father!"

"Of course you can," said her mother.

"But Judith," said Millie. "She's his daughter."

Her mother gazed into Millie's eyes, her face beginning to fade. "Then he'll have two daughters. Two daughters he loves."

"Mum?" said Millie. "What's happening? I can hardly see you."

"The bridge is weakening," said her mother. "I have to go now, but I'll come back as soon as I can. Tell your father who you are, sweetheart."

"Mum?" said Millie. She stared at the empty space before her, tears still falling, and spoke to nobody. "I have a father," she whispered. "I have a father."

Chapter 26

Before Millie could touch the police station door, it swung open, almost hitting her in the face. An elderly woman stepped through it, and smiled at her. "Hello, dear!" she said.

"Oh, hello, Pamela," said Millie. "How's Jack?"

"He'll be out of the hospital by the end of the week, but he won't be doing any marathons for a month or two," said Pamela. "He'll be glad to be out of there — especially since they dumped that terrible man in the room next door. That *murderer*. Jack and the boys wanted to sneak in at night and smother him, they're disgusted at what he did to a fellow member of the metal detecting community. I told them they were hypocrites after the way they treated Tom, and that they didn't have the balls between them to smother a man."

"Oh," said Millie. "Well, that's probably for the

best. We could do without another murder around here."

"That's exactly what I told them," said Pamela. "Two wrongs don't make a right, I said. Jack and the boys agreed, so they've come up with another way of honouring Tom Temples."

"What have they decided to do?" said Millie.

"Pawn Shop Pete came to visit Jack, you see," said Pamela. "And he told them about the gold he had in his safe. Tom's gold."

"Yes?" said Millie, wondering how she was going to tell Sergeant Spencer. Wondering how she was going to tell *David*. Wondering how she was going to tell *her father* that she was his daughter.

"Pawn Shop Pete told Jack that you and young Judith had told him not to touch that gold," said Pamela.

"That's right," said Millie, wondering if her father would hug her or walk away.

"But they came up with an idea, you see, but they needed the police's permission to be able to act on it. That's why I'm here. I came to ask if the boys could auction off the gold and use it for a good cause. Sergeant Spencer said yes, but between me and you," said Pamela, "I think it was the plate of biscuits I brought as a sweetener that sealed the deal. Chocolate chips *and* raisins are a very hard biscuit to resist. Especially for a tubby chap like the sergeant. He was straight into them, like a greedy bugger at a free buffet."

"Right," said Millie, wondering if she would cry or smile when she told her father who she was. "What's the good cause, then?"

Pamela gave a proud smile. "They're building a hall. A community hall. The Tom Temples Hobby Hall, it's going to be named! People can use it for meetings, book clubs – whatever they like, and the boys are buying a few metal detectors, too! They're going to take local children metal detecting! To keep them out of trouble!"

"That is a wonderful idea," said Millie. "And I still have the gold that Jack and the others found in the sand dunes. It's in my cottage. They can have that, too."

"How splendid!" said Pamela. "The boys *will* be happy! Now, you get yourself inside that police station before all those biscuits have gone, you look like the type of girl who likes a good feed every now and again."

"Erm… thank you?" said Millie.

Pamela smiled. "You're welcome." She lowered her voice. "You know," she said. "The policing in this town is very unconventional, but I wouldn't have it any other way. It's not in every town that you can walk into a police station and find a father and daughter having so much fun together! You wait until you see what those two in there are wearing! They had me in stitches! Bye now!"

"Goodbye, Pamela," said Millie, waiting until the smell of cinnamon and brown sugar had dispersed before closing her eyes and taking a deep breath. When she considered herself calm enough, she pulled the door open and prepared herself for the conversation she was both dreading, and anticipating with a happy glow in her stomach.

"Morning, Millie," said Sergeant Spencer, looking up from behind the tall custody desk. "Are you alright? You sounded nervous when you phoned me and asked for a chat. Is everything okay?"

"Everything's fine," said Millie. "I just wanted some… advice?"

Sergeant Spencer gave her a warm smile. "Of course! Come into my office, Judith won't mind giving us some time alone."

Judith poked her head from around the office door, her body hidden. "But not until Millie's seen our shirts, Dad!"

"Of course not!" said Sergeant Spencer. "Our t-shirts from the zoo were delivered this morning, Millie," he said. "You're going to love them! Pamela did!"

"Close your eyes, Millie," said Judith. "They work better when we're standing next to each other."

"Erm.. okay," said Millie, shutting her eyes, anxiety boiling in her chest.

After a few seconds of shuffling feet and a little laughter, Judith spoke, her voice excited. "Okay, open your eyes and prepare to be dazzled by our zoo visiting outfits for next year's father and daughter anniversary trip!"

When Millie opened her eyes, her heart sank. She forced a smile and tried to laugh. "Very good," she said.

"It's not the reaction I was expecting," said Sergeant Spencer, his arm around Judith's shoulder, his daughter's head on his chest. "Maybe we were spoiled by Pamela's over the top reaction. That woman couldn't stop laughing."

"Dad designed them," said Judith. "He chose what to have written on them."

Millie smiled wider, her spirits sinking and her stomach in tight knots of hopelessness. How could she come between them? *She couldn't.* She forced a giggle. "No! They're brilliant! I love them!"

They *were* funny. They were cute, even, but seeing her father's face caught in a mock scowl and superimposed over the 3D features of a grumpy orangutan's face, with the words *father to the best cheeky chimp in the zoo* written below, made her realise she was trespassing. Trespassing on a father and daughter relationship forged over almost three decades. Forged from an awful tragedy, and wrapped securely in bars of the toughest steel.

Judith's shirt, with the words *daughter to the grumpiest great ape in the zoo,* printed below her smiling face, superimposed over the face of a grinning chimp, made her mind up for her. She had no right to change

Sergeant Spencer's life, or the life of his adopted daughter.

"Anyway, enough of that," said Sergeant Spencer. "I'll make you a cup of coffee, Millie. Grab yourself a biscuit or two from the plate which Pamela left for us, and come into my office. Let's have that chat you wanted."

"You know what?" said Millie. "I think I'll give it a miss."

"Really?" said Sergeant Spencer. "Are you sure? You sounded nervous when you phoned me."

Millie nodded. "I'm sure," she said. "I think I was a little stressed out after the murders and the motorbike crash, you know? I just wanted some advice on how to process it all, but seeing those shirts has cheered me up. Laughter *does* seem to be the best medicine."

"That's how I deal with stressful things," said the big man. "By not talking about them too much, and laughing. Are you sure I can't help, Millie? There's nothing wrong with asking for a little help now and again."

"It's fine," said Millie, turning to face the door. "I'll be fine. I'm going to take a walk along the beach. I'm keeping an eye out for Lillieth. I still haven't had the chance to offer her the lighthouse as a home for when she's in these parts."

Judith came alongside her, dropping her voice as she walked Millie towards the exit. "Has George told you who that blonde girl is yet?" she asked.

"No," said Millie. "And I've agreed not to ask until he's ready to tell me. There's nothing going on that I should be worried about. I trust him."

"Good," said Judith, pushing the door open for Millie. "And what about that mystery you and Reuben were trying to solve together?"

"Oh, we solved that," said Millie.

"And?" said Judith.

Millie stepped through the door and into the sunshine. "I'm still trying to work out what to do with the answer," she said.

The End

Also by Sam Short

The Water Witch Cozy Mystery Series - listed in reading order below.

Under Lock And Key

Four And Twenty Blackbirds

An Eye For An Eye

A Meeting Of Minds

The Spellbinder Bay Series - listed in reading order below.

Witch Way to Spellbinder Bay

Broomsticks and Bones

About the Author

Sam Short loves witches, goats, and narrowboats. He really enjoys writing fiction that makes him laugh — in the hope it will make others laugh too!
You can find him at the places listed below — he'd love to see you there!

www.samshortauthor.com
email — sam@samshortauthor.com

Printed in Great Britain
by Amazon